MIND IN THE CLOUDS

The Mind Sleuth Series Book 2

Bruce M. Perrin

This book is a work of fiction.
Names, characters, places, and incidents are products of the author's imagination or are used fictitiously. Any resemblance to actual events, locales, or persons living or dead is entirely coincidental.

Second Edition

Cover Art by Courtney M. Perrin

Visit the Author at
BruceMPerrin.blogspot.com

Mind Sleuth Publications
ISBN-13: 978-1-7320835-5-4 (paperback)

TITLES BY BRUCE M. PERRIN

THE MIND SLEUTH SERIES
Of Half a Mind
Mind in the Clouds
Mind in Chains

STANDALONE NOVELS
In the Space of an Atom
Killer in the Retroscape: A Near Future Mystery

For all the latest on new releases, promotions, and book reviews, please subscribe to my blog: BruceMPerrin.blogspot.com

For my family and
their boundless love and support

TABLE OF CONTENTS

"Success in creating AI would be the biggest event in human history. Unfortunately, it might also be the last ...."

STEPHEN HAWKING
THEORETICAL PHYSICIST, COSMOLOGIST, AND
AUTHOR

TWO MONTHS EARLIER,
THURSDAY, NOVEMBER 12

Information Systems Building, JACC Test Range,
  Nevada, 11:03 PM

A dark shape slid across the desert floor. Alan Garcia watched its advance through a dust-streaked pane of glass. It moved silently, adding no sound to the low moan of the wind across the playa and the swishing of the Indian ricegrass desperately clinging to life below the window. The silhouette dropped into a narrow gulch about twenty yards away, then reappeared a moment later and continued its march. The hair stood out on the back of Garcia's neck. After a moment more, Garcia and the Information Systems Building were lost in darkness as the cloud floated in front of the full moon.

"Damn, I hate this place," Garcia muttered to himself, his mood not lightening as the shadow passed. To him, the desert was inhospitable in the daytime. But now, in this isolated building, alone, in the middle of the night, it was abhorrent.

He turned from the window. His desk sat in a pool of light about halfway across the room. He walked there but didn't sit. He needed something to dispel the pall of the night. Emergency lighting on the other side of the work area backlit three other desks, and Garcia wound his way through them to a bank of switches. He threw the ones he needed, now knowing the set by heart—numbers two, six, and seven. They would light a path to a small galley kitchen where a half pot of coffee sat, slowly turning its contents into a caffeine-based sludge.

If it was up to him, Garcia would have left every bulb in the IS Building blazing. That would help his nerves. But as sure as he did, the new commanding officer, Air Force Lieutenant Colonel Raymond Dempsey, would drop by and he'd have hell to pay. At least, Garcia guessed Dempsey was behind these two-bit, cost-cutting measures on this nearly half-billion-dollar military weapon systems project. Certainly, in the month or so under his command, things had become more shipshape ... or whatever the hell the Air Force equivalent was for anal. Garcia didn't know, didn't care.

He didn't care because he was a subcontractor on a short-term assignment. After another couple of months in nowhere Nevada, he'd be reassigned. Hopefully, it would be to some nice nine-to-five commercial job in a city with a gourmet coffee shop nearby. He was sick of drinking the crap from the communal pot. But until that day, he was working on the software that controlled a military drone, or as his bosses called it, an unmanned aerial system. The official name of the program was the Joint Aerial Combat Capability (JACC), so everyone ended up calling the aircraft Jack.

Jack had been flying for months, and to Garcia, it looked like a half-size helicopter without a pilot. For the first flights, all of its offensive capabilities—missiles, rockets, and machine-guns—had been simulated. Slowly, the real weapons had been brought online, so that the bird currently had both. Jack could riddle the image of a personnel carrier with virtual bullets until it was nothing more than a smoking shell on a computer screen. Or, he could do the same thing in the real world and catch the devastation in a video clip.

The coexistence of real and simulated weapons in Jack's arsenal couldn't remain, of course. Eventually, the simulated weapons needed to become part of training and the real ones part of fighting. But the timing of that work had been a matter of considerable debate. Surprisingly, military leadership, Col. Dempsey, and the civilian JACC Program Manager, Dr. James Marshall from Omega Systems, agreed. With the first live-fire demonstration only a little more than two months away, they felt there wasn't time to modify the software. But Don Williams, the Chief Software Engineer, thought otherwise. The standoff between management and engineer had continued until Williams played the critical-software-issue card. Perhaps knowing that a failed demonstration after overriding Williams could be career-limiting, Dempsey and Marshall dropped their resistance to the change.

With this added pressure on the software team, Williams had scheduled some of the simplest, low-risk tasks for overtime so they could get a head start. And when Garcia saw the job removing the simulated weapons from Jack's arsenal, he was quick to sign up. If he was going to be stuck out in the middle of this godforsaken sandpile, at least he could be well paid. Tonight, Garcia was in his third and final evening. The job was so easy that he almost hated it was over. Almost.

He reached the galley, the acrid smell of stale coffee greeting him. He poured a cup and took a sip. It was even worse than he expected, but caffeine was caffeine. He turned, cup in hand, and started back to his desk only to stop midstride. He'd heard something, like a soft popping. He turned his head, hoping he was orienting his ears correctly, but the noise was gone. He started for his desk, only to have the breeze bring the sound to his ears again. Something was flapping in the wind. He had no idea what it was, but maybe he knew where.

With military projects coming and going from this remote area known as the Nevada Test and Training Range (NTTR), buildings were only partially retrofit for each new occupant. Why tear out good infrastructure when the next project might need it? The Information Systems or IS Building was the perfect example of this philosophy. The office area with its desks, tables, and file cabinets became the domain of the software engineers, while a maintenance bay required by a previous occupant was used for storage and overflow. But occasionally, when Omega Systems had more than four engineers on the premises, Garcia was bumped to the maintenance bay. It was just part of the natural order of things, Garcia had told himself. Prime contractor personnel always trumped subcontractors, even if the former still had trouble spelling RAM.

Garcia entered the maintenance bay and flipped on the lights. On the other side of the space, he could make out a seven-foot-deep trench, presumably used to examine the undercarriage of a vehicle— a tank, truck, personnel carrier. A railing had been placed around it as a safety precaution. Above the trench was an opening with a transparent covering that could be retracted, probably to allow exhaust fumes to be vented to the outside. Garcia knew this specific feature of the room because Col. Dempsey had chewed out the software team after it had been found open one evening. He hadn't left it open, but it made no difference. The maintenance bay had been his assigned workspace, and it had cost him two rounds at the local bar before the rest of the team stopped glaring at him.

Garcia walked to the trench and looked up. "Damn," he said aloud when he saw that his suspicions were confirmed. The vent was partially open, and something that looked like a plastic grocery bag was flapping in the breeze. He found the switch that controlled the vent and flipped it. The opening narrowed and the sound lessened, but some of the noise remained.

He turned to leave and was almost to the door when he stopped. This half measure wouldn't save him from another lecture from Dempsey or the recrimination of his coworkers. He blew a long breath between his lips, irritated because this overcontrolling colonel was getting inside his head. He returned to the vent control and cycled it—open, close, open, close. It didn't help; the bag didn't move. If anything, the noise was louder, and he swore he could feel the cool night air against the back of his now-warm neck.

Turning from the wall, he searched the room for inspiration. He was about to give up when he spotted a stepladder in a corner. He retrieved it and opened the vent as far as it would go. It wouldn't be that difficult to reach the bag from the top rung if he could place the ladder directly below the vent, but he couldn't. It would have to go next to the safety railing, and he would need to lean over the trench if this was to work. Still, he thought he could do it. And even if this bit of gymnastics failed, there was no way Dempsey could fault his effort.

As for the round of drinks for his peers if there was pushback? "Screw 'em," he muttered to himself. He wouldn't be working here much longer anyway.

He climbed to the top, his fingers just gaining purchase on the edge of the bag. But when he tugged, the bag stretched, but it didn't come free. It was stuck. He was about to pull again when motion flashed in the corner of his eye. His head snapped around, and he felt the ladder tip below his feet. Instinctively, his fingers tightened around the plastic, and for a split-second, the bag kept his torso from following his feet in the direction of the falling ladder. Then, the plastic ripped and he began to tumble. The light in the ceiling of the maintenance bay strobed in his eyes as he fell—bright, dark, bright.

His head hit the edge of the trench, and the light turned dark one last time.

THE DAY, THURSDAY, JANUARY 14

Operations Center, JACC Test Range, Nevada, 8:04 AM

She turned her deep brown eyes toward me again, the third time in the last minute. After a final glance at her two striking friends—a blonde and a redhead—and a quick word, she started across the room. Her walk was slow, poised. Her gaze was steady, her lips parted in a slight smile. She stopped before me, the light floral fragrance of her perfume traveling the mere inches now between us.

"Adriana Delgado-Roberts," she said, holding a manicured hand out to me. It was warm, soft.

"Sam Price," I replied.

A few dark curls of her hair fell at the side of her face. They were too randomly perfect to be anything but expertly arranged. She casually brushed one to the side as her brown eyes continued to take me in. Then, they narrowed.

"I heard something I find very hard to believe. Is it really true that you work here eight, ten hours a day, but you have no cell service, no Wi-Fi, and no email? And your landline only goes to the guard station we passed on the way in?"

On the inside, I was smiling. This was the question I knew was coming. But on the surface, I just nodded and said, "Almost. You can send an outgoing email, but they are monitored and attachments aren't allowed. And because they're checked, a message you send today might not get delivered until tomorrow ... or even next week. It's all part of the security measures on the JACC test range."

Next week was an exaggeration, but I couldn't resist stoking the incredulity that had brought her across the room. She paused a beat, her frown deepening. "What if you need to talk to someone? You know, you have a question that no one around here can answer?"

"I could say there's no question someone here can't answer."

She rolled her eyes in a way that could be described as cute but probably meant "cut the crap." I went on. "If you need outside help, you call up the guard station and reserve a conference room. They have two, and from there, you can call anywhere."

A look of pity overtook her features. "How can you live like this? I mean, you'd have to put your life on hold all day, every day."

"Well, I've been here less than two weeks, but that guy over there, Troy Sayers." I tipped my head in his direction. "Over two years." It was too bad she was wearing a wedding ring because, by the look on her face, Troy would have been a shoo-in for a pity date otherwise. With one final pained expression and a quiet thank you, she strolled back to her friends.

I knew what to expect when she approached because Troy and I had watched in quiet amusement as she and her group had milled around the Operations Room, searching for cell phone service and checking for Wi-Fi. After a few minutes filled with failure, they'd discuss the schedule of their outgoing flights, followed by more fiddling with their smartphones. They must have seen the strength of their cell signals fade as they left Las Vegas. The only thing I could figure was that they expected some other accommodation once they got to a military facility. Why the military would make it easier for someone to transmit classified information outside a secure area apparently wasn't a question they'd asked themselves.

Her group—all fourteen of them—were part of the staff of one U.S. senator, one U.S. representative, one state senator, and two state representatives. The U.S. representative, one Arnie Alison, was a member of the House Armed Services Committee. And all of them were from Pennsylvania. The lack of geographic diversity was explained by the fact that the company that built the JACC airframe, Air Dynamics, and the prime contractor that designed, programmed, integrated, and tested everything else, Omega Systems, were both based in Pittsburgh. So, the first live-fire demonstration of this homegrown product had brought out the state's bureaucrats in force. Now, that event was only minutes away.

With the mystery solved, the dignitaries' entourage became eerily quiet. I suppose there is only so much that can be said about who had the best return flight ... best being defined by which returned to civilization the quickest. Fortunately, their uneasy wait wasn't long, and Colonel Dempsey appeared on a large monitor mounted on the wall.

There was something surreal about seeing him on the screen since he was speaking from the Operations Center Conference Room and it was about twenty feet down the hall. Even though the name sounded impressive, the room itself was small. It would be filled to overflowing by the five politicians and three program personnel who sat there. So, video was piped to us as well as two other facilities— the JACC Maintenance and the Information Systems Buildings—so that all the people behind the scenes could be a part of this landmark event.

Col. Dempsey cleared his throat. "Distinguished members of the United States and the Pennsylvania State congresses, ladies and gentlemen, good morning. It is my honor to welcome you to the inaugural live-fire flight of the Joint Aerial Combat Capability or, as we like to call it, Jack."

I had originally doubted that the name Jack would ever make it to the field. It didn't sound menacing enough—nothing like Predator or Reaper, two other unmanned aerial systems in the U.S. military arsenal. I mean, who wants to face the Reaper in combat? But then, when I made this observation to Troy, he said, "You only say that because you don't know Jack." I thought he meant it as a pun, but after I learned more about the program, I knew better. Jack was a stone-cold aerial killer.

I didn't listen to Col. Dempsey further. My shift to mentally reviewing the day's events, however, wasn't in disrespect. If anything, it was the opposite. The man was the consummate spokesperson for a complex program. He'd give his pitch just as I'd seen him practice it three times before, nothing more, nothing less. It was five minutes composed of a welcome, a brief history of the program, and an overview of its position within the U.S. military and the Omega Systems hierarchies.

Then, it would be time for the Omega Systems Program Manager, Dr. James Marshall, to speak. At that point, I would be listening because ... well, I wondered if even he knew what was going to come out of his mouth. I'd heard five rehearsals of his fifteen-minute talk. All had gone over twenty minutes, and they'd all been different. It was as if he was searching for the right mix of bombast and hard sell.

My thoughts were pulled back to the talk by Dempsey's deep baritone. "Ladies and gentlemen, it is my pleasure to introduce the Omega Systems Program Manager for the Joint Aerial Combat Capability, Dr. James Marshall."

Marshall must have been standing shoulder-to-shoulder with the colonel because his face appeared on-screen almost before the introduction was finished. "Well, that title's a helluva mouthful. Anyone need some filibuster material?" There was a quiet intake of breath in the room where I stood, but everyone relaxed when a few chuckles came from the monitor's speakers. If the comment was acceptable to their bosses, it was okay with the entourage.

"Distinguished guests, ladies and gentlemen, I have the honor of leading the United States military into the next century of air superiority. Because make no mistake about it, tomorrow's battle for the skies will be won by the preeminence of our aircrafts' sensor systems and the tactically superior intelligence they carry onboard. Gone will be the days when war is blood and guts. Tomorrow, it will be CPUs and hydraulics, integrated circuits and memory chips acting too fast for a human to perceive, much less react. To assure our place around the table in this new world, I give you the most advanced machine intelligence ever to take to the air—Jack. Jack will take the good fight—no, make that the great fight—to our enemies."

Questions of the validity of Marshall's claims popped into my head. Could Jack's onboard processor actually beat a human's recognition reaction time? After all, computers traditionally had little success in matching the speed and accuracy of human perception. And if the scene was ....

What the hell am I thinking?

My drive to find, weigh, and assess data—some might say obsession—was misplaced when listening to Marshall. The man spoke for effect, not from fact. I knew that from our past encounters, and yet, my tendency was so deeply ingrained, it often seemed beyond my control.

I glanced over at Troy. He was supposed to be sitting down the hall with the big boys to give two minutes on the takeoff and ingress to the target area. But this morning, Marshall had asked him to step down. If Troy held any grudge against the man, however, it didn't show. Perhaps I should have taken him at his word when he said, "Who cares that my part was cut? It was boring. And besides, this gives them more time to blow shit up."

I tuned back into Marshall's talk. "And how are we doing in this race to the next generation of intelligent unmanned systems? Great … if you like looking at someone else's tail, like eating their dust, like being fourth in a three-horse race. I tell you for a fact, our capabilities in unmanned systems are changing at the speed of continental drift." There were a few chuckles in the room, sounding more nervous than amused.

"I, for one, say we must move more quickly and boldly in this game-changing technology. I, for one, say Congress must get behind this program because I, for one, don't want to have to watch as our brave young men bleed out on national television."

It was unfortunate that I couldn't see the faces of the politicians. Marshall had perfected this … well, it wasn't a carrot-and-stick routine as much as a witticism followed by emotional blackmail. But his rehearsals had been increasingly inflammatory, and this one was setting a new standard. Was it possible he was pushing them too hard?

"I was going to start the take-off sequence if you want to watch," Troy whispered at my side. His console had been pushed into the corner to make room for the crowd.

"I could, but I've seen it. How about some of our guests?"

"I don't know," he replied. But I did.

Nothing in the sequence was classified, and I was certain he'd like a little time on stage even if he wouldn't admit it. So I invited the young lady who had asked about the cell phone service if she'd like to watch. She was interested and recruited a friend. Soon, Troy had half the room looking over his shoulder. Even the smartphone withdrawal symptoms waned as talking, smiling, and a few giggles returned to the room. Troy even had Jack perform a few simple maneuvers on takeoff. That would be a serious breach of protocol in the eyes of Marshall and Dempsey if they found out, but I doubted they would.

I, too, became lost in Troy's show and almost missed the five minutes by Brandt Drury, who went by Drew. He was the Omega Systems' pilot who'd fly Jack this morning, and I wondered how he felt after Marshall had denigrated the capabilities of humans in war. And maybe the man's predictions were having an effect; Drew certainly looked grim.

After describing the two missions for the demonstration, Drew asked everyone to move to the cars waiting outside for the short drive to the Mobile Command Center. In a matter of moments, the Operations Room went from pleasant banter, amused titters, and pats on Troy's back to a windowless, eight-by-ten-foot space devoid of all life energy save the two of us. I slumped in a chair next to Troy at his console.

The Mobile Command Center where the politicians were going was a semi-truck trailer equipped with an operator console and video transmission equipment. It was parked near the geometric center of the range, close enough to see Jack in action but far enough away to be safe. The gate to the range was directly to the west—a fact the VIP's entourage undoubtedly appreciated. The placement made for a quick getaway to the airport.

After about twenty minutes, the monitor in the Operations Room came back to life. The camera in the Mobile Command Center had a wide-angle lens, giving the trailer a slightly curved appearance on our monitor. Drew sat in the middle of the picture with the pilot's console in front of him and the dignitaries standing behind. Their position would allow them to watch the console's displays as well as the target area through a large, reinforced window set in the south wall of the trailer. Marshall and Dempsey were on either flank, with the staff members probably standing outside. Marshall held a microphone so that he could narrate the scenarios for those watching online.

Troy set his console to reflect what Drew was seeing. We sat in silence, my gaze tracking between the monitor showing the activities in the van and the console's display. I knew Troy would want to watch because if anything went wrong, everyone would be called on the carpet, sooner or later, to explain what he or she could have done better. But as the action unfolded, I saw no slipups. In fact, it seemed like the best sequences from all the rehearsals had somehow been pieced together for this final show.

When it was over, no one spoke, and I was having a difficult time reading the dignitaries' faces. Maybe they were in awe ... or perhaps stunned was closer. Eventually, one person—the member of the House Armed Services Committee, if I had the players right—turned to Col. Dempsey. Vaguely, I heard, "May I have a word?" Marshall laid the microphone on the console, and he and the colonel escorted the congressman to the far end of the trailer. Everyone else except Drew went outside.

"That's strange," I said mostly to myself.

"What?"

I glanced at Troy. "That no one else stayed for the discussion. It's like they know what's going to happen." Troy tilted his head, empty hands held out in front in a don't-have-a-clue gesture.

We turned back to the monitor. The congressman was speaking; I could see his lips moving but heard nothing. Then, it was Marshall's turn and something came through the speakers, but it sounded more like machine-gun fire than conversation—sharp, loud, explosive. His face was red. One minute he was holding his hands wide to the sides, the next he was pointing at the ceiling. Dempsey, on the other hand, hung his head and stood in silence. I'd never seen him in any poise other than head high, back ramrod straight. This stance was almost as disquieting as Marshall's rant.

Drew was still seated at the console, manipulating Jack's controls. It was, however, easy to tell he was distracted by the verbal skirmish in the back of the trailer; his eyes kept wandering to the group. He stood up, but Dempsey saw him and came over. He guided Drew to the other end of the trailer where they stood with their backs to us, the colonel's hand on the pilot's shoulder.

"You think they're killing the program?" asked Troy.

"I'm not sure," I replied, not wanting to upset him with my surmises that almost universally ran in that direction.

"We showed too much, too fast," he said. "Marshall pushed for that second mission, even though everyone else thought it was over-the-top. Everyone except Col. Dempsey and he was okay with it." Troy paused. "I have to admit, that scenario freaks me out a bit."

A look at the pained expression on Troy's face and I forced a smile to mine. "It's a powerful demonstration. My stomach was in a knot the first time I saw it. Still is. But this isn't over, not by a mile. A lot of people in the Department of Defense and Congress will have a say before the program is terminated."

Technically, what I had said was correct. Practically, however, it was a half-truth at best. This group of legislators couldn't end the program by themselves. Generally, that took time, debates, and votes. But what they could do is put the program in such a bad light that the outcome of all that political give-and-take was a foregone conclusion. After all, if the state's politicians wouldn't stand behind JACC, few others would.

"Yeah, maybe," said Troy slowly. He sighed.

The silence caught my attention as the din of indecipherable verbal shots from Marshall ended. Dempsey left Drew's side to join Marshall and the congressman. But as Dempsey started to talk to the politician, Marshall left to speak with Drew. It was as if they had exchanged roles in whatever drama was being played out.

The four stayed in this configuration for about three minutes—Drew and Marshall huddled at one end of the trailer with their backs to us, Dempsey and the politician in profile on the other end.

Dempsey spoke and the congressman nodded, glancing down at his shoes for an instant. The politician spoke and the colonel stood motionless, staring steadily into the man's face. The pattern repeated. In the absence of words, the picture gave the impression of a father, Dempsey, lecturing his son, the congressman, on the facts of life.

Without warning, both discussions ended. Marshall left the trailer first, followed a few moments later by the congressman. Drew sat back down at his console, his fingers starting to fly over the keyboard. Dempsey said something to him before reaching over to flip a switch on the video equipment. Our monitor went black.

We sat in silence a few more moments while I tried in vain to think of another positive spin on what we'd witnessed. Finally, Troy said, "I'm going to move everything back where it belongs."

"I'll help." We each took a chair and started rolling them into place.

"You gonna come out drinking tonight? Based on the demo alone, I'd say it'd be a celebration. But with that shout-out later, it might turn into a bitching session."

"Sure. I'll see if Jill wants to come along, although she may not. We both have to pack tonight."

"Just throw your junk in a bag and bring her along," Troy replied, and we continued our labors in silence.

As it often did when I had a moment, my mind wandered back to Nicole Veles, a woman I was still getting used to calling my girlfriend. The image of her brought a smile to my face. I glanced at Troy, knowing he'd think I'd lost it if he saw me grinning at nothing, but he was focused elsewhere. Then, I thought about all the phone calls and emails we'd shared over the last few weeks, and I almost laughed aloud. My words were all so far from anything like a love letter. But that, too, was changing.

I broke from my reverie. Troy had turned his console off so we could move it. I grabbed one end, then asked, "You think there's some way we could find out what was going on there at the end? I'm not sure I can wait until tonight."

"I'm not waiting," replied Troy. "I'm just giving Drew a few more minutes to get Jack squared away before I call him."

Troy plugged in his console and started powering it up. I went to get another chair when I heard, "What the heck is going on?"

I hurried back to look over his shoulder. "That's a threat map, with the Mobile Command Center as a high-value target," I said.

"No shit," said Troy. "But what I can't figure ...." He didn't finish as the symbol for a missile appeared, its flyout ending seconds later at the Mobile Command Center. Both disappeared from the display as the rumble of an explosion came through the walls.

"What the hell!" yelled Troy.

"Can you switch to video? Maybe we can get a look?"

"I can't control Jack. We're getting this off a general system feed." Troy started panning and zooming the threat map, then said, "Every building on the range is classified as hostile based on their electronic emissions. But those signals are ours. Jack's coming after us." He sat staring for a moment, shaking his head. "I'm calling the guard station."

I studied the search-and-destroy route plotted across the test range as he got up to use the phone on the other side of the room. "Okay, but don't take too long," I said after finishing a few quick calculations. "Jack will be at its first target, which looks like some people working on the road, in about twelve minutes. I don't think they want to be there when he arrives."

"You and me both, brother," Troy said as he picked up the phone to make his call. "When does Jack get here?" he called over his shoulder.

"About forty minutes." I pulled a chair from the wall and fell into it, staring in disbelief at the display before me.

How the hell had I gotten myself into this mess?

TWENTY-EIGHT DAYS EARLIER, THURSDAY, DECEMBER 17

Ruger-Phillips Building, St. Louis, Missouri, 10:18 AM

Christmas was still a week away, but I'd received an early present. I'd been on what I affectionately called "house arrest" for over three months while the government disentangled the events surrounding my last project. What a disaster it had been. I still had nightmares. But my company, Ruger-Phillips, and my boss, Ken Waters, had stood by me. They put me on some in-house research projects to keep me out of the limelight. On the positive side, the time had given me a chance to work with a few of our more established scientists and get some publications for my resume. But on the negative, I was still saddled with closing out the last project, and this state of limbo had the side effect of keeping Nicole and me apart.

Just about an hour earlier, however, everything had changed. We officially signed off on the project. Soon, I'd have jobs to call my own. And more important personally, closing that window opened the door between Nicole and me. The possibility that our connection might warrant more than a handshake, which was all we had shared so far, was my unexpected, early gift. I was walking on clouds.

Then, in an overlooked report on the last project, I'd discovered the sentence, "R.J. was a 27-year-old male who completed 87 hours of training." That training was what had turned a man into a maniacal serial killer, and I had visions of the nightmare recurring. I called the technology's developer. Fortunately, R.J. was known, was being treated, and had shown no side effects. A morning that had been one heck of an emotional rollercoaster now leveled out, making it feel like just another day at the office. It was time to get back to work, so I headed off to see Ken about my next assignment.

Jobs at Ruger-Phillips were just about equally split between our design, research, and development contracts and validating the work of others, generally known as independent verification and validation. My group focused on training, while I represented a relatively new niche within it—the application of cognitive science to improve learning and memory. So where some of my colleagues could design and test the motion base for a multi-million-dollar aircraft simulator, I could tell them how much movement was necessary for the brain (the vestibular system) and the body (proprioceptors) to sense position and acceleration. Or, where some of my engineering brethren could develop high resolution, three-dimensional models for practicing maintenance skills, I could specify the fundamental, visual properties of these displays to make the experience feel real.

At least, that is what I told them I could do, once cognitive psychology and neuroscience had matured sufficiently. In the meantime, I was making my best guess, testing the results, and tweaking the system until we got it right. And I loved the work—all those data. Strangely to me, even the engineers who worked with numbers all day didn't understand the thrill of forcing a particularly recalcitrant dataset to give up its secrets to statistical analysis. And in some small way—microscopic, if I was being truthful to myself—

I hoped my applied research might further cognitive science because the untapped potential of the field was immense.

As I approached Ken's office, I heard French coming from what had to be a foreign language learning class. So when I reached his open door, I said, "Bonjour."

"What?" Ken said, as his head jerked up. I wasn't sure if my pronunciation was that bad or if he hadn't covered simple greetings yet. "Oh. Hi, Doc. I was just trying to learn a little French before we go there next spring."

"Sounds like a great trip. Just be sure to master the phrase, 'Je ne comprends pas.' It saved me any number of times."

"Okay," he said slowly, perhaps wondering if I had just given him a phrase that would save his bacon or get him slapped in the face. He put the tablet with the language class into his briefcase.

"I just called and left you a message. Is there any chance you can make an emergency business trip to Nevada? It would be right after the first of the year. The guy that was supposed to go broke a leg skiing, and we can't reschedule."

My just-another-day-at-the-office mood disappeared to be replaced by mixed feelings. My ambivalence wasn't because of the location or the timing. It was because on the love-it-to-loath-it continuum for business travel, I wasn't sure where I fell. People at Ruger-Phillips were about equally split, and so far, I'd only been as far afield as the University of Illinois for an afternoon visit with a professor. And then, in a totally unprofessional vein, I wondered how this might affect my chances with Nicole.

"Okay," I said slowly. "How long does this project last?"

"It's short-term. Two months."

Two months? Would Nicole even remember me? Down I went in my emotional rollercoaster, only to rebound considerably with Ken's next words. "Two weeks of it would be on-site and the rest here." That would work.

Ken turned to his computer monitor. "Let me back up and tell you what I know because I'm still learning about this job, too. It involves reviewing some of the training for a program called the Joint Aerial Combat Capability program or JACC. Are you familiar with it?"

"Not really," I admitted.

"That's understandable since it's still in research and development. It's the next variant unmanned aerial system."

"Doesn't combat in those program names usually mean the system has offensive capabilities rather than flying only reconnaissance?"

"Correct," replied Ken. "The primary players on the program are Dr. James Marshall at Omega Systems, Inc., and Lieutenant Colonel Raymond Dempsey on the government side. Our contract is from the JACC office, and the colonel is your Contracting Office Technical Representative, which means ...."

"Col. Dempsey's my boss, push comes to shove," I said, finishing Ken's thought.

"Exactly. Not to make a bad pun at the expense of another Ruger-Phillips employee, but I think you covering this job is a lucky break for the company." I groaned despite his warning. He continued unperturbed. "JACC involves some state-of-the-art artificial intelligence, and as I understand it, Col. Dempsey has some background there, too. Your education will be a plus."

Ken was right. I did have some background in AI. One could hardly study cognitive psychology and not get some exposure, but I had well over the minimum. The idea of creating a machine that thought like a human was intriguing to me, and so I had enrolled in almost every available course.

One, for example, was a class on human problem solving. It described how experts came to recognize patterns and remember specific responses to them. They did this rather than trying to come up with every possible action and figure out its result, an approach that would exhaust their mental capacities in short order. Chess masters were among the first studied, and this ability to learn patterns and responses provided a ready explanation for how they were able to play lightning chess. Later, the same capability was identified in experts across a great number of fields.

Once the psychology in these classes had been covered, they usually provided some rudimentary introduction to how AI had responded. For problem-solving, computer scientists had developed a programming language that could represent pattern-response expertise. What I didn't know, however, was what lay beyond these basic introductions to the AI side? And equally unclear, how did coming at AI from psychology skew what I had learned?

These questions were disquieting, but I didn't find them daunting. Quite the contrary, they were stimulating. They were something that could occupy the time I might have spent on questions such as whether my next-door neighbor should put his house up for sale in the winter or what toilet paper I should buy. I'd be thinking about something. Why not something both challenging and job-related?

"The downside of you stepping into this project," said Ken, "is that the individual who was supposed to go had two months to get up to speed. He also had two meetings with the developer of the training, Omega Systems. You have a week and Omega Systems isn't available. But ...."

Ken paused checking his computer, while I thought, thank goodness there is a "but" to Ken's disclaimer.

"But to help you get up to speed, I've scheduled a meeting with Dr. Mark Dillon at 1:30 next Tuesday. He's from Air Dynamics. They build the aircraft. He's an expert in automatic target recognition, which I guess is part of the AI?"

"Probably." I wasn't certain either.

"Anyway, ATR is supposed to be one of the major strengths of JACC." Ken paused, his brow wrinkling. "It seems a little odd to me that Air Dynamics builds the airframe and puts all this target recognition smarts in it, but the prime contract goes to Omega Systems?"

"I don't know for sure," I admitted, "but one of the major complaints about expert systems, a subfield of AI, is that these pieces of software don't explain themselves well. It's a 'trust-me' from a computer at a time when most people don't. If the target recognition software is like that and the JACC crew has to use it, maybe Omega Systems has techniques that can make the AI more understandable."

"And that's why you're the right person for this job," said Ken.

What Ken didn't recognize, however, was that I could have come up with a dozen more, equally plausible reasons for Omega Systems having the lead. What I had done, rather than list them, was to suggest what I hoped was true because it was an important issue.

There was research on the problem, of course. But you only needed to walk through any office environment using "smart" software and listen to the employees denigrate the lineage of everyone connected with the product to know we hadn't solved it. All too often, the applications that were supposed to save time made the job harder. They interrupted the human by offering suggestions that were neither requested nor wanted. Or worse, they gave advice or made changes that were flat out wrong. I couldn't count the number of times a computer had auto-corrected one of my text documents only to introduce errors that ranged from funny to mortifying.

But while illustrative, my experiences with overzealous, word-processing applications or too-helpful spreadsheet programs were rather trivial compared to what the users of the JACC software would face. In a battle, the advice from JACC's AI had to be precise, accurate, and readily actionable because, as the saying goes, he who hesitates is lost. So, the possibility that Omega Systems had pioneered methods of human-intelligent machine collaboration was exciting. And the chance that I would help configure the training that implemented it was even more so. It was a chance to tackle the question of how one trains a human to collaborate seamlessly with a smart machine on a complex, rapidly changing problem. Few had even asked that question, much less studied it.

"Dr. Dillon won't be able to give you precise information on the aircraft's capabilities, its sensors, or weapons," continued Ken. "That information is classified, and we're still getting you cleared onto the program, but he can give you some idea. Think of it as Unmanned Aerial Systems 101."

"That should work. And you said I'd be traveling after the first of the year?"

"Correct. JACC is being tested on one of the ranges that makes up the Nevada Test and Training Range near Nellis Air Force Base. You start on Monday, January 3. So, with our holiday calendar, you'll have six days to prepare—three days next week and three days the week after. You travel on January 2."

Giving me plenty of time to go out with Nicole.

My completely unprofessional stream of thought had returned, and I pushed it to the back of my mind. "Sounds like a plan."

"Good. On Thursday of the second week, the program will be running a live-fire demonstration for some congressional dignitaries. Since you fly out on Friday, you'll need to brief Dr. Marshall and Col. Dempsey on your findings on Wednesday. No one will be expecting a finished product, just your initial thoughts."

"So, when I return to the office, I'll have another month to complete the project?"

"Correct. The last month is for analysis and report writing. If anything looks amiss, we'll propose an amendment to the contract for the additional work. Anything else?"

"Not that I can think of."

I stood and left his office, as Ken said, "Good luck."

With the possibility of a trailblazing project and time to ask Nicole for a date, life was good. I was once again at a peak on my emotional rollercoaster ride.

Guard Station, JACC Test Range, Nevada, 1:59 PM

Lt. Col. Dempsey parked and entered the JACC Test Range Guard Station. After being directed to Conference Room One, he sat at the table and dialed one of just two phones on the test range with a connection to the outside world. The number he knew from memory. It was his boss's, Colonel Charles "Chuck" Newberry.

Newberry was a "full-bird colonel" in the Air Combat Command based at Langley-Eustis, Virginia. When Jack transitioned from research and development to initial production in a few months, the Air Combat Command would be the receiving organization. Newberry was already on the job, monitoring him and the program's progress.

After six rings with no answer, Dempsey hung up and scowled at the phone. His boss would have someone to answer if he couldn't. If no one was answering, it was at his direction. Dempsey slowly shook his head.

The two men had a history that went back years, and much of it was positive. When Dempsey joined the Air Force, Newberry, six years his senior, had taken him under his wing, giving him career advice. Dempsey had valued the friendship and had usually followed Newberry's counsel. At least he had until about two years ago.

At that time, Newberry had seen no value in a stateside desk job. Rather, he had strongly encouraged his protégé to take an overseas assignment, preferably one involving active operations. Newberry argued that such a move would position him for promotion and greater pay. Dempsey, however, had other ideas. He didn't want to reenlist, higher rank or not. He wanted out.

Dempsey dialed his boss again. Still, no answer. The message, though not spoken, was becoming clear. He leaned back in his chair and let his mind wander.

It had been a little over two years since his wife had left him. It wasn't another man. She had left for a different, more stable life. His decision to leave the Air Force, which had come at the same time, wasn't, however, a last-ditch effort to win her back. Too much had happened for them to get back together. And yet, his leaving the military was due to her because as she walked out of their marriage, he'd gotten a glimpse of himself. Settling for less had become a habit, a way of life that he had hardly noticed until he'd seen it in her eyes. At that moment, he knew his once clear vision of the future was now a mere phantom of a nearly forgotten dream.

By his calculations, however, it wasn't too late. Life outside the Air Force could restore him to the path he desired if he was willing to take some bold steps. So, he'd weighed all the options. He'd evaluated the maturity and capability of many different defense programs. He studied their technologies. JACC was the perfect springboard for his ambitions.

These deliberations, of course, were completed in private, far from the prying eyes and rock-solid beliefs of Newberry. Eventually, of course, his request for posting to JACC had to be submitted, and this was when the schism between these friends first appeared. Newberry was shocked but tried reasoning. When that didn't work, the discussion became more heated. Phrases such as "JACC is career suicide" and "you're a damn fool" had been uttered. Now, those phrases, accompanied by many others more biting, had been repeated more times than Dempsey could count.

But despite both considered arguments and venomous tirades, Dempsey hadn't changed his position. Rather, he'd calmly declared his support for the program and the technology that he would bring to fruition. And until today, he thought this approach was working.

The weekly status calls had become more courteous, although in an overly formal way. "Chuck" had become "Colonel Newberry"; reports had to be printed and mailed, even though the process took longer; his boss required published agendas before every meeting. But until today, Newberry had always been available for a planned call.

Dempsey tried a third time with the same result.

He shrugged, although there was no one in the room to see the gesture. Perhaps there was a reason no one was answering the phone other than the obvious power play it seemed. But whatever the explanation, Dempsey knew he should get used to the silence because when he left the Air Force, the voice of his old friend would be gone forever. That void would be joined by many others—old friends, acquaintances, people he'd never met—who wouldn't understand the road he had taken.

"To hell with them," he muttered to himself, then looked around the room to make sure he didn't have an audience.

Dempsey put the matter out of his mind. He jotted a few notes about the week's activities in an email and sent it. And then, after thinking he "might have better luck next time," he amended the thought. In fact, no answer was the best possible outcome until his time on JACC was complete. And that last day, he knew, was nearly upon him.

Doc's Apartment, St. Louis, Missouri, 6:43 PM

Earlier in the day, I'd decided that 7:00 would be the perfect time to call Nicole. It was early enough that she would be awake but late enough that she should be finished with dinner. But as the clock hit 6:43, I decided that was close enough.

Nicole was a biomedical engineer, and I had met her when she consulted on my first project at Ruger-Phillips in early May. Her involvement in that job had been minimal, and somehow, her presence had escaped my attention for most of the single day she was there. First-job jitters were my guess. But at the end of the day when she summarized her findings, it was like my eyes finally connected with my brain and I was interested. I even knew why. Nicole was incredibly cute.

I understood other men's attraction to the tall, slender models or the statuesque beauties, but something about the direct, wide-eyed innocence of cuteness was my Achilles' heel. And Nicole was the embodiment of all I considered cute. She was about 5 feet, 6 inches tall, with shoulder-length, light-brown hair, and large, hazel eyes. Her eyes, in particular, gave her a look of youthful innocence and naivete. I couldn't imagine an appearance affecting me more at a very basic, visceral level.

While her physical appearance was a powerful initial draw, my transition from interested to captivated followed quickly as I got to know her. Within moments of starting her summary of the project, I knew she was smart. Biomedical concepts that I barely understood rolled off her tongue like they were her best friends. Later, in less formal settings, I marveled at the diversity of her interests, some of which seemed psychologically incompatible to me. As an engineer, she was precise and analytic, but she also had an artistic side that exuded freedom of expression. The bookshelf at her apartment displayed works ranging from nanoscale technologies to light romantic novels. She entertained a diversity of thought, moving from topic to topic without warning. One minute, she was talking about better ways to queue for checkout at the grocery store. The next, she was discussing the colonization of Mars. And then, there were her superstitions. Could finding one or two pennies be good luck, while finding four or more doom your day? Well, she thought so.

So, yes, I was befuddled by Nicole in nearly equal portion to my attraction, producing a concern that the mental flexibility needed to know her was outside my capacity. I was, after all, the guy who couldn't leave an issue until all the data had been gathered, categorized, sorted, weighed, and combined.

That issue, however, was for the future because, in fact, I didn't know Nicole beyond this accounting of my confusion. Over eight months, we had shared dinner twice, lunch three times, had sat in the same working meetings for perhaps 60 hours, and that was it. Why had we had so little interaction over so long when admittedly, I wanted much more? Just about every cliché fit. It was poor timing; it was missed opportunities; it was bad luck.

But I hoped that was all about to change as she answered her phone on the second ring.

"Hi, Sam."

Before calling, I had wondered if she would start to use my nickname, Doc. Nearly everyone did. That mystery, however, didn't last beyond her greeting. But at least my name and number were programmed in her phone.

"Nice of you to call," she said. "I just walked in the door. I've been out doing some last-minute Christmas shopping."

I didn't want to break it to her, but with Christmas still a week away, few people would call what she had just done "last minute." It was, however, part of her passion for organization; I'd seen that side of her, too.

"I'm done, but then, my list is pretty short," I replied. "My brothers and I stopped exchanging gifts a few years ago, so I only have to find something for my mom and dad."

"Ah, I somewhat envy you. Every member of my family gets something for everyone else. That's six people, each bringing five presents. And then, there are aunts, uncles, and cousins. But I also have to admit that on Christmas morning, I love it when the floor gets lost in a layer of discarded wrapping paper and bows. It's a family thing. And this year, we're doing it up right. When we were kids, my parents used to take us to a ski area in Colorado for Christmas. This year, we're all going back and staying ten days from Christmas Eve until after New Year's Day."

"Sounds like fun," I replied. "Before you get out of town, what do you think about going on a hike?"

"You remembered."

"That you listed hiking second, after biking, when we talked about favorite pastimes a few months ago? Yeah, I remembered. And Saturday looks good—maybe a bit cool in the upper 30s, but sunny. And the best part ...."

"No bugs," she said before I could. "Yeah, I'm not much of a summer hiker because of them. Biking's better. I can run away from the mosquitoes on a bike. You have any thoughts about where?"

"Unless you're bored with the place, I thought we could go to Hawn State Park. It's a bit of a drive, but the views from the cliffs are worth it."

"Bored?" she said. "Just the opposite. I've been planning to go there, but I keep making excuses and ending up at one of the city parks. Your company will make the drive down there go fast."

It was the simplest of comments, not even much of a compliment, but it made me smile. And it set the tone for the rest of the call, which focused on the details that normally would seem routine but now felt fresh and new—how far would we go; what was the footing like; preferred snacks; maybe a place to stop for dinner on the way home. It felt great to finally have plans with Nicole that had absolutely nothing to do with my job and too soon, our call was over.

THE DAY, THURSDAY, JANUARY 14

Operations Center, JACC Test Range, Nevada, 9:34 AM

Troy slammed the phone down. "They don't know squat at the guard station."

"Nothing?" I asked, as Troy hurried over but didn't sit.

"Not unless you consider 'keep your head down' helpful." Troy rubbed the back of his neck with a hand. "The good news is that Dempsey and Marshall rode out to the guard station with the big shots. But Drew ...." He slowly shook his head.

"Still at the mobile command center?"

"Yeah. I know he wasn't your favorite person but still."

"I didn't dislike him enough to want him dead," I said in a near whisper, my gaze dropping to the console's keyboard. I looked back at Troy. "Did they know what was going on between Marshall, the colonel, and that congressman after the demo?"

"Something about a stop-work that was already planned, but the VIPs wanted to extend it. Best I can tell, after that it became a shouting match about why and how long." He paused a beat. "The guard station has one of their phones tied up with Maintenance, while Marshall is using the other to talk to Information Systems. He's hoping they can take control of Jack from there. The guards tried to phone the construction crew, but no dice. So, they wanted us to try. You mind calling?"

"They have a phone?" I asked in surprise.

Troy's head was shaking even before I finished the question. "No, but there are emergency landlines located around the range. They're mounted on posts in weatherproof boxes with ringers you can hear a football field away."

"Okay, yeah. I've seen a few of those. I didn't know what they were."

"The number of the closest one is 703." Troy stood staring at me a moment until he recognized my confusion. "I was thinking you could call. After all, they're not going to believe anything I say."

"Oh, right," I said as the light bulb came on. "So, besides the obvious—we're under attack—what should I tell them?"

"Well, this is pretty lame, but Jack has reclassified them as 'unknown.' So, Marshall thinks they'll be okay if they just drive slowly or walk out to the gate. They just have to avoid doing anything stupid, like driving over here and becoming guilty by association."

"Okay. Got it." I stood and started toward the phone as Troy sat.

"Doc?" I turned around. "You could just tell them to jump in their trucks and make a run for it. We could have Jack out of missiles before he ever gets here." Troy tried to suppress his grin but failed.

I chuckled. "Naw, I figured some of them would have rifles. I was going to suggest they just shoot Jack out of the sky for us."

"Yeah, that should do it."

I dialed and let the phone ring—five times, ten times, fifteen times. Finally, someone answered.

"Yes." He didn't sound like he appreciated the interruption.

"This is Dr. Sam Price." I rarely introduced myself as a Ph.D., but I hoped the title might increase the chance that the man would heed my warning. "I'm calling from the Operations Center. Jack is out of control. He's hunting down everyone on the test range. He's already taken out the Mobile Command Center, and we think the pilot, Drew, may have been killed in the attack."

"What?" The man's voice reflected confusion, rather than alarm. But then again, this news was a lot to process.

"I said, everyone on the test range is being hunted. I called to warn you."

"You said you're at the Operations Center?"

"That's right."

"Then tell Troy he's pretty funny, but we gotta get back to work." The line went dead.

"He hung up on me," I called across the room, my voice filled with the disbelief that I felt. Troy just shook his head slowly, looking down at his desk.

"I'm going to call back and let it ring. They'll have to pick up eventually."

"All you can do," Troy said.

After dialing and putting the phone on speaker, I propped my elbows on the desktop and dropped my head into my hands. What could I say to get their attention? And then, a thought flashed into my mind that was so incongruous to my situation that I couldn't help shaking my head in wonder.

What if I never get to know Nicole?

TWENTY–SEVEN DAYS EARLIER, FRIDAY, DECEMBER 18

Doc's Apartment, St. Louis, Missouri, 2:22 PM

Seeing Nicole's name on my cell phone, I answered the call with, "You're not going to let a few flurries scare you off, are you?"

We had made the date to go on a hike less than a day ago, but in those twenty hours or so, the forecast had deteriorated significantly. It now called for light snow and temperatures in the lower 30s. Of course, that news wasn't keeping me from using my afternoon off to get ready.

"No, a dusting of snow's no problem." With that one sentence, however, I could hear the uncertainty in her voice.

"What's wrong?"

She released a long sigh, her breath catching in her throat. Whatever the problem was, it was more than uncertainty. "My mom called. My aunt had a heart attack earlier today. Her condition is serious. Sam, I'm leaving for Kansas City in about an hour."

I felt a little embarrassed about my earlier teasing, even though there was no way I could have known. "I'm so sorry. I hope she'll be all right."

"Me, too. And, Sam, thanks for understanding. Maybe I'll be back before Christmas, but if not, I can't imagine we're going on that ski trip with my aunt in the hospital. I should be back in St. Louis soon and we can go on that hike."

"It's a date ... whenever it is. I'll let you go, so you can get back to packing."

"Thanks, Sam. Bye."

I looked around my kitchen at the empty water bottles and snacks scattered across the counter. "What the heck," I muttered to myself and started putting everything in my daypack. No reason I shouldn't go.

Guard Station, JACC Test Range, Nevada, 2:58 PM

Dr. Jim Marshall was sitting in the same conference room, glaring at the same phone that Col. Dempsey had used the day before. The scowl that was frozen on his face made it clear he was unhappy.

Seated with him were three Omega Systems software engineers. They weren't the source of his displeasure. In fact, once he had been one of them, one of the best and brightest. But that was a long time ago, and now, they were just so much background noise. They were an ignorable means to an end. For their part, the software engineers seemed to feel the same about him. They were talking animatedly about some obscure, floating-point calculation as if he wasn't in the room.

Marshall wasn't looking forward to the content of the phone call. Undoubtedly, the topics of conversation would be as mind-numbingly boring as the floating-point calculation discussion. But that wasn't the primary cause of his annoyance either. He could bear a lot of bickering over these trifles because, in the aggregate, they shaped a piece of software of unparalleled capability and incredible worth.

The reason for his aggravation was the person who would soon be on the other end of the line, Don Williams, the JACC Chief Software Engineer. Williams was brilliant; there was no doubt about that. The man had taken all the inputs and outputs from the Air Dynamics airframe—performance data, sensor information, position and dynamics, communications—and had designed the framework to integrate them. His document created what would become a working—almost living—entity that was Jack. And then as his paper design transitioned to bits and bytes, Williams had maintained a working knowledge of its millions of lines of code. He'd even created some of them. He was an extraordinary individual.

Unfortunately, in Marshall's mind, the man's genius in software design and development was more than offset by his lack of vision for the future of warfare. Given a tough choice on the battlefield, Williams much too frequently opted for human intervention. He would leave Jack hovering in the line of fire while human operators debated the appropriate response. Simply put, Williams had no appreciation for the speed of battle and the need for decisiveness.

So, again today, he was about to clash with Williams so that Jack would have a fighting chance when the real shooting started. The conference room phone rang, and Marshall answered, "Hello."

While to the outside observer the greeting might seem inappropriately informal, the program used it as a simple, everyday security precaution. By randomly dialing the exchange of a military installation, program rosters could be pieced together by unfriendly intelligence services if people answered, "This is Dr. Jim Marshall, JACC. How may I help you?" A simple "hello" could avoid such a possibility.

"Hi, Jim. It's Don and two members of my software team. Thanks for taking some time today to discuss these parameter updates."

"No problem, Don. There's three more of your guys here."

All of the engineers identified themselves, followed by a few minutes of small talk. Marshall disliked this part of the calls even more than the business—was the fact that it was colder in Pittsburgh than Nevada worth talking about every week? But he played along, all in the name of maintaining an open work environment.

"Today, we're going to look at the algorithm that controls the inheritance of threat level due to association with known threats," said Williams after the pleasantries were completed. "The current algorithm increases the level of threat for an unknown target according to the duration of contact with a known threat and according to the number and combined threat level in the group. The basic idea is that ...."

Marshall's attention was already starting to wander. Early in the program, he had debated these details with Williams *ad nauseam*. After what seemed liked hours of Williams adding and subtracting 0.01 to a weighting factor, several of the calls had ended with Marshall shouting something like, "Just how many freaking hours does it take you to order a cup of coffee in the morning?" Then, he'd slam the phone down.

But all his outbursts gained him was a less cooperative chief software engineer. Williams could be quite obstinate when pushed. Then, about a year and a half ago, Marshall discovered that Williams could be manipulated.

The insight had come one day when Marshall was arguing that Jack should be given greater latitude over its self-defense, one of his common themes. With its bursts of speed and sudden changes in direction, a human would hit it only by chance. Concessions from Williams, however, were coming slowly, if at all. Then, one member of his team asked, "How long would a boxer last if he had to ask the corner if he could duck a punch?" Surprisingly, Williams capitulated relatively quickly after that and Marshall saw his opening.

Within a week, he had found an individual on the software team who shared his way of thinking. Later, this person converted a second engineer. Now, for his part, Marshall only needed to sit quietly, wait for Williams to become excessively conservative, and then offer a mildly-worded opinion to the contrary. His two disciples inside the group had been told to use their judgment on these issues and support the alternative only when they believed it was the better option. And maybe they did. But so far, their opinions had been identical to his.

From his occasional sampling of today's discussion, Marshall had picked up on the fact that Williams was about to hamstring Jack again. He was suggesting that the threat level shouldn't be changed based on where a target had been.

"Are you sure we can't deduce anything about threat from location?" asked Marshall, trying to sound uncertain about his position.

Silence followed. Marshall wasn't sure if Williams was actually thinking about the comment or if he just wanted to give that appearance. He'd never know because right on cue, one of his cohorts in the software group ventured an observation. "So, if there are cars parked outside a McDonalds, who would you expect the occupants to be other than customers or workers?"

For reasons Marshall couldn't fathom, Williams preferred these everyday analogies. And he hadn't even had to instruct his compatriots in their use; they seemed to know that already. The software engineer continued his thought. "So, is it that much different to conclude that vehicles parked outside a known military facility are probably driven by military personnel, all other factors being equal?" A few minutes later, Williams conceded the point.

The call ended after another half-hour without Marshall needing to exert his invisible influence again. Progress had been made, and it happened without veiled threats or muted profanity. Marshall hung up from the call, wondering how it could be so easy to manipulate someone who was otherwise so brilliant.

Operations Center, JACC Test Range, Nevada, 3:11 PM

Col. Dempsey was seated behind the desk in his closed office reviewing the personnel time reports he'd received from Marshall. Managing the day-to-day activities of Omega Systems people wasn't his job; that responsibility belonged to the civilian program manager. But in his current situation, poised to make the leap from the military to his life after, Dempsey needed everything on JACC to run smoothly. He'd already weathered one storm when the subcontracted software engineer, Garcia, died on the range. Fortunately, the military police had found nothing suspicious and eventually ruled it an accident, but when he replayed it in his mind, he'd seen the end to his plan much too frequently. The whole thing was too damn close.

After studying the first dozen or so reports, it was clear to Dempsey that there were gaps in the work hours of some of the Omega Systems people. Mostly the missing time was just an hour or two during a day that was otherwise fully covered. It was probably innocent, but it was careless. And that attitude would have come from Marshall. He wouldn't push his team for greater diligence because that took time—time that he wanted for proselytizing his vision for unmanned systems.

But reasons less innocent than indifference were also on the table. With program logistics under his control, Marshall could be involved in any number of illegal activities—drugs, moving stolen goods, human trafficking. What JACC vehicles and personnel did off the range was recorded, but it wouldn't be difficult for them to pick up a little extra cargo, make a slight, unplanned detour. And some of the missing personnel times corresponded to vehicles being off-range.

The correlation wasn't perfect, but it was good enough to be troubling.

He leaned back in his chair, a sardonic smile coming to his face. "Glad I'm past timesheets," he muttered to himself. If he wasn't, his pattern of absences would raise red flags in just about anyone's mind. Most of the time he was gone were half-days or less, and he made up for it in the evenings. He wasn't shortchanging the Air Force, but the holes in his work record were unusual for a desk job.

He glanced at the reports again. He'd have to get Marshall to sit down and go through this mess. Of course, he'd been trying to do that for weeks, but the program manager always had an excuse. This delaying tactic, if that was what it was, had to stop. As he reached for the phone, it rang with an incoming call.

"Hello." Even though this line didn't reach beyond the guard station, it was easier to maintain the habit of a simple greeting.

"Colonel, Guard Allen Lewis at the JACC range entry gate. I have a request from Col. Newberry for a teleconference at 3:30."

Dempsey glanced at his watch. As the gate was only about a ten-minute drive, the timing was fine. Perhaps Newberry was calling to apologize for being a no-show for their planned call yesterday, although Dempsey strongly doubted that was the reason. "Sure. Tell him I'll be there."

Dempsey cleared his desk, packed a few papers he wanted to review at home this evening, and left.

* * *

"Afternoon, Allen," Dempsey said when he entered the guard station. "What room do you have me in?"

"Two, sir."

Dempsey seated himself and placed the call. It was answered on the second ring.

"Col. Chuck Newberry, Air Combat Command," said the man on the other end of the line. Long gone were the days when he would have answered the phone with, 'Hi, Ray,' even though he knew quite well who was calling at this precise time using this exact exchange. At least Newberry didn't have someone else answer the phone, only so that person could put him on hold for a five- or ten-minute wait. That had happened too often for Dempsey to believe it was just his boss's hectic world.

"Hello, Colonel. Ray Dempsey here, calling as requested."

"Glad I caught you before the end of your day," said Newberry.

The snub—that Dempsey's day ended at the same time as Newberry's even though he was three time zones later—was subtler than most. Dempsey didn't correct him because today it would be true. He had a lot to do, so he was leaving as soon as this call was over.

"I have some intel you should hear, assuming it hasn't made it out to the range yet," continued Newberry. "The Turkish army was running some training exercises, quote-unquote, near the Syrian border when some Harpies got out of control. Took out a couple of television stations. I thought you should know since you're making unmanned systems your career."

Okay, that jab was a little less subtle. But when he considered the message, he nearly fell out of his chair. This was significant to him but in ways that Newberry could never guess. He needed to get to the bottom of this story. "When?"

"Minor story about nine hours ago. Verified in the last couple."

"Can you tell me the source?" asked Dempsey.

"Initially, one of the national news agencies, but it's been corroborated by assets at our bases. And if you're thinking that what we have is just the version of events that the Turks want to share with the world, I agree. But there's no doubt about the locations hit or that the weapons were Harpies."

Because few connected the name to the mythological bird of prey, Harpy sounded somewhat innocuous. But as a modern-day weapon, it wasn't. It was a first-generation, autonomous smart weapon—a fire-and-forget missile. It loitered in an area, waiting for an enemy radar installation to activate its systems. Once it did, it would follow the signal back to its source. It was the lack of human involvement that put Harpies in a class different from anything currently in the U.S. military arsenal. All US weapons required—or at least provided an option for—human input in the attack decision. Harpies didn't.

"And definitely TV stations?" asked Dempsey, surprise registering in his tone. "How the heck did they get those missiles programmed for a television signal?"

"Who knows? They're claiming no knowledge, but mistaking a TV signal for a military fire-control radar can't be an accident."

"Agreed, sir," replied Dempsey. "So, let me guess. We're thinking that the Syrian stations got a little too vocal for the Turks. So, they re-programmed a couple of Harpies to remedy the situation, with an army training exercise as the standard smokescreen. Of course, why would you ever fire a Harpy during a ground exercise? Not the most convincing cover story."

Newberry chuckled. "Yeah, spinning a story's not their strong suit. Ground troops would hardly know a Harpy was in the air till it struck. But you have one thing wrong. It wasn't Syrian stations that got hit. The stations were in Turkey."

Dempsey took a moment to ponder that information. "Some of the locals getting out of line?" he asked slowly.

"That's what we're thinking. We're still trying to locate the news broadcasts they were running before the attacks, see if there was anything that would have caused the government to retaliate. And I guess there's also the possibility that the missiles were supposed to hit Syrian targets but got activated before they crossed the border."

For Dempsey's interests, it made little difference which story was true. It was the incident itself that he needed to factor into his plans. For once, he was glad that Newberry had called.

"So, what about your own unmanned systems accident?" asked Newberry.

This accident, rather than the sloppy record-keeping, was the primary reason why Dempsey had been seeking a meeting with Marshall. And since he was derelict in this inquiry even in his own eyes, he was due the dressing down he was about to receive.

"Sorry, sir, but Dr. Marshall hasn't been available to review all the personnel records with me. I was just about to schedule another meeting."

There was a pause. Dempsey thought he could almost feel the tension coming over the line. "You need to remind that prima donna who the hell signs his checks," snarled Newberry. "Get him to the table immediately because I want a full report on that incident. Understood?"

"Yes, sir."

Newberry paused before saying, "Okay, next Thursday at the regular time." It wasn't a question.

"Yes, sir," said Dempsey again, surprised at the brevity of his chastisement but not in the lack of an explanation for his boss's absence at the last call. The men hung up.

Dempsey remained in the guard station conference room considering his options. Things were moving fast. The world was changing quickly. Maybe he should accelerate his meetings with Steve Gerhardt? But when he considered the possibility in detail, he knew that his actions depended on other events over which he had no control. No, better to let things play out as planned. It would all be over soon anyway.

THE DAY, THURSDAY, JANUARY 14

Operations Center, JACC Test Range, Nevada, 9:36 AM

A break in the repetitiousness of the ringing phone was followed by an annoyed, "Hello."

"Don't hang up," I blurted, my hand shooting out for the phone only to jam my finger on the edge of the table. I swore, mostly under my breath, because I hadn't needed to jump. It was already on speaker.

"Easy there, Doc. You okay?"

"Yeah," I said slowly. "Larry? Is that you?"

"Yep, the one and only ... at least 'round these parts."

I knew Larry—well, his first name anyway—from evenings drinking in the local bar. There wasn't much else to do at night, so I knew a lot of first names and little else except drinking stories.

"Bart told me what you said. You're not screwing with us, are you?"

"No, no way. We're being hunted by Jack. The Mobile Command Center's already been hit. According to the threat map, you guys are next and he's nearly there. Col. Dempsey and Dr. Marshall thought you should just walk or drive away slowly. And whatever you do, don't go near IS, Maintenance, or Ops. All those buildings are classified as hostile military targets."

"Well, damn," Larry replied. "And that's the only word from the brain trust? Walk away? Don't they have a self-destruct button or something?"

"They do, but Jack isn't taking orders from us. And, by the way, if anyone brought a rifle along, drop it and walk away. Otherwise, Jack might misunderstand."

"You know rifles on the range are against the rules," Larry replied, the irony apparent in his tone. It was a regulation occasionally ignored because of both the peril of the desert and the force of habit. "Okay. Better go. I'll spread the word."

He hung up before I could even say, "Good luck." I started across the room to where Troy sat staring at his console. "How's it look for them?"

"We'll know soon."

I started to sit down but decided that looking over Troy's shoulder was the better option. Whatever happened, I'd need to pace when it was over. I looked at the display. Jack was close. A knot grew in my stomach. The clock on the wall that I'd never heard before now counted out the seconds like someone was tapping on the back of my skull. One, two, three.

Jack slowed as it approached the construction crew and then stopped. It had some of the best sensors and fastest processors in the world. Couldn't he get the information he needed any faster and move on? The clock continued counting. Nine, ten, eleven.

For their part, the crew was acting exactly as I had asked. Two trucks were slowly driving away. Two other people had set out on foot.

"Crap," said Troy. "Jack's following that one truck."

I leaned in and stared. There seemed to be some change, but was it a movement? Troy had zoomed in so far that we had to be at the limit of the sensors and the resolution of the screen. Now, slight variations in the readings from any number of factors that had nothing to do with Jack's position might cause some pixels to change. "Honestly, I can't tell."

"Yeah, now I'm not sure either," replied Troy.

What was clear was that the unknown targets—the men of the construction crew—were moving ever so slowly. "What was that joke Marshall made about things changing at the rate of continental drift?" I asked, blinking in an exaggerated way to get my eyes to refocus on the screen. "That's about the speed of the road crew."

Troy gave a single, soft snort. "Yeah, and let's hope that's a nonthreatening pace in Jack's mind."

The clock continued counting, each tick tightening the knot in my stomach. Fifty-three, fifty-four, fifty-five. The crew moved farther away. Jack held his ground, watching, thinking.

And then it was over. Jack moved on. I released a breath I didn't realize I was holding. Troy's reaction was much more demonstrative as he whooped once, then yelled, "Score one for the good guys."

"Or four," I replied and then thought better of it. If we were counting bodies, that would make it four to one.

Maybe Troy had the same thought because he was more subdued when he spoke again. "I'm going to check in with the bosses, see what they have in mind for us."

He crossed the room, dialed, and was soon talking to someone. I paced. Occasionally, I'd stop and listen, but other than Troy sounding incredulous from time to time, I couldn't tell much about what was being said. Finally, he hung up and walked back over to where I had been doing laps near the console.

"Lots of stuff happening, most of which sounds like fantasy to me. First off, they said the shot at the mobile center might have been a one-off glitch that won't happen again." I knew disbelief was registering on my face even before Troy confirmed it with his response. "Yeah, sounds like they're smoking something to me, too.

If it's a one-off, why is everyone still showing up as hostile on Jack's threat map?"

"That almost has to be a 'don't lose your head' message."

"As if that helps," replied Troy. "They're working on some fixes, too, but the first?" He looked up at the ceiling and shook his head. "It sounds about as likely as the one-off thing. They've got Don Williams trying to regain control over Jack."

"But I thought ...."

"That Don was the JACC software guru?" Troy finished the statement for me. "He is. But the reason it isn't going to work is because all he has is a coordinator's console. That's like trying to break up a concrete sidewalk with a fly swatter."

In any other situation, his comment might have been funny. Now, it was just sobering ... and confusing. "They have a console at the Guard Station?"

"Nope, he's in the IS building with a bunch of others who wanted to watch the demo from there, which means he's second on Jack's list. Jeez, talk about pressure. Fix it or else. And those fake threat maps of the range?" I nodded. "He seems to think the software that lets Jack run those simulated search-and-destroy routes may be the source of the problem. Some corruption or bug in them."

I nodded. I knew all about those search-and-destroy maps, my car being classified as a "hostile military transport" on the second day I was here. Of course, on that day, there was no chance that it was about to become a burned-out shell. Today, things were different.

"Don have any way to check that out?" I asked.

"He won't know till it works or doesn't, but Dempsey may have a fix sooner. Something in our signal enables Jack to classify us as the good or the bad guys. Hardware from another program wouldn't have that extra bit. So, he's getting some small robotic units being tested on another range—something that does bomb disposal. They're going to run them out, see how Jack reacts. If that works, they load a jeep with non-JACC transmitters and come to the rescue."

"How long?"

"Don't know," Troy responded. "But not fast enough if you ask me. And then, we have the final line of defense. They're scrambling some Apache helicopters. There's no talk ... not yet, anyway, of them coming onto the range. But worse comes to worst, Jack won't be leaving here."

"And us?" I asked. "What do they want us to do in the meantime?"

Troy looked at me a moment, then raised two empty hands. "Keep our heads down. What else?"

TWENTY-THREE DAYS EARLIER, TUESDAY, DECEMBER 22

Ruger-Phillips Building, St. Louis, Missouri, 1:27 PM

It was difficult to keep my mind on work. I told myself it was because Christmas was just three days away, but eventually, I always stop lying to myself. I couldn't focus on the job because thoughts of Nicole kept popping up.

We'd traded calls and emails, and it looked like she would be back from Kansas City soon. Her aunt was doing better. And since she'd scheduled vacation for her ski trip and Ruger-Phillips was closed during the week between Christmas and New Year's Day, I could foresee lots of opportunities to invite her to dinner, to catch a movie, to ... well, that was why I was finding it difficult to keep my mind on work. I could imagine a lot of things.

But I was still at work, and today was an important day. Today, I had Unmanned Aerial Systems 101, as Ken had called it, from Dr. Mark Dillon at Air Dynamics. In preparation for the meeting, I had read everything I could find about JACC. There wasn't much. It was about to enter the last phase of R&D and due for initial production shortly thereafter if everything went according to plan. So far, it hadn't; it had gone better than plan. It had stayed a bit ahead of schedule without any cost overruns and no accidents—at least none that had made the news. Consequently, the program was almost totally under the public's radar.

"Doc." I knew from the voice it was Ken, and I turned around to find him coming down the hall. "You're off to meet with Dr. Dillon?"

"I am," I said as he dropped in beside me. "I'm heading to Building 1 now to pick him up if you want to join us."

"Sorry, I can't. I have a meeting on next year's raise review processes. But let me know if you see any issues for our contract."

"Will do." He continued down the hall while I exited the building to cross a parking lot to Building 1.

Liz, who was staffing the reception desk, gave me a wave and dipped her head toward a man sitting on one of the chairs along the wall. He appeared to be in his early 40s, making him younger than I had expected for an expert on aircraft sensor systems and artificial intelligence. He stood as I approached.

"Dr. Dillon?"

"Yes," he said, extending a hand. "And it's Mark, please."

"I'm Sam. Sam Price."

"Or Doc, as I understand it from Rick."

"Rick Johnson?"

Dillon nodded. Someday I needed to explain to my coworkers that half the people I met with had a Ph.D. They might find it odd to call me Doc when they were also docs ... although none had complained so far.

"I've reserved a small room where we can talk." We passed through a set of double doors leading to a work area. "My boss said Rick knew some of the people on JACC but not that he knew you."

"Technically, I'm not on JACC, although Omega Systems uses some of the capability I've worked on. I understand you're heading to the test range soon."

"First of the year," I replied. "Supposed to be there for their first live-fire demo."

"Jack will put on a great show," he said, as we entered the conference room and sat.

Jack?

"Okay, I know that any acronym that can be pronounced will be. So, J-A-C-C becoming Jack for the program makes sense. But the way you said that makes it sound like they call the aircraft Jack?"

He grinned. "They do. And they also call the aircraft a 'he,' which might be a bit strange since most other weapons from ships to rifles are usually female. But so far, it's Jack."

"Good to know. At least I won't look like a complete outsider when the first question out of my mouth is, what can this J-A-C-C unmanned system do anyway? And that, by the way, is my first question. Maybe you can give me something in the way of a general overview?"

"Love to," replied Dillon, "although as I understand it, I'll need to keep this unclassified."

"Correct," I replied. "My clearance will be in place for the visit, but for now, just the white-world version." And with that, Dillon launched into what was obviously a carefully developed and well-practiced talk, complete with printed copies of his slides.

Omega Systems, working with Air Dynamics as their principal subcontractor, had won the JACC research and development contract after a fly-off with two other competitors. The winning design resembled a helicopter except that where the tail rotor should have been, there was none. That was because these rotors could become entangled in obstacles and Jack usually operated near the ground. So, for the program, Air Dynamics had worked with Boeing to adapt one of their commercial helicopters known as the "Notar" for no tail rotor.

In a sentence, Jack was a low-altitude, long-endurance unmanned aerial combat system with a primary mission of close air support. He flew anything from humanitarian to attack operations where ground forces were vulnerable. In most respects, he served the same functions as a military helicopter but without endangering a pilot. And because Jack was unmanned, he could use rapid evasive maneuvers that no human could withstand. While Jack was dodging and weaving, dropping behind cover and popping back up, he was also calculating a launch point for his self-defense. Only a moment's hesitation was necessary for Jack to deliver its counterpunch. At one point in the talk, Dillon showed me a video of Jack in action. The closest thing I had ever seen to its ducking and darting was the behavior of a dragonfly. It was impressive indeed.

Like an Apache Attack Helicopter, Jack bristled with externally carried weapons—a 30 mm chain gun, Hellfire missiles, and Hydra 70 rockets—making it capable of taking out most ground targets and a formidable adversary against air threats. Although classification issues prevented him from giving me precise numbers, Dillon provided enough information from less capable systems to more than satisfy my thirst for data. And facts like the sensitivity of the infrared system of the Predator—it could detect the heat of one person at nearly 40 miles—made my head spin. And Jack was even more capable. When I considered Jack's weaponry and sensor capabilities, the phrase "nowhere to run, nowhere to hide" came to mind.

After 45 minutes, Dillon finished and it was just in time. No more data would fit in my brain, and my hand was cramping from all the notes I was writing in the margins of his charts.

"Thanks, Mark. That was great. Just what I needed."

"My pleasure," Dillon replied.

While my head was filled with facts and figures—all the stuff I love—it still had some room for impressions. And the ones I wanted were Dillon's take on my new customers if he was willing to share. "I'm going to be presenting my initial findings to Dr. Jim Marshall and Col. Ray Dempsey. Any chance you know one or both of them?"

Dillon didn't hesitate. "I know Jim Marshall pretty well. Before Omega Systems, he was at DARPA. You know, Defense Advanced Research Projects Agency?"

"Yep. They came up once in a while when I was in school."

"Yeah, they would," Dillon replied. "Anyway, Jim was in unmanned systems software development. Way I heard it, he was a real whiz kid. But then, he got tired of the bureaucracy. He used to joke that he had typed more characters into DARPA forms than he ever put into the software. So, when Omega Systems came along, promising breakthroughs in the field, he joined them."

Dillon paused, chuckling to himself. "You're probably going to doubt that 'whiz kid' comment when you meet Jim. Now, he's all about showmanship, and technical detail can get buried in that world. But in his current job, a vision is crucial. As for Col. Dempsey, I heard his name mentioned some time ago in connection with another unmanned systems program, the MQ-1 Predator. But other than that, I don't know him."

"Both with some background in unmanned systems," I said, mostly thinking aloud. "Good to know."

I considered calling the meeting to an end. I'd asked all of the questions I'd prepared. But then again, the chance to talk with someone with Dillon's background didn't come along every day. "We've still got some time. And since you're an expert in artificial intelligence, I was wondering if I could go a little off-topic and ask a few questions about that field?"

Dillon smiled, holding up a hand. "I appreciate the compliment, but AI is extremely broad. So, an expert? Not really, although I do know a few areas pretty well. But before we get into that, your background is cognitive psychology, right?"

"Correct."

"Then, your study of AI has most likely emphasized the relationship between human and machine intelligence?"

"I'd guess so, but that was part of my question. For example, I remember one professor who said that the goal of AI was to make machines think like humans. But that seems ... well, frankly, ridiculous."

Dillon laughed. "I'd agree. But out of curiosity, why do you feel that way?"

"Well, perhaps I took the prof's comments too literally, but there are a lot of reasons. For example, people forget things. So, are we supposed to design computer programs that randomly drop data records from time to time?"

Dillon chuckled again. "I doubt there'd be much demand for that. Talk to most practitioners and they'll tell you that the definition of AI is a moving target. Twenty years ago, a computer that could answer a few simple questions would be considered a marvel of AI. Today, no one thinks anything about asking their phone to find the nearest seafood restaurant ... although that might be a fish sandwich at a burger joint."

"Yep. Seen my phone do that and worse. So, does Jack do anything you'd call AI?"

"Well, I wouldn't but only because the term has become such a catch-all. The core of what I do in automatic target recognition is to try to get a computer to find the tanks, artillery, aircraft, and so on, whether they're sitting on a runway or camouflaged under some trees. That capability has some parallels to human vision, and vision is often considered one of the defining challenges of AI. So, if we get there, we would have reached a milestone."

"And Jack doesn't find military equipment as well as a human?" His comment seemed strangely at odds with a machine that could see a human's heat from 40 miles.

"Well, yes and no. If we limit Jack to the part of the electromagnetic spectrum that's visible to the human eye, then no, he couldn't. It would take him quite a while to piece together enough from video to figure out he was looking at a person. But, of course, we don't limit Jack that way. He gets returns from a wide range of sensors that gives him size, shape, volume, materials, and so on. With all that, Jack does well compared to humans. And at a distance, he's the hands-down winner."

"Okay, the inputs would be different," I said. "What about the processing of them? Is there anything in Jack that would be considered a simulation of human visual processes?"

"I'd say, little if anything. You're familiar with those processes?"

"The basics," I replied. "If I looked at a street with people and cars, parts of my retina would detect features like lines, colors, and angles. Other parts of my brain would aggregate those features into larger groups until I perceived objects, like a person or a car. Then, there are depth perception processes that tell me if I'm looking at a child nearby or an adult farther away since both would take up the same area on my retina. There are also attentional processes that affect how fully each object is processed. If I attend to an object, I'll attach meaning to it. So, I end up recognizing a friend standing in front of her new silver two-door."

"A much better description than I could have given off the top of my head," said Dillon, causing my face to warm. And while his praise was part of my embarrassment, some was because Nicole's car was a new silver two-door. She was invading my thoughts, even in this meeting.

"Perception was part of my oral exams ... not all that long ago," I replied to explain my somewhat technical answer. Two years from now, much of that would be lost to forgetting and I'd be searching my college texts for the details.

He nodded. "So, if you take those human processes and looked at all of Jack's internal machine logic, you'd be hard-pressed to find anything similar, except in the most general sense. Yet, Jack will take his sensor data from the same street scene and identify the humans and the cars ... but not that one of them is your friend. Well, that's unless he or she is in a database of high-value targets."

I drew back, looking at Dillon closely. "High-value targets? Like terrorists?"

"That would be an example," Dillon said.

"And Jack has such a capability?"

"He could. His sensors can pick up various biometric information such as height and weight, and several behaviometric traits such as a person's gait. Take those data and check for a match in an onboard database, and you have it. But whether Omega Systems has made provision for doing that, you'll have to ask them."

He paused, rubbing his forehead for a moment. "You mentioned attention as one of the processes that affect perception."

I nodded.

"There's a very rough parallel there to what Jack does. He'll look at an overall situation and plan how to allocate his resources. He'll start with a rapid scan, relying heavily on infrared to find warm-blooded animals of a certain mass. In other words, animals that may be adult humans. If he finds any, he'll allocate more resources to figure out what they're carrying, what or who they're near, and so on. In other words, he gives them more attention. It's a rough comparison to human perception, but that's as close as I can come ... at least without giving the question some more thought."

"It makes sense he'd need to do that because humans certainly have to tune out a lot of information. Just sitting here, I've stopped hearing the hum of the lights over our heads, the smell of the coffee from the galley down the hall, the slight noise from conversations outside our room."

"And now that you've mentioned them, my attention has shifted and the noise in the hall is all I can think about."

I smiled, feeling some pleasure in finding common ground between AI and the psychology I knew. And while I could have asked any number of other questions about human learning, memory, and reasoning and what Jack did, it was time to move on. "So, how does the Operations Coordinator fit into all of this?"

"The coordinator? He doesn't."

Perhaps my face fell because my emotions did. Dillon got a sheepish look, which confirmed my feelings were appropriate. "Don't get me wrong," he said. "Everything we've talked about will help you understand what Jack is all about, but the coordinator's not involved with most of it."

"Then what does he do?" I asked.

"Coordinators will fly groups of aircraft to the operations area, usually four to six of them. But it's not flying like you may be thinking. It's more like drawing a line on a map before the mission. When the mission is run, the route is flown automatically. Jack flies the takeoff and ingress, then a pilot takes over for the operations, whatever they are. Then, it's back to automatic, as Jack flies the egress and landing. If anything fails, coordinators can fly Jack manually, but that doesn't involve much of the advanced processing we've talked about."

Dillon hesitated, the sheepish look returning. "You're going to hear this anyway, so I might just as well tell you. Around the program, they say the pilots are the fighters and the coordinators are the babysitters."

Training for state-of-the-art human-machine collaboration? Hardly!

"Not exactly what I was expecting," I admitted. "But coordinators are still part of getting the job done."

"Absolutely," said Dillon. "If they can't get the aircraft to the battle, people die."

The conversation was starting to sound like a pep talk, and that wasn't necessary. I knew training problems often hid in some of the most unlikely spots—even in "babysitting" jobs—and I wasn't about to let one slip through if I could help it. I checked my watch.

"Sorry, but it looks like I got carried away with the AI questions. We've run over a bit." Dillon waved a hand, dismissing my concern. "The overview was great. And the connections between AI and my education as well as the lack of them was telling."

"Glad I could help," Dillon replied. "Look, if anything comes up on the project, don't hesitate to give me a call. My part's finished, but for personal and professional reasons, I'd like to see Jack flying one day."

"Thanks. I will."

I walked Dillon to the reception area where we said our good-byes. On the way back to my office, I replayed all I had learned about automatic target recognition and the AI built into Jack. Even if it wasn't relevant to the Operations Coordinator's job, it was still fascinating stuff, at least for a techno-nerd like me.

Of course, it wasn't like it was ever going to save my life.

Operations Center, JACC Test Range, Nevada, 2:07 PM

Dr. Jim Marshall strode down the hall toward the Operations Center conference room, the soles of his shoes clicking on the tiled floor. He was late for his 2:00 meeting with Colonel Dempsey, but he didn't hurry, didn't worry. His tardiness was by design. As a negotiating tactic, keeping someone waiting had its risks. But while he didn't know Dempsey well, Marshall felt the potential for backlash was small. Better to let the man stew, distracting him from the discussion to come.

As for the talk, Marshall was certain it would focus on Brandt Drury, or Drew as everyone around the range called him, and the so-called 'Wiley case.' The colonel had been insistent that they meet immediately to discuss personnel matters. What else could it be?

He would cooperate in the discussion, of course. That is, he would if re-stating his oft-repeated position could be considered cooperation. He would echo the official report from the Air Force, which had ruled that the incident was the result of human error with extenuating circumstances. The factor that excused Drew's mistake was the centering of the weapon loadout display; it wasn't centered. True, the misalignment was nearly imperceptible to the human eye, but it was there. And he'd repeat those facts as many times as Dempsey wanted to hear them.

To Marshall, it was Drew's exuberance that was a bit off-center, but he'd never admit that. Nor would he discuss the steps he'd authorized to discover the problem with the display. It had taken a handful of his best software and hardware engineers nearly a month to find it, but the effort was worth it. It would keep Drew on the program. Long-term, he didn't need the pilot, but in the immediate future, the man was irreplaceable.

Marshall's contrived apologies for being late were forming in his mind as he stepped into the conference room, but he didn't need them. Dempsey wasn't there. He wasn't sure what to make of it. He started for a seat, then turned to leave, only to spin around once more and sit down. But no sooner had he leaned back than he decided he wouldn't be the one kept waiting. He stood to leave. At that precise moment, Dempsey opened the conference room door. Seeing Marshall on his feet, Dempsey said "Great timing, Jim. Looks like you haven't even had a chance to sit down."

Marshall sat and rubbed a hand over his forehead, smoothing the frown that was forming there. "Yep, great timing," he replied, trying to make it sound like he meant it. If this was one-upmanship, Dempsey had played it masterfully. But one game doesn't make a match and Marshall had all his distractions in a row. He carefully laid out his notebook and pen on the table in front of him, then nudged the edge of the book as if assuring it was perfectly aligned with the world. The attention, however, belied the book's contents; it was empty. His rule of thumb was never bring anything to a meeting that is not specifically requested, and Dempsey had only said personnel reports. That could be almost anything from work logs to annual reviews. "You have questions of me?"

"Yes, I do," replied the colonel as he opened his notebook and read. "I'd like to talk about Jesse Morgan."

Marshall felt himself fall back against the chair as if the question had pinned him there. He'd thought about subordinates other than Drew, of course, but Morgan? How had Dempsey even heard the name? And with that question coming to his mind, Marshall knew it was a second game lost in this match. Worse, he was certain the colonel was reading the frown he could no longer massage away.

"I'm not sure I understand. Jesse Morgan was a JACC test pilot in the last Research and Development phase. He's been gone from the program for more than two years now and certainly long before you arrived two months ago." It was a none-too-subtle attempt to make Dempsey feel like a latecomer, an outsider who lacked the background he needed to criticize actions completed before his tenure.

"I've been here for three months. It's been two months since I first requested this meeting, which probably explains your confusion."

Game-set-match, Marshall conceded in his thoughts. He wasn't going to distract Dempsey with minor slights or push him to a more tentative position. If this pattern continued, they would end up so strongly polarized on an issue that was largely inconsequential that compromise might become impossible. And in the end, he reported to Dempsey. So, for now, he had no option but to be straightforward in his comments ... or at least, some of them.

"Yes, sorry, Colonel. It's taken a while to find a time when we're both available. But now, we have one. What can I tell you about Jesse Morgan?"

"Well, for one thing, I understand that he left the practice target area pretty much in shambles when all he was supposed to be firing was simulated weapons. What can you tell me about that incident?"

"With the information you just mentioned, you must have the incident report. I can't expand on what it says."

"It says nothing. It says maybe software, maybe human error, but something happened that resulted in Morgan firing a live missile at one of the demonstration buildings. I guess the report rules out sunspots, but not much else. Why don't we know more about the root causes of this accident?"

"Again, that's covered in the report."

"Summarize it for me."

"Okay," said Marshall slowly. "The playback files were corrupt. Jesse said he was sure the JACC loadout screen showed only simulated weapons. Don Williams and the software team were positive that the loadout display was accurate. In the end, it was a 'he said, he said' situation, without any records to prove who was right. And since no one was hurt and not even any permanent structures were damaged, the no-fault decision was appropriate in my judgment. My legal people said that a resolution of that type was within the scope of our contract. I forget just what section they referenced, but I can pull up the document and we can find it if you want."

"It's not the opinion so much as its timing that bothers me," said Dempsey, again failing to take the bait he'd offered that could have sidetracked the meeting. "It came at the end of the previous phase and just before a system maturity review. The findings of that review were to determine whether JACC was to move forward or not. It, of course, passed. Jesse Morgan, on the other hand, was terminated.

That doesn't sound like what happens when there are equal weights on both sides of a question."

Morgan's termination was information that had been carefully buried. The ex-pilot had first been transferred before being terminated at a location where he knew few people and had no real friends. Most of his previous coworkers in Pittsburgh didn't even know what had happened to him. The action, of course, was taken in defense of the JACC program. Why let one malcontented, ex-employee scuttle a game-changing program with unfounded claims? Even rumors, if they came to light in the media, might have killed Jack at that crucial juncture.

So, how did the colonel know? Had Omega Systems simply handed over Morgan's employment records? Most private, commercial companies would surrender this type of data to the government in cases of national security. Certainly, those involved in government contracting would. But the stakes weren't that high. Had Dempsey obtained the ex-pilot's current status from some other government agency like the Internal Revenue Service? Whatever he'd done, he was quite adept at rooting out the information he wanted. Marshall wouldn't underestimate the man again.

Knowing there was no other option, Marshall said, "Omega Systems did what it could to protect Jesse Morgan's reputation. In the end, we re-administered our pilot selection tests—twice as a matter of fact—and Jesse couldn't pass them. Those two failures, along with the incident on JACC, suggested he was ill-equipped to be a pilot. The fact that he originally passed also suggested that the tests needed improvement. Since then, they have been completely overhauled by our Personnel Department."

Marshall wasn't certain how much had been done, but creating legally defensible tests was their job. And besides, if Dempsey was looking at the Personnel Department, he wasn't looking at what was going on at the range.

"Given all these circumstances and since we had no other positions suitable to Jesse's skills, we had no option but to let him go," said Marshall in a summary he hoped would end this part of the meeting.

"I see," said Dempsey, tenting his fingers in front of his chin. "Can you tell me why the report for this incident isn't kept on-site in our archives?"

Damn, Dempsey wasn't going to let this go. "Well, as you know, these reports lose their validity over time. If there was any fault with the JACC software—and I'm not saying there was—but if there was, all of that code has been reviewed and refined. Not a single line of it remains untouched." Again, Marshall wasn't sure of his facts and with some digging, Dempsey might prove this claim inaccurate, but he doubted the colonel would go to all that trouble.

"So, with the selection instrument most likely at fault and with the age of the software being used during the time of the incident, the report was removed from the archive because it was no longer relevant to the program."

"So, you're blaming the Omega Systems pilot selection tests, clearing JACC programming and its readiness of all responsibility?"

"That's not exactly what I said," replied Marshall. "After a thorough review, we believe the tests are the most likely cause. And if they were out-of-date, they're state-of-the-art now. Our upgrade was patterned on the pilot selection instrument used in the Air Force."

"I want the official Omega Systems report on the incident replaced in our archives," said Dempsey, matter-of-factly. "And, if it's not already described, I want an addendum added that lists the possible root causes—software readiness and human error, the later possibly enabled by limitations in the selection test. I want those possibilities assessed quantitatively, along with a description of your methods for evaluating them. Any questions?"

What an ass. The program is on the cusp of a breakthrough in unmanned systems technology and he's giving me this make-work study of inconsequentialities. But it's not a problem. I'll just get some flunky in Personnel to prepare his useless addendum.

"None, sir. Anything else on Jesse Morgan?"

"No, I think we see eye to eye on that matter," replied Dempsey.

Marshall dropped his gaze to the tabletop and then berated himself for a gesture that implied they hadn't reached common ground. But by the time he brought his eyes back up, the colonel was busy reading from his notebook.

After about twenty minutes of what Marshall considered innocuous questions, Dempsey said, "I think that's about it. I just need to record the last of our action items." He bent to jot something in his book.

Marshall couldn't believe his good fortune. Nothing about Drew had come up. But then, without looking up from his work, Dempsey said, "Oh, by the way, I took the liberty of putting the incident report on Brandt Drury back in the files. I found it about a month ago. Seems it, too, had been misfiled."

Marshall could feel the blood drain from his face. When the colonel looked up, he said, "Something wrong, Jim?"

Marshall chastised himself for letting his emotions show ... again. "Just upset that our record-keeping seems to be so sloppy. I'll speak to the responsible parties. And I'll meet with Drew again, go over the lessons we learned."

Not a bad recovery, he granted to himself. And with some reflection, he even realized where Dempsey might have gotten the report. The incident wasn't a secret around the range—just the opposite—and the home office would still have the report on hand. If he had asked for a copy to correct what he described as a routine, clerical error, they would have handed it over. He made a mental note to tell them that he should be informed of all of the colonel's requests, formal or informal.

"Speaking to Drew isn't necessary," said Dempsey with a slight wave of a hand. He jotted something else in his book. "We've had a few chats about it."

"Without anyone else present?" Marshall snapped without thinking.

Dempsey looked up, his stare icy. "As long as he's on my program, I don't need your permission."

"Sorry, Colonel. It's just that Drew's a bit touchy about what happened, and I need him at the peak of his game for the live-fire demo in three weeks. I didn't mean any disrespect."

Dempsey continued to stare for a moment, then closed his book and stood. "None taken, Dr. Marshall," he said, although his tone implied otherwise. He walked out of the room and closed the door behind him.

Marshall slouched back in his chair, muttering, "What the hell?" He had been certain Dempsey would want to have Drew reassigned if he ever found that incident report. Maybe that was still coming? Or maybe he bought the display misalignment explanation? But what was even more startling to Marshall was the fact that the colonel and Drew had talked. What had Dempsey said to the kid? Maybe his comments were harmless. But every way Marshall turned the thought in his mind, he never found a good side. It looked ugly from every angle.

* * *

Dempsey left the meeting and drove directly to the guard station, as Col. Newberry would be awaiting his call. Once seated in the closed conference room, Dempsey dialed his boss.

After the hellos, Dempsey said, "It's exactly like you suspected, Colonel. Omega Systems did terminate Jesse Morgan, although we don't know what part Marshall played in it."

"That's not necessary," replied Newberry. "The mere appearance that they got Morgan out of the picture to keep him quiet about the software is good enough for now. How'd you find out?"

"I have my ways," said Dempsey, not wanting to get into how he had tricked Marshall into confirming their action. "By the way, he's blaming their selection tests, which of course, points the finger back at pilot error as the root cause. If they'd gotten a better pilot, none of this would have happened."

"Also, of no importance," said Newberry. "This information raises enough doubt to suspend the program for a month while we run an independent software readiness review. If Marshall wants to drag their company processes through the mud at the same time, let him. Even if he wants to hunt down Morgan and run him through the Air Force tests to prove he's not pilot material, more power to him. By the time he's done with that, I'll have the data I need to let the program go forward or pin his hide to the wall for rushing it to the next phase."

"Sounds good, Colonel," replied Dempsey.

"Now, about the live-fire demonstration. By the time the government gets there, they'll know about the temporary stop-work. I know you won't mention it to Jim Marshall until it's official, but I have no idea what the politicians might say. You should be ready for some fallout if it comes up."

"Thanks, but you should know—the stop-work rumor has been circulating for a while. I've even addressed it at a staff meeting, just as a possibility, not a certainty. So, the whole team probably has their grievances well prepared."

"That's unfortunate. Just keep them in line." There was a pause of several seconds, accompanied by the sound of shuffling paper over the telephone line. "So, what the hell is up with this second scenario?" Newberry asked without preamble. "Did you agree to it?"

"I did."

"And you don't think it's highlighting a worst case, a balancing act that would give anyone nightmares? Why shove it in the government's faces when things like that don't happen very often?"

"But on occasion, they do," replied Dempsey. "The way I see it, we could hide this weapon system's capabilities, but sooner or later, someone would put it together. I'd rather it was us that showed the government what they're buying rather than some talking head on the ten o'clock news."

Dempsey could hear his boss release a long breath. "Okay. Just make sure they know it's not all or none," said Newberry. "We could use a dumbed-down version of Jack in the military. He could be a real asset if we put a pilot back in control."

But you can't keep the weapons dumb forever, thought Dempsey, although his words were quite different. "True. But the program is still working their R&D agenda, so being clear to the government now will get them prepared for what comes in the last phase."

"Yeah, the last phase," said Newberry, pausing a moment. "I suppose they should see it all now because there's no way to sugarcoat what's coming. Carry on."

"Yes, sir," replied Dempsey, barely finishing the words before the line went dead.

Catching Marshall and Omega Systems pushing JACC forward before the software was ready had been Newberry's obsession for the last couple of months, and Dempsey was glad it was. By the time his boss had run the readiness issue to ground, his plan would be in motion, and there'd be no turning back. The die would be cast.

As for the software itself, Dempsey knew with certainty that his boss was wrong. True, at the time of Morgan's debacle, it was probably marginally acceptable. Don Williams, whose ability and professional ethics he had come to admire, had admitted as much. But that was then.

During his watch, Dempsey had monitored the software closely. He had held several telephone conferences with Williams, coming to recognize the man's brilliance. He knew the team the chief software engineer had assembled—bright individuals who shared their supervisor's vision, perhaps even pushed his envelope. He wondered if the latter was the influence of Marshall, but if so, perhaps it was for the best. If Williams had any failing, it was that he could be a bit conservative.

Over those months on his watch, the software had moved from marginal to exceptional. In some areas, he would even say it was astonishing. Now, even if the millions of lines of software code that gave Jack his intelligence were etched on stone tablets, it would still be worth its weight in gold.

Doc's Apartment, St. Louis, Missouri, 7:22 PM

The smell of an already forgotten meal hung in the air. I might have questioned whether I had eaten it, but the feeling of satiation told me I had ... as did the dirty dishes sitting on the kitchen island. This wasn't like me. Eating while lost in thought was common enough, but half the time, I cleared the counter as I ate. That routine, however, had been disrupted by the thought of calling Nicole and I had spent the last ten minutes pacing. I was already on the fifth variant of our conversation in my mind.

Maybe this degree of anticipation was ill-advised—I hardly knew Nicole—but there was no denying my gut. And frankly, even my head agreed. She might well be the unique mix of order and spontaneity, science and art that complemented my logic-driven persistence. So, after our call yesterday, when it was clear that her aunt was rapidly recovering, I started anticipating the magic words I hoped to hear from her today, "I'm headed back to St. Louis."

I sat down at my kitchen island and dialed her cell phone.

"Hi, Sam." Unfortunately, the tone of her greeting said not everything was going to plan. But as to the nature of the hiccup, I had no idea.

Rather than trying to guess, I kept my reply simple. "So, how's everything going there?"

"Good. My aunt's doing great actually." She paused, giving my heart time to drop. If her aunt wasn't the problem, what was?

"She's doing so well that everyone thinks we should go on our ski trip. Well, everyone but me." My mood rebounded some. "The plan is to make a stop in St. Louis, but only long enough to pack. Then, we hit the road. I hate to ask, but can we put hiking off for another week? I'll be back on January second, and any weekend after that should be fine."

I pulled the phone from my ear and stared at it wordlessly for a second. My ninth month of trying to get with Nicole would be like the last eight. It was poor timing, missed opportunities, bad luck, or whatever cliché you preferred. I returned the phone to my lips. "Sorry, but I'm going to need a couple more weeks after that. I'm leaving on business travel the same day you're returning. I'll be back on January 19."

"Oh."

"Nicole?" I asked after a period of silence.

"Still here. Just thinking. The middle of the month may be getting a little cold for hiking ... or not. Missouri's weather is so unpredictable. But I'm sure we'll find something to entertain ourselves."

Something to entertain ourselves?

For the second time in this short conversation, I pulled the phone from my ear to stare at it. Was that a bit of playfulness I heard in her tone? The options that came to mind for a reply ran the gamut from sappy—looking into your eyes is entertainment enough for me—to an escalation of the sexual overtones—you mean like strip poker at my place, house rules? I went with a middle of the road response. "Sure. Might be a better time for hot chocolate and watching a movie. I'll let you get back to your family and give you a call when I'm back in town."

"I see them all day. Are you busy? You want to talk for a while?"

Hang out on the phone? I hadn't done that since high school. It was a bit what ... old fashioned? And yet, the idea was intriguing. Apparently, Nicole didn't let poor timing, missed opportunities, or bad luck stand in her way.

"Yeah, sure. Want to tell me more about your visit to KC?"

"I've had enough sick talk for a while. What about the hike we had planned? Did you go?"

"I did," I replied. And over the next few minutes, I gave her the summary: covered the north and south loops of the Whispering Pines trail making it about ten miles; saw a deer—not unusual—and a raccoon—a lot less common; enjoyed the solitude as everyone else had been scared off by the light dusting of snow. Then, it was her turn.

"You had me looking forward to our hike so much that I went on my own. And besides, by the time I went, my aunt was chasing us out of her room and visiting with my cousins was getting old.

"I went to a park about ten miles out of town. It had a half-inch or so of new snow, but the sun came out when I got there. Everything with color—the birds, the evergreens, even the rocks—seemed to jump out of a background that was brilliant white. But it was the waterfalls that were really spectacular. I suspect there wasn't more than a trickle of water in the streams, but over the days, it had frozen, layer on layer, into a cascade of ice several inches thick. And when the rays of light hit them, it was like a column of shimmering diamonds. Unfortunately, I'm not enough of a photographer to capture their beauty, but I did take a lot of pictures."

"I'd love to see them sometime," I replied.

"Maybe we can look at those before the movie while we're wrapped up in that blanket enjoying hot chocolate?"

I hadn't said anything about a blanket, but I didn't correct her. I liked the image that went with the words. "Absolutely."

"Well, unfortunately, you have to work tomorrow. I should let you go."

Whatever reservations I'd had when she asked if I wanted to talk on the phone had been irrevocably erased from my thoughts. "Is it okay if I call you from the road?"

"I'd like that, Sam. I'll talk to you later. Bye."

THE DAY, THURSDAY, JANUARY 14

Maintenance Building, JACC Test Range, Nevada, 9:41 AM

The smell of exhaust and unburned gasoline hung in the air as Marv Richter pushed more fuel into the engine of his 1971 Ford Mustang than it could handle. He eased off the pedal before revving the motor again, feeling the deep-throated rumble in his chest.

At the same moment, Jack was a little over three miles from the JACC entry gate and moving away from Richter's position toward the far edge of the range. Soon, however, the aircraft would be turning back. It would be following a search-and-destroy route that would take it directly over the Maintenance Building, directly over Richter. At that point, he and his passenger would be dead. That is, they would be if Richter stayed, but he had no intention of hanging around.

Richter pressed down on the accelerator again, the mixture burning more cleanly now. Warming up his car was a calculated risk, although slight if he understood the geometry correctly. The heat signature of the car's exhaust should be hidden from Jack by the Maintenance Building. That fact, however, could change without warning.

"Jack climbs and we'll stick out like a new zit on a teenager's face," he muttered, glancing sideways at his passenger. "But I'm bettin' he won't before we make our break."

The driver looked at his instrument panel. Everything there was fine, but it didn't contain the information he'd need during his sprint to the JACC guard station—how much more abuse could the engine take before he threw a rod, how much more heat could the radiator handle before a hose burst, how hard could he hit the next rut without bending an axle? No display held that kind of insight into their fate.

Richter had already picked their route to safety. It wasn't the smoothest, but it was the shortest. By his calculation, he could cover the distance in about a minute and a half if he could hit 70 miles per hour in the straightaways over the rutted, gravel road. And that was the idea. If he'd gone earlier, back when Jack was on the far end of the range, his need for speed would have been less. But he hadn't. Instead, he'd wasted time arguing with his boss about their options. The man wanted them to take cover inside the building, try to withstand Jack's onslaught from there.

Richter, however, was certain his supervisor was wrong. He simply didn't understand what they were facing. He hadn't been the one standing in the desert when Jack popped up out of a dry gulch fifty yards away and closed the distance to ten yards in a blink of an eye. He hadn't stared down the barrel of Jack's chain gun as the aircraft hung menacingly in the air, twitching side to side as if its onboard intelligence could hardly hold the violence at bay. No, his boss hadn't witnessed all of that. Richter had, and the images still haunted his sleep.

Drew had been on duty that day, and Richter accused him of flying a morbid practical joke. Drew, of course, denied it. He said Jack was just running some ground-following exercises. So, Richter had said nothing more. After all, he had no proof. And besides, Drew was the brass's golden boy. Morgan had screwed up and he had disappeared. No one knew where he was. But when Drew messed up, they promoted him to JACC lead test pilot.

And if his run-in with Jack out in the desert hadn't been bad enough, Richter had also witnessed the aircraft's machine guns coming online. The entire JACC Maintenance team had been treated to the inaugural firing, watching as a blistering stream of tracer bullets leaped from the muzzle of the gun. The whole thing reminded Richter of a frog flicking out its tongue to capture an unsuspecting fly. It was that fast. And when the dust settled, there sat the chassis of an old truck, cut in half by the barrage.

With the shortcut he had picked and pushing his car to the limit, Richter figured they'd escape, barely. But what if his guesses were wrong? What if he needed two more feet? Two more inches? To lighten his load, he'd already thrown all his tools onto the gravel parking lot. Now, the only extra baggage he was carrying was his passenger. He looked over at her. She looked scared, even though she had no idea what Jack could do to them. Maybe he should kick her out. If his supervisor was right, she'd be better off here anyway.

But Richter was sure the man was wrong and leaving her behind was sentencing her to death. He couldn't do that. He threw the Mustang into gear and floored it, leaving a trail of flying gravel and dust in his wake.

* * *

Richter's 1971 Mustang sat 7,521.3 feet from the JACC Test Range entry gate. Jack was 11,784.0 feet from the car, flying 37.3 feet above the desert floor. As Richter had hoped, the Maintenance Building had shielded him from Jack's infrared sensors and would continue to do so for the first 11.7 seconds of his run. At that point, the car emerged from the shadow of the building.

At 18.4 seconds, the car was traveling 67.2 miles per hour. Any faster and Richter and his passenger would probably end up dead or injured in a ditch at the side of the road. They were 5,906.6 feet from the gate when Jack detected the car and classified it as "unknown" transport. The aircraft paused the current leg of the search, turned, and sped toward the heat source. The gap between them was 12,072.4 feet.

After 29.2 seconds, Richter was pushing his car and his luck even more, now reaching a speed of 72.1 miles per hour. Negotiating every curve and dip in the road had become a death-defying experience. The Mustang was now 3,146.7 feet from the gate, and the gap between the hunter and the hunted had grown to 12,767.3 feet.

At the same moment, Jack completed the analysis and determined the car to be a hostile, military target. A Hellfire missile leaped from the aircraft's undercarriage. The particular variant of the Hellfire that Jack carried had a maximum speed of Mach 1.3 or about 1,462.9 feet per second. The missile reached the Mustang in 8.7 seconds, allowing the car to travel another 802.9 feet. Then, the car and its passengers disappeared in a ball of flame.

Rather than the two-inch deficit Richter feared he might have, or even two thousand inches, he was still 2,343.8 feet from the guard station when the Hellfire caught up with him. He had, however, fallen even shorter of his goal than he had imagined because of a misunderstanding of Jack's tactics. If Richter had made it to the gate, the missile wouldn't have stopped, wouldn't have self-destructed just because it had passed an imaginary line on a map. Rather, it would have followed the car for over another mile into the desert beyond the gate before it ran out of fuel. Richter and his rider never had a chance.

Operations Center, JACC Test Range, Nevada, At the Same Time

When the Mustang appeared on Troy's console, I was pacing near the operations room telephone, willing it to ring with the good news that we were safe. That wishful thinking was shattered, however, when Troy yelled, "What the hell is going on?" I spun around to look at him, just in time to see his head drop into his hands. He held the pose only a fraction of a second before looking up at his console, his head slowly shaking, an expression of pain on his face.

"What is it?" I called, jogging across the room to where he sat.

"Someone at the Maintenance Building thinks he can outrun Jack in a car. What an idiot."

I soon found the aircraft and the ground vehicle on the display. More symbols appeared. "Look. People are running out of the guard station." I pointed at four contacts who were moving away from the building.

"Probably Marshall, Dempsey, and the guards running for cover," replied Troy. "If the vehicle makes it that far, a missile from Jack might take them all out."

The symbol for the vehicle turned from unknown to hostile. Then, a second symbol appeared. It was a missile in flight. "But the vehicle's not going to make it that far," Troy said, his tone now flat.

We watched in silence as the vehicle moved a mere fraction of an inch on the screen while the missile covered the entire distance between Jack and the car in the same few seconds. Both symbols disappeared, followed later by a low rumble like distant thunder.

"A fricken, one-time glitch, is it?" Troy was yelling again, even though I was standing right behind him, looking over his shoulder. "Then what the hell was that?" He turned to look up at me. When he saw my face, his eyes narrowed then went wide. His voice dropped to almost a whisper. "Sorry, Doc, but she's okay. She'd never do anything that stupid."

I knew who he meant without asking. She had been one of two surprises I'd received during my first day on the JACC test range.

TEN DAYS EARLIER, MONDAY, JANUARY 4

Operations Center, JACC Test Range, Nevada, 7:23 AM

I have my suspicions that during the period between Christmas and New Year's Day, my clock was running at half-speed, maybe quarter. The days dragged horribly. That was, all of them except the thirty minutes or so when I called Nicole or she called me. That half-hour, which nearly became a daily ritual, went by in a blink of an eye.

It somewhat surprised me that two people who knew so little about each other could find so much to talk about, but we did. Not that the talk was earth-shattering. We didn't solve world hunger. We didn't come up with a plan for world peace. But we did share a lot about our daily lives: opening presents, skiing, snowball fights, and verbally sparring with cousins for her; football, Christmas dinner, visiting with parents, and more football for me. So, while she was enjoying some fresh air and exercise, I was sitting on my rear, eating, and watching television. It led to more than one playful taunt from Nicole of the ilk, "I'm going to walk you into the ground when we finally go on our hike." She got me worried enough that I went out for a couple of jogs during Ruger-Phillips's break between Christmas and New Year's.

But two days ago, the slow march of time finally came to an end, and it was time for me to start my business travel. After a long flight into Las Vegas, I had made an even longer drive into the desert to The Golden Nugget Motel. It was to be my home for the next two weeks.

The motel's rooms were in a U-shape, with a parking lot around the outside and a pool in the middle. On one side of the motel were a convenience store and gas station. On the other, a pawn shop, then a hardware store. Across the street, there was another service station, an empty lot, a Chinese restaurant, and a gun store. Similar collections of business concerns continued for another half-mile or so when this varied commercialism gave way to military order at the main gate to the Nevada Training and Test Range. NTTR, in turn, was composed of smaller ranges, each devoted to the test and development of a specific, military weapon system.

After an uneventful and extremely early evening at the Golden Nugget—I hadn't even ventured out to explore eateries—I had gotten up at 5:00 AM and was out of the door by 5:30. I thought that should be plenty of time to make my 6:00 AM appointment. I was wrong. I'd underestimated both the number of contractors who were coming onto NTTR and the scale of the individual ranges there. The JACC range was a rectangle of about three by five miles—testing an unmanned aerial system didn't require that much room. The areas used by other weapon systems, however, were an order of magnitude larger.

When I reached the JACC guard station, I was given a map to the grounds. The entry gate was near the midpoint on the east side of the rectangle with my destination, the Operations Center, in the northeast corner. A structure identified as the Information Systems Building was in the northwest corner, with a Maintenance Building a bit south of it but still in the northern half of the range. Near the southern border was the demonstration area, composed of a half-dozen buildings. If it was like other demo areas I'd seen, the structures would be ramshackle. Why build them better when you were just going to blow them up?

After the short drive from the gate to the Operations Center, I found a one-story, concrete structure I later learned was called "The Cinder House" by the residents. It was about thirty by forty feet of drab, gray walls with a single, darker gray metal door centered on the side facing the parking lot. There were no windows. The lot looked sufficient for a dozen cars but currently held only four. I parked and stepped out, only to be reminded of how cold the mornings in the desert could be. I doubted it was much above freezing.

I walked to the door. There was a video camera above it. On one side, there was a keypad and a single button with a sign that read, "Push for Entry". So, I did. After considerable scrutiny of my papers at both the NTTR and JACC gates, I was expecting the same at the Operations Center, so I held them out when the door opened.

"Dr. Sam Price?" asked the man standing there.

"That's me," I said.

He nodded, hardly looking at my face and ignoring my documents entirely. Instead, he folded a paper he had in his hand and stuck it into a pocket. "This way."

He was about 5 feet, 8 inches tall with red, somewhat unruly hair and slightly protruding ears. He had brown eyes and a trace of freckles on his cheeks and across the bridge of his nose. I couldn't help thinking that if those freckles had been more prominent as a child, he could have been the real-life equivalent of Alfred E. Neuman but without the gapped tooth grin. As for his age, I was stumped. He could pass for mid-20s, but for some reason, I suspected he was older. He was dressed in tennis shoes, jeans, and a T-shirt. I was almost surprised it did not feature Neuman's signature presidential election slogan, "You could do worse ... and always have!" Instead, it read, "University of Hawaii Drinking Team."

When the man reached the second door, he punched in a code and entered. The room was dominated by a narrow wooden table circled by eight chairs. A tabletop lectern, keyboard, and telephone rested on one end. A large flat panel display hung on the wall behind the lectern. The other end of the room was filled with a rolling cart holding computer equipment and a video camera. Even empty of people, the room felt crowded.

"Welcome to the JACC Operations Center Conference Room. I'm Troy Sayers, and as I understand it, I'll be your guinea pig for the next two weeks."

People I worked with often called themselves my "guinea pig." I was never enamored with the term because it implied some sort of obsequiousness on their part. Actually, the opposite was generally closer to the truth. Success in my job depended more on Troy's willingness to be open and candid than anything about my position or authority.

"It's a pleasure," I replied. "I'm looking forward to learning from an expert about what an Operations Coordinator does."

The comment had the desired effect as he drew back slightly, his brow wrinkling. Perhaps finding no trace of insincerity in my expression, he finally said, "Sounds good, Doc."

Now, it was my turn to be taken aback by a comment. "How did you know my nickname?"

He grinned. "Didn't. I call all you Ph.D.'s Doc."

"Oh, okay. Sam or Doc. Either is fine. You go to the University of Hawaii?"

"Nope, just like the shirt. And drinking. I'd say, take a load off, but we've got places to be. We have a live-fire demo in a couple of weeks, and one of the first, dry runs is starting in a few minutes. Any questions before we go in and watch?"

"Just a quick one. What about the codes for getting around the building?"

He gave me the Neuman grin again, making me wonder if, by the end of the trip, I'd be able to picture him any other way. "I took the liberty," he said, fishing a slip of paper out of his pocket. "Here are the access codes for the front door, the Operations Room, and the room we're in now, the Conference Room."

He handed me the paper with three 4-digit numbers on it. Beside each was two letters—OC, OR, and CR.

"You have an Operations Room in the Operations Center?"

"Yep. No expense was spared in coming up with the names."

"I can see that," I replied. "And you can just have these codes written on a piece of paper?"

"Absolutely not." His indignation was feigned but not bad. "You need to memorize them, eat the paper, and only take a dump when you're here. Wouldn't want those to get out into the public sewer system."

I couldn't stop my guffaw. If I had any doubt before, I was now certain—Troy was the office joker.

"Just be careful with them," he said more seriously though still smiling. "There are too many codes around here to remember, so everyone has them written down in some form. Just don't tell the security guys; they'd have a cow. So, ready to get your first peek at Jack?"

"Absolutely."

"Okay. When we go in, we'll stay by my console on the near side of the room. That way, we'll be out of the way. Drew—that's Brandt Drury—will be flying Jack on his system. Dr. James Marshall, who would be doc if you weren't here ...." He paused, probably to make sure I caught the reference. "He'll be providing the commentary. Everything they do today is simulated, but in a couple of weeks, it'll be live. Then, they'll run it from a trailer called the Mobile Command

Center. The government big shots will be there, too. It's far enough away from the action to be safe but close enough they'll feel the ground shake. You ready?"

"You'll be at the Mobile Command Center, too?"

"Naw, no room. I do my stuff before the firing starts. We'll watch the action from a video feed to this building." He raised an eyebrow in question.

"Yeah, I'm ready. Nothing like starting with the whole nine yards."

"We aim to please, Doc."

Just as the words left his mouth, a bell rang somewhere in the building. Troy frowned, turning first to the door and then back to me. "Someone's lost. The only other visitor is supposed to go to Maintenance." He walked over to the flat panel display, activated it, and pulled the paper I'd seen before from his pocket. "Let's see who we have now?"

But when I looked up at the monitor, I couldn't believe my eyes. Before I could think, the answer to his question escaped my lips. "Jill?"

His gaze made the circuit from the screen on the wall to my face to the piece of paper and back to me. "You know Jillian Henshaw?"

Yeah, I knew Jill Henshaw. Actually, I knew her quite well. She and I had been in graduate school together. She was in a two-year master's degree program in Industrial Psychology, while I was in the four-year doctoral program in Cognitive Psych. We started the same year, but somehow, our paths never crossed until the second. But when that happened, there was—for me at least—an immediate attraction.

Jill looked like the all-American tomboy with a trim, athletic physique and an easy, friendly smile. She had short brown hair, brown eyes, and a dusting of freckles that she was always trying to hide. I, however, found her freckles one of her more endearing features and completely consistent with her tomboy image. Her look of athleticism, however, was a complete illusion. Jill wasn't agile, was hardly coordinated at all. To say she had two left feet might be an insult to left feet.

The first time I asked her to play frisbee, she declined. I thought she might be trying to spare my feelings, so I persisted and eventually, she relented. Then, I watched as the disc slipped off her fingertips or she grabbed a handful of air again and again. So, I made sure to toss one directly at her. It went through her hands and hit her in the face.

That was the last time I tried to talk her into sports, but we soon found another physical activity that we both enjoyed ... in the bedroom. It surprised me how quickly we became intimate. I was equally surprised, however, when it all disappeared so quietly about seven months later. As best as I could figure, we just drifted apart because that was the easiest option. She was finishing her program of study and looking for a job. I had two more years to go on mine. It was as if we'd both conceded in our minds that there was no future for us. And after that concession, questions like, will we get together in two years, never got serious consideration.

At least, that was how I recalled it. But by this point in my life, I knew how flawed memory could be. Did we argue and I had forgotten? Did I ask her to wait for me and she had laughed in my face? No, that one I would have remembered. But the chance that my recollections of her were incorrect in the details was a near certainty. I just hoped those details didn't add up to a slap in the face.

After stating simply that Jill and I knew each other from graduate school—because to say more would be to open the door to all kinds of innuendo—Troy left to give her directions. I followed to say hello.

When Troy opened the door, he was met by, "Hi. I'm supposed to be meeting with personnel involved in maintaining the J-A-C-C Unmanned Aerial System, but I think I may be in the wrong place."

Before Troy could say a word, she glanced over his shoulder and saw me. Her eyes widened as a hand came up to her mouth.

"I think you already know Doc." I couldn't see Troy's face, but by his tone, he was enjoying Jill's shocked expression.

She dropped the hand, revealing the smile I remembered well. "I do," she replied, "but not by that name." She leaned slightly to the side to look directly at me. "So, I take it you finished your Ph.D., and now, it's gone to your head. Doc, is it?"

She raised an eyebrow. The tease was a much better reaction than a face slap.

"Are you here long enough to discuss it over dinner?" I asked.

"Till Wednesday of next week. You?"

"Two days longer, but you might want to ask about extending your trip. They have a live-fire exercise on Thursday. Since you have the clearance to get in here, I doubt there'd be a problem sticking around. And Jack should put on a good show."

She laughed. "Ah, you're on a first-name basis already." She paused a moment. "I'll look into that. As for dinner, sure. I'm in the Golden Nugget Motel, but I have no idea what's around."

"Same place," I replied. "And I'm in the same situation on restaurants, but we can figure that one out. Call you around 5:30?"

"Sounds great. But now, I better get going." She shifted her look to Troy. "Can you tell me how to get to Maintenance?"

Troy gave her directions and she left.

"School friends, huh?" he said as we walked back to the Operations Room. "Both in the Golden Nugget, too. How convenient."

I didn't respond beyond a shrug, figuring innuendo dies of starvation, not denial, and soon, we were at the Operations Room. Troy stood aside, so I pulled the paper from my pocket and entered the code on the keypad.

"Still don't have those memorized?"

"I just had breakfast. Figured I'd save them for lunch."

Troy chuckled and slapped me on the back as we entered the room. He was going to be easy to work with.

Operations Center, JACC Test Range, Nevada, 7:57 AM

As Troy and I stepped into the Operations Room, I could see it was filled with three pairs—two desks, two equipment consoles, and two people. The desks were battered, gray metal with equally worn chairs. The top of the desk closer to the door was clear, save the nameplate that identified the occupant as Troy. He had a side table that held an old rotary-style phone and a sheet of paper with the title "JACC Range Phone Numbers." The other desk was equally tidy and sat across the room. Under its side table, I could see an aging tower computer, while a keyboard and monitor sat on its top. It, too, held a piece of paper I could read even across the room: "No Classified Email."

Next to each desk were two identical racks of equipment, strikingly new compared to the ancient desks and computer. Other than a shelf holding a keyboard, joystick, and trackball and two large display screens above it, I recognized none of the hardware. It was all boxes with readouts, switches of every variety, plugins, and dials. While these setups lacked all the glitz of a polished, commercial console, you could sense the raw computing power they held from the smell of warm electronics and the hum of cooling fans. I even felt a charge in the air ... or at least, imagined that I did.

"Two screens?" I whispered to Troy.

"Completely reconfigurable. Right now, Drew's has simulated video on the right, the threat map on the left. The video screen can show the output from any of Jack's sensors—camera, infrared, and the like. The map gives Drew overall situation awareness, showing him where everything is and Jack's assessment of the contacts—friend, foe, or unknown. Drew can put up other information there, like a weapons loadout. And he's got systems status in a small window on the video side. He can pop it up if the situation calls for it."

It wasn't difficult to see how Mark Dillon's work on target recognition fit into this scheme. His technology identified the humans, the trucks, the tanks, and so on from sensor data. Omega Systems' contribution was collecting and organizing all the rest of the information—the who, where, and what—in order to assess and display the threat they posed.

One person sat at a console, while another, older man stood at his side. Both turned to look when we entered, but neither moved to introduce themselves. Any doubt that I might have had about their identities, however, was removed when the older of the two said, "Just ease in there a bit more, Drew, and we'll get started."

"You got it, Jim."

One of the first things that caught my attention when I glanced toward these two wasn't either of the people. It was Drew's chair. It was equipped with enough knobs and levers to adjust every aspect of the seated position known to man: height, recline, recline tension, rotation tension and lock, back support, and who knew what else. But I guess if you spend your workday on your rear, it pays to invest in the best ergonomics available.

"Yeah, something, isn't it?" whispered Troy, clearly not surprised I was gawking. "Custom. And it cost him a small fortune."

"He could live in that thing," I replied under my breath.

"He almost does."

That fact, too, seemed apparent when I looked at him closer. On one hand, Drew's face and arms were lightly tanned. He wasn't a complete stranger to the outdoors. But on the other, whatever muscle he'd developed there or in the gym was well hidden by pudginess.

Adding the fine, light brown hair that was making a rapid retreat from his forehead and Drew reminded me more of a middle-aged banker than a young pilot.

Dr. James Marshall, on the other hand, was quite distinguished-looking, fit, and trim. He appeared to be in his mid-50s with slightly wavy, black hair and a dark mustache on a weathered face. He was a bit taller than I, at probably 6 feet, 2 inches or so. From appearance alone, he could have been anyone from the foreman of a vast, Texas cattle ranch to a four-term Senator from one of our Western states. The cowboy boots and jeans completed that illusion, although the shirt he wore was pure white and looked like it was starched enough to stand up on its own.

"That's good," said Marshall. "Ready?"

"Always."

Troy gestured toward his unoccupied console and we sat. A moment later, he had it up and running. "I've got my console linked to Drew's, so you'll see everything he does. You also have a video stream on the wall monitor behind Drew. He'll be toggling through different windows to show up there."

Marshall cleared his throat, walked to the wall monitor, and stood a bit taller. "Ladies and gentlemen, I give you Jack with Mr. Brandt Drury at the controls in the live-fire scenario we call The Street Ambush."

From that point forward, Marshall's comments became much terser, even sounding somewhat off-the-cuff. "You'll notice some friendly forces coming up the street," he said, pointing at the video display. "Our job is to protect them."

"Fantastic sim," I whispered to Troy. "Very realistic." In my job, I'd seen a lot of them and it was among the best. "You reuse any of it for the live-fire demonstration?"

"No way. Everything is real that day. We just make the sims look good for contractors like you and that cutie friend of yours." Troy failed to get the line out without a grin, so I didn't bother with a response.

"After all, the higher the fidelity of the sim, the better the pilot is prepared for the fight," Troy said after a moment. He glanced at me and added, "Marshall's law."

Marshall's law, however, was probably wrong ... or at least, incomplete. Most of the research indicated there were diminishing returns from increasing low-level detail in simulation-based training. Their effect might even become negative if they distracted the trainee from more general principles. But the research was complex and not definitive, making Marshall's position a common stance when you were on the selling side of a government contract.

"And here's the bad guy," Troy whispered in his best game-show-host voice.

A man with some type of shoulder-launched weapon appeared on a rooftop in the corner of the screen. Simultaneously, an open circle appeared on the threat map. The symbol quickly morphed to a triangle, first unfilled but rapidly darkening.

"Circle for friend, triangle for foe?" I asked.

"In part," said Troy. "Circle is friend while the shading shows how confident Jack is. No shading, no certainty. Totally dark and he's willing to bet the farm. So, an unfilled circle is technically a friendly with no certainty—pretty much the same as unknown. The dark triangle is that bad guy on the rooftop ... which is pretty much a no brainer since the guy's pointing a gun at the friendlies."

There was a flicker on the screen, and I looked more closely. "Is that video from Jack?"

"It is," replied Troy. "That's a shot of Bogey Town, as we call it, the town that gets to bite the dust on the live-fire day. And yeah, I know. Bogeys are usually hostile aircraft, but this is what you get with the Air Force leading the program. Anyway, Drew and Marshall are just checking that all the troops are showing up on the threat map correctly."

"And those are what, manikins I'm seeing in the video?"

"Yep," he whispered back to me. "See them popping up on the threat map? Jack takes them to be human because of a small transmitter on each. Then, he uses the rest of the data to classify them, friend or foe."

Sure enough, each manikin in Bogey Town got translated into a good or bad guy on the threat map. Then, something strange happened—strange for manikins anyway. "Some of them are moving? Are you mixing virtual and real somehow?"

"Nope," he replied. "You're still seeing nothing but manikins. Some of them are mounted on a small four-wheel dolly with a motor. If you watch closely, they always move in a straight line."

After a moment switching my gaze between the threat map and the video, I said, "Very impressive." The correlation of the physical manikins and the symbols on the threat map was a basic requirement. Having a contact appear at the wrong place or not at all wasn't acceptable. But the realism of the figures I saw on the video and the addition of motion made the illusion complete. Sure, only some of the manikins moved and always in a straight line, but in the context of a complex, evolving scene, the overall effect was compelling. I felt I was there.

Drew switched the display back to simulated video to take his first shot. It was a hit, and the man with the shoulder-launched weapon went down. After that, the enemies' attention shifted from the ground forces to Jack. That made sense; they wouldn't last long if they didn't remove the danger in the air.

Their change in tactics, however, did nothing to change their fortunes. Calmly and with great skill, Drew eliminated each would-be attacker. One moment, he had Jack hovering behind the corner of a building. The next, Jack dashed from cover to dispatch a hostile.

Drew's shot on a sniper was particularly impressive. He positioned Jack behind a partially demolished wall and then popped up to launch a simulated Hellfire missile through a window and into the room that held the shooter.

"Did you get any training on Jack's offensive capabilities?" I whispered to Troy.

He frowned slightly and said, "Nope. Just flying in and out, watching that nothing breaks."

"What if a pilot gets sick or something like that and can't finish a mission?"

"If there's no backup pilot, we get the hell out of Dodge." I wasn't going to use the term that Mark Dillon had mentioned, but Troy did. "We just babysit. The pilots do the fighting."

I nodded. Troy's version of his responsibilities matched those described by Dillon. Of course, it would be easier to get out of Dodge if you could take a couple of shots at the bad guys chasing you. Presumably, that alternative had been weighed and fleeing was the better option. And yet, that was an assumption. I decided to ask and be prepared with arguments for some rudimentary weapons training for coordinators, just in case.

When the first scenario ended, it wasn't difficult to pick the winner. The enemy had been decimated and the friendly ground forces were unscathed, moving forward on their mission. It was an unlikely outcome during actual hostilities, even given overwhelming firepower; things never went exactly to plan. But still, it was an excellent demonstration of Jack's capability.

It also wasn't difficult to tell that Drew was his own biggest fan. Troy admired his coworker's skill and I could tell that Marshall was a supporter ... but not like Drew himself. Throughout the event, there had been a flair in the way he manipulated the controls, like the flourishes of a world-renowned concert pianist after a particularly challenging passage. After several shots, he had paused and glanced our way as if expecting us to applaud. And after taking out the sniper, he had pumped his fist. My thought was petty, I admit, but it seemed he might be taking too much pride in his work.

Troy leaned over and whispered in my ear. "You're going to want to watch this next scenario closely. It shows as Marshall puts it, the future of unmanned systems."

What was the last one?

I nodded, figuring I'd get an answer to my question by watching. When Marshall retook center stage, he reiterated Troy's words. "Ladies and Gentlemen, it is with great pleasure that I present to you a mission that highlights the future of unmanned aerial systems. I present to you, Jack flying The High-Value Target scenario."

Something in his introduction didn't seem quite right. It wasn't the mention of a high-value target. Dillon had already introduced me to that concept. But what it was escaped me.

"You've got it backward," said Marshall, sounding none too pleased with his pilot. "I want the simulated video of the street first, then the infrared sensors."

"Right. Sorry." Drew did something on his console, and the street scene appeared on the monitor on the wall.

"Ladies and gentlemen, let me set the stage for you," Marshall continued, now reverting to his formal, presentation tone. "In the course of close-air support for a U.S. Seal team pursuing members of a terrorist cell, Jack has identified a high-value target—the terrorist cell leader. The man is responsible for the deaths of hundreds, troops and pro-Western civilians alike, and his denunciation of us escalates by the hour."

After the talk with Mark Dillon, I had some understanding of how Jack might have made that identification. I looked closer at the screen, which was now showing the returns from Jack's infrared sensor—human forms in glowing red and yellow on the top floor of a three-story building. It was a gathering of some sort, and some of the ghostly forms were small.

Children?

Troy leaned over toward me again. "The high-value target is the five-pointed star on the threat map. It's dark because Jack's sure he's the guy."

I'd been ignoring the threat map, still wondering if those little glowing blobs could be kids. Their behavior fit. They were dashing back and forth between a couple of rooms. But with Troy's words, I looked down from the wall display and studied the threat map on his console. It took me a moment to make the connections between the symbols on it and the infrared forms, but when I did, I said, "Oh, shit." It was supposed to be under my breath, but apparently, it wasn't. Marshall glanced at me and smiled.

The scenario was one of those nightmares of war. A murderous terrorist was meeting with his cell members amid children and other innocents, perhaps women, all represented as unfilled circles on the threat map. It was the kind of situation no one wanted to face. And yet, it happened, and when it did, someone had to make a gut-wrenching call. Let the leader escape to kill again or risk the loss of innocent lives in an attack against him. And unfortunately, our track record on situations like this one wasn't perfect. In 2013, an unmanned system strike in Yemen was responsible for the deaths of several members of a wedding party, including some civilians.

I felt like someone had put a belt around my chest and was slowly tightening it. Even reminding myself this was a simulation didn't help; my heart was still drumming in my ears. Why had Marshall made this part of his campaign to keep the program sold to the government? What was he thinking? And how would Drew react when it was over? Even if it was a complete success—the terrorist was eliminated and no innocents were harmed—I couldn't see Marshall and Drew bumping chests afterward.

I'd been so stunned by the scenario that I'd almost forgotten that Marshall was still talking. I tuned back into his words. "Success in this simulation of the High-Value Target scenario would be easy to guarantee, of course. While Jack is a real unmanned aerial system, the behavior of the targets and the innocents have to be preprogrammed. It would be simple to add a little computer code to Jack's software that said, wait until two minutes, seven-point-three seconds into the scenario and then you'll have an open shot. But we're not cheaters."

Marshall looked slowly around the room that was now empty, perhaps imagining the audience he'd soon have. "No one knows just when the kids might leave ... or if they will at all. And to further increase realism, their movement is based on observations of children at play, rather than the guesses of a 20-something-year-old software engineer about what a five-year-old might do."

I was impressed with the attention to detail Omega Systems had taken, but that didn't make the situation any easier to watch. And as I did, the civilian adults moved to the second room—perhaps the women leaving to let the men discuss business? It was easy to weave a story around what I was seeing. The children, on the other hand, continued to dart between the rooms. One minute, a child was there with the terrorist leader; the next, he/she would move off to the adjacent area and join the others.

Over time, however, the children migrated to the adjoining space until only one was left. Just as the last child departed, the targeting display appeared and a missile was launched. At the distance Jack was operating—about 1000 yards—the missile reached the target in approximately four-tenths of a second. It was long enough for the child to clear the room, but not so long that he/she should return. Simply put, the shot had been expertly placed and timed perfectly. The innocents would be hurt by the blast wave, but unless they were also hit by some flying debris, they should survive.

Even though the mission was technically a success, my body did not register it as one. I felt exhausted and a bit shaky, like I had just finished a half-marathon. I wondered how often unmanned system operators found themselves in situations like this. Unfortunately, I suspected they were all too common. Wouldn't there often be civilians or culturally significant structures near targets? Wasn't that a tactic that was often used by terrorists? The saying, war is hell, felt very real to me in the aftermath of this scenario.

Marshall turned to Drew. "Taking out the sniper was great but a couple of those rooftop shooters just about picked off a friendly. Want to run over the ambush scenario again?"

"Yeah, sure," Drew replied, more unemotionally than I thought possible. But then, I suppose Drew had flown the second scenario enough to have acclimated himself.

"Can I talk to you in the hall?" I whispered to Troy.

"Sure. Let me get something first." He opened a drawer in his desk and pulled out a document that was perhaps three inches thick. It was entitled, *JACC Operations Coordinator, Training Needs Analysis and Curriculum Development.*

When we were in the hall, he gave me the document. "It doesn't mean anything to me, but I guess it's your thing. And since I'll be a little late coming in tomorrow—I have a dentist appointment—this will give you a little light reading."

I took it, doing one of those fake almost-drops from its heft. "Yep. Not the first one of these I've seen. Not likely to be the last, either. But what I wanted to ask about was Drew in that last scenario."

"Drew? Why?"

"Well, for one thing, he didn't get into it like the first one. No fist-pumping or anything like that ... not that I expected it, given what it's about. But I didn't even see him bring up the targeting display or launch the missile. Does Jack have some kind of snap-shot setting?"

Troy chuckled, saying, "Yeah, snap like off the top of his head."

That seemed to answer the question in Troy's mind, but I still had no idea how Drew had done it. Sure, I'd seen him toggle among Jack's different tactical displays, giving Marshall a constantly changing scene on the wall that followed his commentary. But I'd seen none of the steps necessary to launch a missile. "I'm serious. How did he pull off that last shot?"

Troy drew back and looked at me closely. "You're not screwing with me, are you, Doc?"

I slowly shook my head, not knowing what more to say.

"Drew doesn't do anything in the second scenario. Jack was flying."

With those words, I knew why Marshall's introduction to the second scenario had seemed strange. He'd said Jack was flying, and at some level, the implications of that statement must have registered. It just hadn't been at the conscious level. And now that it was conscious, it was hard to believe. "Jack is collecting the information? He's evaluating it to determine who's a threat? And he's initiating an attack based on that assessment?"

Troy had been nodding his head emphatically during my entire sequence of questions, causing me to pause in disbelief. "And there's no human intervention in the process?"

"A pilot could decide to keep Jack out of the autonomous mode. But once he flips the switch, no one's fast enough to stop Jack. By the time the pilot recognizes the targeting display, the missile's in the air. But then, that's the only way to go with that scenario. Hesitate and the bad guy's gone or the kid's back."

Now, Marshall's decision to use the High-Value Scenario made perfect sense. Initially, there had been widespread concern that unmanned systems would make war too impersonal, too sterile. The people who were targeted were just blips on a screen. Isolated from the horrors of war, the operators of these systems would become unthinking and unfeeling.

The truth, however, was often the opposite. In many cases, the operators of these systems observed their targets over long periods; they came to feel that they knew these people. Or they found them surrounded by innocents or priceless cultural artifacts. And rather than being isolated from war's horrors, they often saw the effects of the attacks they initiated. As a result, the incidence of posttraumatic stress disorder among unmanned systems pilots was quite high compared to other occupations in the armed services.

In the High-Value Target scenario, Marshall had found the perfect case for unmanned systems, the perfect catch-22. Human hesitation could cost the lives of others, but action risked the psychological life of the actor.

"Is this a classified capability, this autonomous mode?"

"How it's done, the algorithms and all are," replied Troy. "But the JACC program will tell anyone who'll listen that it's being developed. It's the foothold it has on the future of warfare."

Foothold on the future of warfare?

Troy was starting to sound like Marshall, leaving me feeling a bit disoriented. "Where can I make a call to someone outside the range?"

"Call the guard station. They'll set you up with a phone and a time. Is there something wrong?"

I didn't answer before I left other than to say thanks. My head was too full of questions vying for attention for more than that.

Guard Station, JACC Test Range, Nevada, 8:30 AM

"Hi, Mark, it's Sam Price," I said when Dillon answered his phone. "Thank God you're there."

There was a moment of hesitation, making me realize that not only was my call without warning, my comment was without context. Additionally, some quick mental math told me it was around his lunchtime. The fact that none of this had popped to the surface of my mind on the drive to the guard station told me how consumed I'd become in my thoughts—not that this state was unusual for me.

"Hi, Doc. Problems?" he asked.

"Not exactly problems," I replied. "But first, sorry for calling out of the blue. I need a sanity check and was hoping you could provide it."

He chuckled. "A psychologist asking for a sanity check. That's a new one. But your timing's good. I was just grabbing a bite at my desk between meetings. You're at the test range, right?"

"Yeah, first day and already, I'm feeling a bit ... well, for want of a better word, ungrounded. Apparently, Jack has an autonomous mode. It can reach its own conclusions about contacts. And if any are threats, it can initiate an attack. Is that common in programs like JACC?"

"Sure," replied Dillon without hesitation. "For many, autonomy has become the Holy Grail of next-generation warfare. I just finished a book called *Wired for War*. Ever hear of it?"

"No, can't say that I have."

"You might want to take a look sometime. It talks about five US military programs that are researching autonomous weapons. And I'm talking about serious, well-funded efforts, not your academic studies with a few hundred thousand dollars. It was published around 2010, and the emphasis has only grown from there. I'm not sure you're going to find any unmanned system programs that aren't researching machines that think and act on their own."

Well, so much for the foundation I had from my academic studies of artificial intelligence. The discipline was thriving in areas that had hardly been mentioned in class. But maybe this work wasn't in textbooks because they had failed? Technically, research that didn't find an effect was publishable; it just didn't happen very often. "So, any of these programs come up with anything?"

That caused Dillon to pause but not for the reason I hoped. "Yeah, but most of the break-through stuff is classified."

Why I had seen so little of this research in my classes now seemed obvious.

"Hold on," came Dillon's voice over the phone, followed by the sound of some drawers opening and closing. "I just wanted to make sure I remembered the name right," he said when he came back on the line. "Have you heard of a DARPA program called HART?"

"No, sorry."

"No need to be," replied Dillon. "The tech developed under the program never got used, didn't even get that much press. But it raised the bar significantly on machines that could act on their own. The drones DARPA built under HART could conduct aerial surveillance without human pilots. They could coordinate their flight paths so that they covered an area efficiently. They could decide if an individual was acting suspicious, and when they found someone, they'd assign several units to keep him from slipping away. If they got enough dirt on a guy, they'd notify law enforcement who could come in and arrest him. But like I said, it never got fielded."

"Issues of privacy?" I asked.

"Pretty much," replied Dillon. I heard papers shuffling again. "Homeland Security tested HART drones for border protection and general public surveillance. And both the Miami–Dade and Houston Police Departments tested them for things like traffic control and SWAT operations. There are countries where technology like HART would be more acceptable, but in the U.S., it just didn't fly ... pun intended."

"Okay," I said slowly. "You've got some route planning like a GPS could do. And HART drones spot people who are acting strange, trying to hide or whatever. But that doesn't seem anywhere near as complex as Jack. He's hiding .... Damn, now I'm calling this machine a 'he'."

"Hard not to," said Dillon.

"Anyway, Jack's ability to hide behind things, how it snaps off its shots. It just seems worlds away from what we see in the commercial market ... like self-driving cars. They can park themselves or keep you in your lane on well-marked roads. But speeding down a winding, country road during a thunderstorm, hands off the wheel? No one is claiming that kind of capability."

"You can degrade Jack's performance, too," said Dillon, "if you make the environment unforgiving enough. But your point is well taken. The difference is largely in what a company can afford to put into a car they want to sell to a well-heeled private citizen compared to what we can put in a weapon system that could save hundreds of lives. Much the same technology that allows cars to self-park, for example, lets Jack hide behind a wall before taking a shot. But we give Jack a lot more sensors to pick up what's around him and a helluva lot more computing power to understand the environment. Jack's a self-driving car on steroids."

It all made sense the way Dillon explained it. Jack's abilities didn't even seem that controversial. But as I dissected the issues in my mind, I hit on the crux of my worries. "It's Jack's latitude to use deadly force that makes me uncomfortable."

"But the pilot can still intervene."

"In theory," I replied.

"What does that mean?" Dillon asked slowly.

So, I described the High-Value Target scenario and the conundrum that Dillon would easily recognize. "If a pilot had to approve that shot at the terrorist, the opportunity would be lost. So, he's forced to decide before he knows exactly what Jack will be facing and how risky the shot will be. And by moving the decision away from the battlefield ...." I wasn't certain how to continue without stepping on Dillon's professional toes.

"We would isolate the human from the consequences of his actions, and he could become a monster," said Dillon, finishing my thought more bluntly than I would have. "We all know there's that possibility, Doc. And unfortunately, I don't have an easy answer. Some AI researchers believe that we should be systematically reviewing and strictly limiting the skills we grant to machines, and I'm sure that some of Jack's abilities are on their to-be-banned list.

"But on the other hand, there are those who believe that the sense of self and the ability to reproduce are the primary poison pills of AI. A machine that could build copies of itself and that saw value in doing that could evolve into something evil. Both of these capabilities are being studied in labs, but neither would be given to Jack."

Dillon was silent for several moments, then said, "I can see why you called." He sighed, loudly enough that I could hear it over the phone. "Col. Dempsey's giving the government something between a hard sell and an ultimatum with this scenario. It exposes the tradeoff between human judgment and cold machine logic better than anything has in the past."

"Col. Dempsey? I thought Marshall and his team made the call on these demonstrations?"

"The colonel was probably involved in the planning. But even if Omega Systems came up with it on their own, nothing gets shown to the government without his okay."

Another pause was punctuated with another sigh over the phone. "Damn, I've made things sound bleak, and they probably aren't for a couple of reasons. First, just because a capability is being researched doesn't mean it'll make it into the field. Weapons that have emerged from military R&D programs have had most of their autonomy stripped away. What remains, if anything, is an ability to attack specific, well-defined threats. Jack may be nudging the state-of-the-art on hunting and prosecuting targets, but those advanced capabilities will probably never see the light of day.

"And the other thing—I won't use the phrase 'smoke and mirrors', but the scenarios that are used in demonstrations are selected for a reason. Every system has limits. Jack has boundaries where it operates less efficiently or not at all. Demo scenarios avoid those areas like the plague. Additionally, the methods Jack is using may have been built specifically for the demo, and those methods may not easily extend to broader problems. Jack is probably not as capable as he appears in the High-Value Target scenario."

Now it was my turn to release a long breath. "Thanks, Mark. I needed your perspective. The research is a lot further along than I had imagined, but as you said, it's still research. And it's still in the lab ... assuming you can call the range a lab. Anyway, thanks and I'll let you get back to your lunch."

"No worries. I've got a return trip to St. Louis in early March. How about lunch, and you can regale me with the stories of your time in Nevada?"

"Absolutely. My treat," I replied. We said our good-byes and hung up.

I headed back to the Operations Center, still somewhat disquieted by the breadth of Jack's responsibilities. But as I drove, I took comfort knowing that until the government fully vetted Jack's capabilities, he was a prisoner of the JACC test range. Looking out over its beautiful but barren terrain, I muttered to myself, "And not much he can hurt out here."

The Golden Nugget Motel, Nevada, 3:14 PM

Back at home in St. Louis, my days always started with a jog. Those runs were my time for pondering the minutia of life and planning my approach to its numerous but generally minor snags. But with days starting at 6:00 AM on the JACC test range, that schedule wasn't workable. About the only exercise I'd be able to fit in the morning was bending my elbow to get the cup of coffee to my lips.

That left the afternoon for my runs, which had its good and its bad points. On the plus side, with January temperatures hovering around 60 degrees in the afternoon, the whole desert was my gym; at home, I was usually stuck on a treadmill. But the plus side of Nevada's open spaces was also its downside. There were no sidewalks through quiet residential neighborhoods. There were no meandering paths through shady parks. My impression, sitting in my motel room, was that civilization was hardly wider than the two-lane highway out front and the collection of businesses on either side. But then, I hadn't tried to find more.

I donned a pair of shorts and a long-sleeved T-shirt. Stepping outside, the highway option immediately looked less promising than even I'd thought. There was no sidewalk. The parking lots of some of the businesses were connected, but most weren't. That left running on the untended ground between the businesses or running on the shoulder of the highway until I reached the driveway of the next lot. The latter option, in particular, seemed foolhardy. Though the speed limit around the motel was 50 miles per hour, most of the drivers were going 70, staring out of a dust-streaked windshield ... or so it seemed. And the shoulder was fair game if someone had stopped on the road for a left turn.

Fortunately, I found a second option I'd completely overlooked — side roads. The one next to the motel was hardly more than graded desert. It didn't warrant a stop sign on the highway, much less a traffic light, which explained why I hadn't noticed it. And while people were still driving fast, traffic on this street was quite light. It would work, so I set out on my jog.

Forty-five minutes later, I returned. Had it not been for the buzz in my legs, I would have thought I'd strolled the whole way. The sign of a vigorous workout in the Midwest—a T-shirt soaked through in sweat—was largely missing due to the low humidity levels in the desert. And also missing, unfortunately, was the mental harmony I sought from running. Simply put, I'd spent too much time staring with wonder at the unfamiliar terrain and too little on organizing my internal world. That problem would pass, however, as I became more acclimated to the surroundings.

After a shower, I checked the time. There was still enough to call Nicole on the landline before dinner with Jill.

The thought brought a stupid grin to my face—I could tell even without looking in a mirror. There had been plenty of times in my life when I didn't have one attractive female to socialize with, and now, I was juggling two? Well, not really. I would be spending a quiet evening with an old friend with no thought of a future with her after I called a new acquaintance, hoping we might have one.

The calls between Nicole and me had become something of a daily ritual, or worst case, every other day. But despite their clockwork regularity, they were never planned, never scheduled. They just worked out.

And the content of these calls? Let me just say that in the extremely improbable event I became a presidential candidate in the future and the media got hold of them, they would probably conclude we were passing state secrets. How else could one explain Nicole's range of topics: trying Plein Air painting to document her travels, which might include anything from Paris to old-town St. Charles across the river; controlling room temperature by thought using neural implants; restoring an old Victrola for an accent piece in her apartment; becoming irritated by the main character in her latest romance novel because the woman lacked common sense. In truth, however, the breadth of topics was just a reflection of her nearly boundless curiosity.

What I talked about in turn was focused and analytical ... or if you prefer the negative phrasing, narrow and obsessive. I observed with a microscope and assessed with a micrometer, turning my mental gaze to things that mattered to me. What mattered changed over time, of course, but not with the rapidity of Nicole's mental life. And what mattered to me right now? Jack and Nicole, not necessarily in that order and obviously, not for the same reasons. But as I dialed her number, I resolved to steer clear of any talk of Jack. After all, I was still looking at the aircraft through my microscope, taking measurements with my micrometer.

"Hi, Sam. I thought you might call this afternoon. So, first day in the Nevada desert. What's it like?"

"Cold in the morning, warm in the afternoon, and always dry and dusty. But I have to admit, it has a rugged beauty. I went out earlier, looking for a jogging route."

"Looking for one of your pondering paths? Or is it a reminiscing route?"

I chuckled. At some point, I'd mentioned to her that while jogging was my preferred way to exercise, I also valued it as time alone with my thoughts. She'd obviously remembered the comment. "So, what have you been doing besides spending hours coming up with clever alliterations for my pastimes?"

"That was off the top of my head," she replied, her indignation sounding like what it was—feigned. "Actually, I've been reading up on JACC."

So much for my plan to skip that topic.

"It's not exactly in the headlines," she said, "but I did find a couple of articles online. One called the aircraft, and I quote, one of the most advanced implementations of artificial intelligence not on a supercomputer anchored to the ground. It sounds like quite an opportunity for you."

Having not considered what to say about Jack in advance, the first sound from my lips was a sigh. Nicole, however, had no trouble attaching meaning to the exhalation. "So, concerns about the program."

"Well, not exactly concerns," I replied. "It's just not what I expected."

"How so?"

No turning back now.

"Well, first, I'm not working with the guy who interacts with the advanced artificial intelligence in the aircraft. That would be the pilot and my guy ... well, he calls himself the aircraft's babysitter. But that's not the real issue."

Over the next ten minutes, I described what I'd learned about Jack's autonomous capabilities. When I finished, I said, "I know it's stupid to worry about Jack taking over the world. After all, he'll run out of fuel eventually." The quip didn't elicit a response, however. She probably knew I wasn't ready to laugh off my disquiet just yet.

"You mentioned those other programs that had researched autonomy, and none of them introduced this level of self-control into the military, right?"

"That's what Mark Dillon told me," I replied. "And where I've found information, that seems to be the case."

"Don't you think this one will turn out the same?"

"Probably. Between the Congress and the Department of Defense, every aspect of this program should be examined and re-examined. I mean, capabilities like this just don't pop up on the battlefield, right?"

Nicole laughed. "I don't recall reading much about the lifecycle of a U.S. military weapon system in my medical journals. Are you thinking you should say something about it ... when you give your talk to the leadership out there?"

"Frankly, I have to figure out what I think before I can say anything to Col. Dempsey or Dr. Marshall. I mean, putting Jack into our military arsenal could save lives. But at the same time, isn't this just one step closer to the dystopia some futurists predict? We hand over more and more responsibility to machines until one day, we wake up and they have the upper hand?"

"Well, I'm sure on your pondering path jogs, you'll figure out how you want to handle it. You always do."

"Thanks, Nicole. Thanks for listening to my rambling."

"That's what girlfriends do."

It was a simple word, a common word—girlfriend—but it stole my breath, perhaps because it was the first time either of us had used it. I wanted to think of Nicole as my girlfriend, hoped I would someday. But I wasn't there yet. So, how was she? Or was I making too much from what was a simple slip of the tongue, an unguarded comment?

And yet, in the split-second I had to absorb her words, I knew it wasn't a mistake. I, too, felt the closeness. Even though I had never hugged her, never walked hand-in-hand with her, never kissed her, I knew we were building a shared world of the little things in our lives, as well as the pivotal ones—our values, our hopes, and our dreams. That common reality would have grown had we been together, but it seemed to have blossomed more quickly in the absence of the physical.

All in all, the realization was startling. I hadn't anticipated it, but I knew it to be true. I wanted to talk to Nicole about it. And yet, words would fail me. I needed to look into her eyes, hold her hand in mine, and then talk would do what it does best—confirm what I knew to be true from the unspoken. For now, however, that talk must wait.

"How's your aunt doing?"

"Really well," replied Nicole. "She's getting her strength back, looking forward to going home and getting back to her hobbies. She's been talking about gardening in the spring so much, I started thinking about joining my neighborhood group that does the plantings around our entrance."

For the next ten minutes, she spoke with passion about the pros and cons of various types of borders—shrubs vs. grasses—and mixing annuals with perennials to get color all year long. I mostly explained that growing up on a farm in the Midwest meant I knew something about corn, wheat, and soybeans, but little else. And yet, I knew if she continued in this interest, in a few weeks I'd be speaking with some authority on the varieties of boxwood shrubs and enjoying the challenge of finding the perfect one with her.

Too soon, my call with Nicole was over, and I went to the motel lobby to meet Jill for dinner. I sat in one of the armchairs along the wall but only to stand before it had even warmed to my touch. It was as if my unconscious was trying to make a lie of my earlier thought, that this was just a quiet evening with an old friend. The problem was, not getting slapped earlier in the day had eliminated only one possibility—she didn't hate me enough to make a public display. But everything else from a serving of silent disdain for dinner to seduction and a wild night of sex were still on the table. And it didn't help that the feel of her soft, warm body, the smell of her hair, the taste of her lips weren't buried as deep in my memory as I expected.

Logically, I believed she'd be happy to see me, as I was her, but nothing more. Jill and I had gone our separate ways, and neither of us had looked back. But not knowing for certain was having its way with me. So, I paced the lobby, alternating between staring out the front door into the desert night and checking the wall clock that never seemed to move.

Eventually, she appeared at the door—it felt like "eventually" even though the recalcitrant clock said she was two minutes early. And when she appeared, my tension vanished. The grin on her face, the same one I remembered from college, and the way she turned a cheek to me so I could plant a kiss there told me all I needed to know. We were good with each other. She even started using my nickname, picking it, I supposed, as a good compromise between the intimacy we had known and the friendship we had now.

The rest of the evening was spent scouting out a restaurant and dining, interspersed liberally with stories of our lives. She was happy in her job but wasn't sure about the advancement possibilities. And she had a boyfriend who had recently become a fiancé. I watched her eyes twinkle as she talked of her husband-to-be. Then, she invited me to her wedding, and I accepted, not just from common courtesy, but because I was happy for her. And I was looking forward to meeting the guy who had captured her heart ... and to warn him about frisbee, if he didn't know already.

After several minutes of her fiancé-talk, she stopped almost midsentence and blushed. "I'm sorry. I'm dominating the conversation. Are you seeing anyone?" I surprised myself by telling her about Nicole, almost as if we were as close as she and her intended. And when the evening was over, the only strained part had been when I had to fight to keep the stupid grin off my face every time I used the word "girlfriend".

THE DAY, THURSDAY, JANUARY 14

Operations Center, JACC Test Range, Nevada, 9:47 AM

After watching as someone tried to outrun a Hellfire missile in a car and fail miserably, Troy tried to phone JACC Maintenance. He wanted to know who was in the car. I, on the other hand, didn't just want to know; I was desperate for that information. "Still no answer," Troy called across the room to where I paced behind his console. I was watching Jack returning to his search-and-destroy route as if nothing had happened. In three minutes, he would pass just north of the Maintenance Building coming from the east.

"I'm going to try the guard station."

No answer at Maintenance made perfect sense to me, I thought as Troy dialed the phone. Now, no one would be trying to claim that Jack's destruction of the Mobile Command Center was a one-time glitch. He was systematically hunting us, and the people in the Maintenance Building, whoever was left, would be preparing for the onslaught.

Someone answered at the guard station, and I listened to one side of the conversation, learning little from the occasional "Us, too," "The two of them?" and "No shit."

"What's the news?" I asked as Troy walked over and took his place at the console. I still couldn't sit, all the extra adrenaline in my system keeping me from landing in one spot for more than ten seconds.

"Well, one good thing," said Troy. "Your friend, Jill, wasn't in the car that got blown away."

"I didn't think she would be. She'd know better." The statement was true, although until Troy's report, I'd found no solace in the logic.

"It was Marv Richter. Him and his dog. You know him?"

"I know him from one of the bars. Seemed like a nice guy."

"He is ... was," said Troy, slowly shaking his head. "Otherwise, the guard didn't have much. Marshall and Dempsey don't have the bomb disposal robots yet, but they're on the way. And Williams is still trying to regain control but with no luck. But I saved the best for last. Dempsey got a couple of Apaches in the air, although they're keeping them off the range ... which I don't understand. I mean, one little jog into Jack's airspace, and we'd have our answer. If Jack's good with them, they could come on in and blow him out of the sky."

I understood the sentiment, but it didn't seem that simple to me. "The colonel's probably worried about what might happen if Jack sees them as hostiles. He could go off the range, chasing them, and who knows who wins that fight?"

"So, you'd just sit back and let your friend die?"

The comment hit like a punch to my stomach. "No Apache's going to get to Jack before he gets to Maintenance," I said softly. I looked down, squeezing my eyes closed against the pain that was coursing through my mind.

"Doc, I'm sorry. I didn't mean that."

I looked up, trying to swallow the lump in my throat. "Jill would be safe at home with her fiancé if I hadn't talked her into staying. I've messed up a few times in my life but never anything like this."

Troy shook his head. "You forget. I was there. All you said was that Jack would put on a great show, and she's probably heard that a dozen more times from a dozen other people since she's been here."

But not from a former lover.

And that was the flaw in his argument. But there was nothing to be gained from correcting him, so I said, "Thanks," and resolved to wall off my emotions for now. If I survived and Jill didn't, I'd have a lifetime to regret my words. And I would. They would echo in my memory until I died.

I might have had more difficulty getting Jill out of my head now except a glance at the console filled my thoughts with a new set of questions. "How many people are watching from the Maintenance Building?"

Troy looked at the screen. "Whoa. I wouldn't think more than four or five, but that's a crowd."

As Jack neared the building, a large area of heat had resolved into a dozen or more individual returns. At the moment, all of them were in one spot. "Is that part of the building reinforced?"

"Not sure," said Troy. "Wait a second. I might have the building plan." He went over to his desk and started digging through it. After a moment, he pulled out a sheaf of papers and quickly flipped through them. "Sorry, I must have pitched that stuff."

I turned back to the console. "Looks like they've spread out and there's more like fifteen of them."

Troy walked back over, looked down at his console, and frowned. Then, he slapped his forehead with an open palm and dropped into his chair. "Damn, I'm such an idiot. Those aren't people. Well, some of them are, but most of them are manikins."

"Targets for Jack?" I asked. Troy nodded.

"I should have watched them spread out," I said, pointing to one area of the building. "Then, we'd know if that big bunch of contacts is manikins or humans."

"Trying to draw fire there?" asked Troy.

"That's what I was wondering. Anyway, at least they're fighting back." It was the first ray of hope I'd experienced in the last ten minutes.

"Yeah, right," Troy said. "Nothing like fighting one of the most advanced killing machines in the world with a bunch of dummies who can't even pull a trigger. Besides, Jack will just blanket the building in missiles. Nothing's getting out of there alive."

"Most likely," I conceded after a moment. "It's just too bad they .... Never mind."

"What?" asked Troy.

"Well, if they'd put those manikins out in the desert, Jack might have wasted a bunch of missiles. It might have cut down on what he could throw at them."

Troy's face screwed up like he'd taken a bite of lemon, his head slowly shaking. "Not likely, Doc. He'd just carve them up with the chain gun, and he's not likely to run out of bullets."

"Then, make them a harder target. Put them inside a car or truck. Stick one or two in a cave. Whatever."

Troy's head stopped shaking, and he was staring at the wall. "Maybe," he admitted after a moment. "I'm pretty sure Jack had a full load of Hellfires for the demo—sixteen, with only two fired so far. But if they got him to waste a half dozen or so, that might help."

"Maybe we could do something like that?"

"No manikins here." Troy held up a hand before I could object. "I know what you're going to say. Yeah, I'll give it some thought." But before I could concur, he shouted, "Damn! Jack's firing on Maintenance."

I looked on in horror as the symbols for three Hellfire missiles appeared on the display, each ending its flight a half-second later at the Maintenance Building. Legs that only moments before had been so restless I couldn't stand in one place now failed me. I dropped into the chair next to Troy and hung my head. Would I be toasting Jill and her new husband at their wedding in a few months ... or would I be explaining to him how I had drawn her into a killing field during her funeral in a few days? The pain and guilt I felt threatened to paralyze me.

The sounds of an explosion reverberated through the building. I raised my head and stared at the display. Only a glowing blob from the fire remained where the structure had stood. A thin trail of heat stretched to the south, forming an infrared return that looked a bit like a tennis racket.

That's a strange shape.

"Is there any breeze out there?" I asked, thinking the racket handle might be heated debris carried downwind.

Troy tapped a few keys then said, "Nope. Completely calm. Why?"

But I didn't answer. My thoughts were consumed by the final moments of the Hellfires' flyout. I replayed that split-second in my mind. After a second mental replay, I said, "See how most of the heat is on the north end of the building? When I think about the attack, it seems like none of the missiles went more than about halfway across the building."

"Maybe," Troy said slowly, a hand rubbing his chin. "But we're zoomed out quite a bit. I'm not sure you can tell exactly where the missiles hit or what's left."

Perhaps Troy was right, but I wasn't convinced. But before I could muster my mental data, pro and con, a second explosion shattered our moment of silence.

"What the hell was that?" asked Troy. "I didn't see a shot on the screen."

"No fuse is delayed that long, is it?"

"Nothing in our stores," he replied. "I guess it could be a misfire of some sort."

I turned back to the display. Whatever damage the last explosion had inflicted, I couldn't see it in the size, shape, or intensity of the infrared return that had been the Maintenance Building. And Jack? He had returned to his hunt as if nothing had happened, as if he hadn't left four or five people dead in his wake. And unless the programmers in the Information Systems Building came up with something soon, they'd be next. And then, us. We needed to work the problem.

"I can't see we have anything to launch an offensive against Jack, which leaves fooling him somehow, right?"

Troy stared at me, then rubbed his forehead with enough vigor to turn his fingertips nearly white. "Doc, I've been thinking. I hate to say this, knowing how you feel, but there's a chance Jack isn't stuck in autonomous mode."

"What do you mean?"

He released a long breath. "I mean, it could be Drew."

NINE DAYS EARLIER, TUESDAY, JANUARY 5

Omega Systems Home Office, Pittsburgh, Pennsylvania, 8:07 AM

Dr. Harold Brinkley, Vice President of Research and Development at Omega Systems unlocked the door to his office, entered, and tossed his coat on an empty chair. He moved to the window and stared out, running his fingertips over his graying mustache mindlessly. He should be dialing his phone. After all, he was late for his 8:00 call. "And I really don't give a damn," he muttered, thinking he was alone.

"What was that, sir?"

Brinkley spun around. A woman had followed him in. "I'm sorry, but you are?" he asked.

"Willamena Luke, sir. Dorothy's been delayed by the weather. But she called, asked me to see if you needed anything this morning."

"Oh, okay." Brinkley started toward his desk, collecting his thoughts, then glanced back at the woman. "Please excuse my earlier language." She just smiled, pressing her lips together tightly as if locking a secret behind them, then nodded.

"If you would get me Jim Marshall on the phone, I'm good for a while. Use the number for the guard station at the JACC test range in Nevada."

"Yes, sir. And just dial 137 if you need anything else."

"Thanks. I will. And please close the door when you leave."

Brinkley didn't care what Marshall thought because, in his mind, the man was a self-promoting opportunist who didn't care who got in the way. But, no, that wasn't quite right, was it? Marshall didn't just take opportunities, he made them. He manipulated people and events, doing whatever it took to further his agenda. This call was a good example.

Four days ago, when the time was set, Marshall had offered to come into his office at 4:30 AM, a full hour and a half before their standard start time. Eventually, they'd agreed to 5:00 AM—8:00 AM local—but only over his subordinate's objections; Marshall complained that the call would cut into his time to prepare for the live-fire demonstration. Perhaps the man was making a sacrifice, but more likely, it was another chance for self-promotion. In a day or two, he'd find an off-hand reference to Marshall's tireless dedication to the company in a report that somehow had made it to the CEO's desk.

Brinkley walked back to his office window, stuffed his hands in his pockets, and stared out over the cityscape. His normally impressive view of the downtown and the Monongahela River beyond was rendered a blank, white canvas by the swirling snow. Much more of this and those few who had fought their way into work this morning would be turning around to make the perilous trip back home. Even so, that drive was better than being trapped at work.

Brinkley wondered if Marshall had agreed to this time slot because he'd seen Pittsburgh's long-term forecast. It was a petty thought, but the long-standing pattern of Marshall's behavior had killed every inclination he had to be charitable.

"Sir, I have Dr. Marshall on the phone," came the voice over his intercom.

"Thanks, Willamena."

Brinkley dropped into his chair and hit the speaker button.

"Morning, Jim."

"Hal. Looks like you're up to your ass in snow back there. Sorry to see that."

Brinkley didn't care for the man's feigned familiarity either; he'd never asked anyone to call him Hal. Even his family called him Harold and he'd told his subordinate as much. But those protestations had no effect. Marshall continued to use the shorthand as if he needed to be on a different footing than everyone else in the company.

"Yeah, a virtual whiteout. So, let's get to the heart of this call. You've got some very influential members of Congress visiting Thursday—the second in command of the House Armed Services Committee, Representative Alison, no less. I just wanted to make sure you're ready."

"Good to see you're reading my status reports," replied Marshall.

Brinkley could feel his blood pressure go up but decided it wasn't worth his breath to reply.

"I have indeed secured Representative Alison's commitment. As for being ready, Jack's always ready. And I've got the team shaped up. The pilot's practicing nonstop. Whether or not he has a bad day? Well, that's up to the demo gods."

"Good," replied Brinkley, ignoring the man's posturing mixed with the foundation for an excuse should things go sideways. "When can I expect to see the scenario descriptions? You're flying two, right?"

"Correct, but you should have them already. They went to our customers a week ago."

That was too much for Brinkley to ignore. "Dammit, Jim. I should have seen those before they went to the government. What the hell are you trying to pull?"

"Easy, Hal. You know I don't have an assistant out here. Everything runs through the colonel's flunky. If he screwed up, I'll ask Col. Dempsey to ream him a new one. But as for their content, you have nothing to worry about. Our pilot flies a bread-and-butter, close-air support mission in an urban environment. You know, protecting the good guys coming down a street on their way to liberate a captive. And the second scenario features Jack's unique capabilities for timing and precision. It'll have them pulling out their checkbook before they leave the range."

"You're at the guard station. Send them in an encrypted email before you leave."

Marshall paused a moment. "You know it doesn't work that way, Hal. Even from here, the content has to be reviewed, and then, they encrypt it for transmission. The military has this range sewed up tighter than a gnat's ass, and I can't fault them. We're sitting on a weapon system that will change the world's balance of power."

Brinkley oversaw projects at a dozen bases and had forgotten how tight security was there. But there was no reason to admit that to Marshall.

"Just get me those damn descriptions ASAP," he snapped over the line.

"Will do," replied Marshall, sounding a bit too pleased considering the situation. "If that's all you have, there is one topic I want to raise with you."

"What's on your mind?"

"These two civilian researchers? I thought you were going to hold off giving them access until after the live-fire demonstration?"

They had discussed the timing of the contractors' visits, and he had considered a delay. But in the end, approvals from the commands that would receive Jack were crucial, and they had questions about the program's support foundation—was the training ready, could the aircraft be cost-efficiently maintained. A desire to put Marshall in his place, to show him who called the shots hadn't played in his decision to allow the contractors on the range now ... at least, not much.

"There's more concern about Jack's readiness than you like to admit. People haven't forgotten that black eye you got when your pilot blew a hole in the desert." Perhaps he should feel guilty about the pleasure he was feeling by bringing up the incident, but he didn't.

"We've been down that road," replied Marshall, smoothly. "Personnel selection isn't an exact science, and we got a bad apple. Meanwhile, we have a gal looking at maintenance tasks and a guy looking at the coordinator's training. We've had no issues with maintaining our test fleet, and the coordinator's job is nearly irrelevant to flying Jack. I could put everything he needs to know on a Post-it Note."

"We build total systems," Brinkley snapped, angered almost as much at himself for his outburst as his direct report's words. "Weakness in any part is a weakness of the whole."

"I agree," said Marshall. "But you could pull them out for a couple of weeks. I don't need any clueless civilians running around my range right now."

Marshall let the silence grow, probably hoping that he'd see the wisdom of the suggestion. But Brinkley didn't. Funding decisions loomed. The work needed to be done, and if the program was as far along as Marshall claimed, it shouldn't be a problem. He'd also heard some rumors that the military was still looking at the incident from the last phase, and because of it, they might issue a temporary, stop-work order to verify the facts. If true, that action had the ring of the government flexing their oversight muscle more than any real threat to the program, but you never knew. And having those two civilians on the range sent the message that Omega Systems was being responsive to every concern.

"Sorry, Jim, but they stay."

After several moments, an audible sigh came through the speaker, and Marshall continued. "Okay. But preparation for the demonstration comes first. Those two contractors get what's left and live with it."

"As it should be," Brinkley replied. "If they don't get everything they need this time, they can come back. Or maybe extend their stay." He figured the threat of a return visit was enough to pry some cooperation from the man. "Anything else?"

"Just one other thing," said Marshall. "Any rumblings about trouble spots where Jack might be needed?"

Brinkley sat back hard in his chair, staring at the phone. "What did you say?"

"You're sitting there near the capital and travel to DC all the time. I was asking if there are any rumors about hot spots around the world where the unique capabilities of Jack might be needed."

In the few seconds it took Marshall to clarify, Brinkley had considered the possible reasons for the man's question. One—and the one he considered the most likely—made him see red. "Don't tell me you're hoping for bloodshed, just to get Jack into the field," he snarled.

It had happened before, Brinkley knew. Experimental weapon systems had been rushed to the battlefield when the need was pressing. And if the system performed well—and especially if it could be shown to save lives—it often became part of the military's arsenal with little additional deliberation.

"Whoa, hold on, Hal. It's not even my question. Colonel Dempsey wanted me to ask. But if it was my question, I'd want the opposite. Jack gets fielded and I ... we lose control. It becomes a support program, not research and development. And while Jack is extremely capable now—miles ahead of anything else the military has—he can be more. He will be more when we've completed the final phase."

"Colonel Dempsey? Why the hell would he ask us that? He'd be closer to the source than us."

"I wondered that, too. He said something about the best clues about politicians' future actions often came from public opinion. He's a bit of a strange duck if you ask me."

Brinkley wasn't sure what to make of the question. A Lieutenant Colonel in the Air Force asking a civilian about political opinion was certainly odd. And the topic was even stranger. By the time any politician in DC was ready to throw water on a smoldering world issue, the military would know all about it. What did Dempsey really want? Or was Marshall trying to cover up his interest by claiming the question wasn't his? With nothing else to go on, he'd just have to take a wait-and-see approach.

"The colonel's probably being cautious," Brinkley allowed. "And I appreciate you wanting to see the research completed and not have Jack rushed to the field." He mentally added the phrase "if you're telling the truth" but didn't voice it. "As for the colonel's question, the only thing I can think of is the accident Turkey had with their Harpies. If that grew into open hostilities and we got involved, there might be a call for Jack. Pit one unmanned system against another, so to speak, though a Harpy wouldn't stand a chance. But in any case, that whole scenario seems pretty unlikely."

Brinkley could hear Marshall blow out a breath before responding. "Yeah, I have to agree. And since I mentioned that incident to the colonel already, I'm done unless you have something else."

He didn't, and the men ended their call.

After the goodbyes, Brinkley sat staring at his phone a moment. He couldn't shake the feeling that there was something wrong at the JACC test range. Was Marshall pushing the technology too far, too fast? Or was it Dempsey who wanted it out of the lab? He didn't have a legacy to secure by rushing Jack to the field, but he could have a profound effect on the course of history with Jack on our side. And lopsided victories never hurt the career of a military man.

Then again, maybe the outlook for open hostilities was important for other reasons. But what could they be? Perhaps he should pull the civilians off the range until after the demo. They'd be safer elsewhere.

"What the hell am I thinking?" he mumbled to himself. "They're in one of the safest places on earth."

Operations Center, JACC Test Range, Nevada, 5:53 AM

Yesterday, after I learned that self-governance was standard research fare for unmanned systems during the phone call with Mark Dillon, I had gone back to the Operations Center. To me, the ten-minute drive over dusty roads had lasted but a blink of the eye. The terrain that the day before had captured every bit of my attention now passed without notice, so busy was I reconciling my previous beliefs with what I now knew to be true.

Some of the pivotal capabilities of artificial intelligence—the ability for machines to think and act on their own—were not just the domain of bespectacled old men tucked away in the far reaches of the halls of academia or deep in the bowels of industrial research laboratories. Rather, those abilities were the focus of numerous, everyday efforts, not to extend theory, but to find practical uses for them. It was the focus of JACC.

But hadn't I already known this? For a completely trivial example, the lights at work came on when I entered my office. Or, to make it sound like AI, the lights thought, "Hey, there's a human here according to what my eyes (sensors) are telling me. I should illuminate my space." Was that different from Jack thinking, "Hey, there's a human here with a gun according to my sensors. I should remove him from my space." What was being controlled and the consequences of error were quite different, of course. But in the reasoning of each, there was a great deal of commonality.

That point was as far as my thoughts ran before I reached the Center. And while Troy might have joined in further discussion of these ruminations, I still had a job to do. So, I pulled out the training needs analysis document, and we started discussing what he did for a living. His first summary was, "I just fly Jack in and out, watching that nothing breaks." We covered several tasks before I realized just how comprehensive that one-sentence summary was.

"What do you do during a takeoff?" I had asked.

"Monitor performance and watch for system abnormalities that require manual intervention," Troy replied.

"Is that phrase from the training?"

Troy grinned. "Yep, word for word."

"Have you ever had to intervene because of an abnormality?"

"Nope. Not in real life, but there are training scenarios where I fly a take-off with some type of malfunction."

"These scenarios are in the simulation, right?"

"Correct. Flying the sim is a blast, especially with a fault. Without it, the training would be deadly dull."

The same pattern emerged again and again—he was waiting and watching for something that never happened except in the simulation. And since the sim was the same as that used by the pilots, the handling of the aircraft and its behavior during a malfunction had been thoroughly vetted by experts. Even if I had the skills to test a sim—and I didn't—it was extremely unlikely I'd find a problem there.

That left the computer-based training, screen after screen of text and graphics that described what was to be done when and how. And since the Operation Coordinator's job was all so simple, all so cookbook, if every task was covered in that material, I would be done. As for the chance that the training developers had overlooked a task entirely? The risk of that was both small and easily checked. My analysis job now felt like something a novice could do in his or her sleep.

After the workday, I'd gone back to the motel and gone through what already seemed a familiar pattern—jog, shower, call Nicole, and have dinner, this one with Jill. Sometimes I wondered if I fell into routines easily so that my mind would be free to churn through the events of the day. That was the case yesterday, as no sooner was the glow from talking about fiancés and girlfriends fading than I realized something was bothering me about Troy's description of his job.

I started replaying the discussion in my mind. It was about the time we got to the task of landing when I found the source of my disquiet. Troy was still using the same phrases—"monitor performance and watch for system abnormalities." It wasn't what he was saying but how. His enthusiasm had been spent. His elbow was on the desk, his head propped up on a fist. He'd even stopped making wisecracks ... and I didn't think that ever happened. In a phrase, he was talking but not thinking. And therein might lie a rub. Omega Systems had made Troy's job so repetitive and tedious that it now seemed inevitable that his attention would wane. And if true, that's when things could go sideways.

Of course, audible warnings could and had been added to the system, but why should I advocate adding more? They'd just be computer code added on top of code, and I could see no reason why the additional software would be any more effective at drawing the coordinator's attention than the first had been. It held no new information. And worse, trying to fix automation with more automation often annoyed the user and all of it got turned off. To cure this problem, we needed something besides more lines of software code.

Before I started trying to solve the problem of boredom on the job with training—no easy feat I might add—I had to make sure it was, indeed, a problem. And that was why I was getting to the Operations Center almost an hour before sunrise, already thinking that the day was wasting away.

When I pulled into the parking lot, Dr. Jim Marshall was there. He was pulling a garden hose across the gravel toward a car with its hood up. I knew who he was from the practice session the day before, although we hadn't been introduced. So, I walked over to correct that situation. Apparently, he knew who I was as well.

"It's Doc, isn't it?" he said as I approached, sticking out a hand. "I'm Dr. Jim Marshall."

"It's good to meet you, Dr. Marshall. Car trouble?"

He harrumphed. "With Jack, we're flying processors that can diagnose complex, rapidly changing situations in the blink of an eye. And yet, I haven't been able to find a mechanic who can diagnose my car in a month. I thought maybe they had it fixed. It looked pretty good on the drive in, but it overheated when I drove from the guard station to here. Fortunately, I have another car I can take tomorrow because this isn't the place to be on foot."

"I'd say not," I replied. "Your demonstration scenarios yesterday were quite impressive."

Marshall waved a hand in front of his face as if shooing an invisible insect. "We enjoyed considerable synergistic collaboration with the manufacturer, Air Dynamics, in the development of the situations. But AD's concepts for self-direction to deal with them ranged from Neanderthal to nonexistent, which is why we took the lead on this dog and pony. Saved them from embarrassing themselves ... or worse, embarrassing Jack."

Does he really talk this way?

Probably, he practices his catchy turns of a phrase on passersby before springing them on his customers, and I just happened to be in voice-range. But more importantly, does he think Jack's feelings—as if the machine had any—outweigh the effect on Air Dynamics? That concept was the perfect segue to a question about Jack's machine intelligence, but when I played the conversation in my mind, it seemed pointless. "Do you realize that Jack can make decisions and launch attacks on his own?" To which he would reply, "Well, duh" ... or something to that effect. After all, he'd merely smiled when I was staggered by the second scenario. So instead, I said, "I'm sure you'll have some impressed government representatives next week."

"That's the plan," he replied.

I nodded and turned for the Center.

After I let myself into the Operations Room, I found Troy's console empty, but Drew was at his. Like Marshall, we hadn't been introduced, so I walked over. After I stood off to the side of his console for a moment, he glanced at me.

"Hi, I'm Sam Price, here working with Troy Sayers."

"Yeah, I know," he replied. "His desk is over there." He nodded toward it with his head, his eyes back on the display.

His dismissal seemed a bit rude, but he was also busy with Jack. And whatever the reason, it was fine; I didn't have to work with him. I sat down at Troy's desk and pulled out the needs analysis notebook to study it further. After forty-five minutes, however, Troy still hadn't shown up. I walked back over to Drew.

"Sorry to bother you, but do you know when Troy will be in?"

Drew looked up, staring at me blankly. Then, he tapped his forehead with a couple of fingers. "Oh, shoot. I forgot. Troy had a tooth pulled yesterday. He called this morning. Said he wouldn't be in till around 8:00."

"Okay," I said simply. I was a bit irritated he hadn't told me earlier, but if he had, I would have spent my time reading anyway. I turned to leave when his voice came from behind me. "You go by Doc, right?"

I turned back. "It's a nickname from work. And you go by Drew?"

"Correct. I've just been flying some night ops. Gotta keep my rating current. Anyway, sunrise is at 6:52, so that's done. You have any interest in watching a bit?"

"Sure." There was some overlap between his job and Troy's, mostly in emergencies, so this was job-related. And to be truthful, it was like Troy had said—the sim was a lot more interesting than the rest of the training.

"Whenever we have fuel left at the end of an exercise, we have a standing order from Dr. Marshall to set all our systems to hostile and fly Jack in either the simulated reconnaissance or simulated search-and-destroy modes. This lets him compile new threat maps. You may not think much changes on the range, day-to-day, but it does. We've found quite a few minor bugs just by throwing a real-world environment at Jack, over and over. He just passed over the Ops Center."

I looked at the threat map. "Is that a bug? That Jack thinks my rental is a hostile military target?"

"Nope. Not an error," said Drew, matter-of-factly. "By the way, did they tell you to get the special rental car insurance? It covers Jack turning your drive into a burned-out shell."

I chuckled, though my question remained. "You're saying that Jack's target recognition thinks my car is a tank or something similar? Mark Dillon gave me the impression that Jack's more accurate than that."

"Dillon and the Air Dynamics gang did the easy stuff. Based on what they did, yeah, Jack knows your rental is a small capacity transport. But with all the intelligence added by us, he also knows that"—Drew started shaking his head, tsking with each shake—"you're obviously in cahoots with the enemy. Therefore, you and that car of yours have to go."

"I don't get that. How am I being connected with the enemy?" I had my suspicions, but the guess was tentative enough that I wanted confirmation.

Drew stared at me, his eyes narrowing. "Your car is parked outside a hostile military facility. Jack knows that from the Ops Center's electronic emissions, as well as other information. You're a human of a size and age appropriate to a soldier. What the hell is Jack supposed to think? You're dropping off lunch?"

"I could be," I replied, immediately regretting the comeback. Drew's frown had morphed into a glare. My learning opportunity would be over if I couldn't reverse his growing ire. "Of course, in an area of open hostilities, Jack's interpretation could be spot on."

And a bit scary, too.

The relative comfort I had felt after Dillon described his work on automatic target recognition faded to near irrelevance with Drew's description of the work split. Air Dynamics' products were just the starting point for deriving much more complex conclusions based on subtleties and logical but fallible reasoning. I felt a mix of intellectual curiosity and amazement against a backdrop of dread. And because AIs had to deal with the full range of real-world complexities, validating their databases and their inferencing processes was orders of magnitude more difficult than any other software product.

"Yeah, Jack's amazing," Drew said. He went back to flying as I looked over his shoulder. After several minutes, he removed the threat map and replaced it with a different display.

"Are you showing infrared now?"

"Yeah," replied Drew. "Thought I saw something, but we're getting into shadows. Infrared might give us a better picture."

"What did you think it was?"

"I'm not sure," he said slowly. I bent in closer behind him. "There. What do you think that is?" He pointed to a softly glowing figure near the center of the display.

"It looks like a person." His or her knees were drawn up toward the chest, as if in a fetal position. One arm was extended out from the body; the other was hidden, perhaps below the torso or tucked in close.

"Oh, shit," said Drew. "I think you're right."

"What's Jack think it is?" Drew spun around to look at me. Did I have it wrong?

"With Jack's range of sensors and onboard processing, I thought he could figure out things like that."

Drew turned back to the console, talking over his shoulder. "Generally, and over time, yes, but I'm not sure we have time. Whatever it is, it's hardly warmer than the rocks around it. And that's not a good sign for anything living." He brought up several, unfamiliar displays and flipped through them quickly. "There's something that's not rock down there. Maybe plant. Maybe animal. Hard to say."

Drew's commentary didn't match what I'd come to expect of Jack. Dillon had made him seem nearly infallible and extremely fast when it came to classifying objects, and that was all Drew was asking—animal, vegetable, or mineral? But maybe his performance degraded under early morning conditions? I'd certainly never asked anything that specific. But there was another issue with this guess.

"But a person? How could anyone get out there with all the security?"

Drew shook his head. Since he was still looking away, I couldn't tell if the gesture was accompanied by his eyes rolling in annoyance or gazing off into the distance in contemplation. When he spoke, however, I guessed he was closer to irritated than thoughtful.

"It's tough getting past the main gate, true. But after that, it's not hard to jump a fence or find a gully where you can go under one. And since several of the adjoining ranges are being set up for new projects, the place is crawling with civilians these days."

It seemed unlikely to me that the government had lost track of who was on the range and had left an unauthorized individual out there overnight. But on the other hand, it wasn't a time to confuse unlikely with impossible and leave someone there to die.

"Look, Doc, I'm going to contact Security, get someone to go check it out." Apparently, I had pondered the issue too long, as Drew was clearly irritated now. "But that'll take time. If you wanna be useful, grab a blanket and a canteen from that closet over there and go take a look."

"Okay, sure. How do I get to where Jack is?"

"Easy," he said, his tone returning to matter-of-fact. "If you turn right as soon as you go out the front door of the Ops Center and walk along the edge of the building, the body is straight ahead, about a mile out. It's on the edge of a gulch." He pointed to a darker, jagged ribbon cutting across the display. "It's 7:12 now. If you don't find a body and no one shows up by 7:45, just head back. There's no way I can contact you if this is a false alarm. But, no worries. Jack will keep an eye on you."

I found the last comment both comforting and concerning, the latter emotion driving my response. "Just make sure Jack knows I'm a medic now, not a soldier." Drew just nodded as I turned to get the blanket and fill the canteen with water.

As I exited the front door and turned right, I took a sighting along the side of the building to a jagged peak probably three or four miles in the distance. Its top formed a rough 'M.' If I walked directly toward the middle of the notch, I would be traveling in a straight line.

After about twenty minutes, I reached the edge of a small gulley. It was not very deep, perhaps five or six feet in most places, but the bottom was still cloaked in darkness; it would show up as a cooler band in an infrared display. There was, however, no body on its banks. Knowing that I could not have possibly walked in a perfectly straight line—and that the heading was an approximation anyway— I turned and walked about 150 yards along the edge of the gulch in one direction. I found nothing but rocks and sand. So, I returned to my starting point and then continued another 150 yards in the opposite direction. Again, nothing.

Either I had wandered off course more than I thought or this was a false alarm. And since it was 7:52 and no one had appeared, it was probably the latter.

I returned to the point where I had originally intersected the gully, turned back toward the Center, and found a landmark in the distance. Just as I started walking, I heard a high-pitched humming. In the Midwest, I might have thought "mosquito." And even in the desert, that was possible if there was any water, fresh or salty, nearby. But the sound wasn't quite right. I stopped and looked up into the sky, but much like this search for a body, I saw nothing. I finally decided that my imagination was getting the better of me and I continued. The rest of the trek back to the Center passed without incident.

When I entered the Operations Room, Drew greeted me with, "And here he is, the star of that sensational new snuff film from JACC productions, Doc Price." His tone reminded me of a DJ introducing records in a low-rent bar.

Troy had come in to work during my absence, and he was standing behind Drew. His hands were stuffed into his pockets. He mouthed the word "sorry," then stared at the back of Drew's head, his own shaking slowly.

I looked back at Drew. "What's going on?"

Rather than answering, he said, "Shall we take a look at the movie trailer? I'm sure it'll go viral the moment it hits the web."

With that, he hit a few keys on his console, and a video clip appeared on the monitor hanging on the wall. It was a split-screen shot with the feed from Jack's front-mounted camera on one side and a tactical threat map on the other. From the map, I had no trouble recognizing the location—the edge of the gulch where we had spotted the human-shaped return.

Having decided this was Drew's idea of a joke, I was surprised when I noticed that the threat map was showing a black star for a high-value target. Was it me? It would take a considerable amount of work to get my particulars into Jack's database. But all doubt was removed by the video from the camera. There I was, trudging across the sand, stepping around the rocks. I stopped and looked up, searching the skies for the source of the sound I'd heard.

I was about to tell Drew how lame this joke was when the targeting display appeared—a circle with short lines intersecting on the right, left, top, and bottom. The lines didn't meet in the center, but rather stopped about three-fourths of the way there. But if you extended them, I was in the middle of the cross-hairs they would form. The circle flashed, indicating that a firing solution had been achieved. The pulsing stopped and then flashed once more; a missile had been launched.

On the wall-mounted display, I could see the missile in flight on the threat map, straight and true toward the high-value target, straight toward me. The video on the other half switched to a simulated camera in the nose of the weapon. The image of me standing in the desert grew slowly at first and then began to accelerate rapidly as the missile homed-in. In the final instant before impact, my face filled the screen. There was a flash of brilliant red, then nothing but static and electronic white noise.

The video changed back to Jack's camera, looking down from a cloudless sky to the point of impact on the barren desert floor. About the only thing that destroyed the illusion that I'd just been assassinated was the lack of blast debris—no charred vegetation, no crater in the sand, no burnt clothing or severed body parts. I didn't need that bit of realism, however, for my anger to erupt.

"What the hell are you thinking?" I snapped. "You're using a classified, military weapon for your personal entertainment?"

"Just following the boss's orders," Drew replied, crossing his arms over his chest, his chin jutting.

In the background, I could see Troy holding up a hand. But if he wanted me to stop, it didn't work. "So, Colonel Dempsey wants you simulating my death, does he? What you did was no better than a police officer pointing his gun at a civilian and laughing when the man ducks."

"It's more like pointing his body cam at someone," said Drew, his sneer remaining. "Don't be such a pussy. Jack's not carrying any real missiles."

"So, your gun's not loaded, is it?" My tone dripped sarcasm. "Wanna tell me how often that's the excuse after someone dies?"

"To hell with you," growled Drew. His hands balled into fists. I realized mine were doing the same at my sides.

"Doc, let's talk." Troy had advanced to my side. I stared at him, almost without recognition. "In the conference room," he added. But I couldn't seem to move as if my anger had commandeered every neuron in my being—even those that I needed to walk. Finally, Troy put his hand on my shoulder and guided me out of the room.

Operations Center, JACC Test Range, Nevada, 8:17 AM

Troy didn't stop leading me down the hall until we reached the galley. "Jeez, Doc. I didn't know you had a temper."

"I don't." I paused, knowing I couldn't defend that claim after what had just happened. So, I admitted, "Not much of one, anyway.

But that has to be one of the most asinine things I've ever seen. Who in their right mind uses a real military weapon and an actual person in a simulated murder for a joke? That's crazy."

That last word slipped past my lips before I could stop it. Besides being an unfortunate and inappropriate choice of words, I didn't have the background to render any judgment about the state of Drew's mental health. I'd never taken even a single class in abnormal or clinical, opting instead for the study of cognitive psychology. And the latter deals almost exclusively with typical mental processes in the general population.

Of course, in the candor of my private thoughts, I wondered if Drew's stunt was more than just a warped sense of humor. For all I knew, he was drunk on the power Jack gave him. "For all I knew," however, was the telling phrase. I didn't know and didn't have the training or education to find out.

"You really think Drew's lost it?" asked Troy. "I mean, he's said some strange things like ...."

I held up a hand, needing to wave it a bit to get Troy to take a breath. "Sorry, I didn't mean it that way. I just meant his stunt is way out there for a joke. Who does something like that?"

Troy shook his head. "Yeah, I'm supposed to be the prankster around here, but I cringe every time he does it."

"Every time? You mean this is not a one-time, total lapse in judgment?"

Troy looked trapped, his eyes shifting back and forth across the galley. Finally, he said, "No, unfortunately, he's done it a few times. He calls it his Deadman's Gulch scenario. He stumbled on that spot one morning, and since it fooled him, he figured it was the perfect practical joke."

"And Marshall hasn't gotten wind of this? Or the colonel?"

"One guy tried to report it," said Troy, "but flying Jack around the area is authorized. Of course, firing the fake missile isn't, but Drew claimed he was just zooming in on the guy's face. He said it was all a big misunderstanding, and there's no way to prove otherwise. No one's ever going to find the video clips from those attacks."

I took a couple of paces around the galley before turning back to Troy. "This image that looks like a body—it's a natural formation of rock?" Troy nodded. "And it fools Jack?" I asked.

"No way. Drew wasn't showing the tactical map, or you would have seen there was nothing alive down there. And after the sun gets a little higher, the image disappears, too."

With my adrenaline rush starting to abate, I felt a bit nauseated, and the stale coffee in the galley wasn't helping. "Mind if we step outside for some fresh air?"

"Sure."

The walk gave me more time to think. "I suppose, as a joke, it wouldn't be that bad except for the shot. In the final system, I'm sure it will be nearly impossible to mix up real and simulated weapons, but how about now?"

I glanced sideways to see Troy's forehead wrinkle. "Not sure?" His expression changed to a grin, and he leaned closer to speak softly. "I did pirate the screens a pilot uses to change from sim to real weapons, but I haven't studied them yet. Gotta do that on the q.t. since it's none of my business."

"Well, that needs to change. Coordinators should know how to use Jack's weapons in self-defense, if for no other reason."

I had gone from asking about the lack of coordinator training on weapons to telling Troy it was a mistake. It was probably my ire at one of the pilots speaking, but it wasn't smart. After all, I was only a little over a day into the job. And when I looked at the grin that was spreading even further on Troy's face, I was certain I should have kept my mouth closed. If I had to change my position again, I'd have one disgruntled coordinator on my hands.

"I'm not saying you'd be a fully trained pilot, but it seems like you should know a few, basic self-defense maneuvers."

"Absolutely, Doc." His grin didn't fade with my clarification. "I need to be ready. It's like the bumper sticker says, shit happens. And in war, it happens faster."

I stopped at the front door to the Ops Center and looked back at him. "Not sure I've seen that one," I said, although I suspected he'd made it up. "But that's the idea. Anyway, the next step for me is to study the incident and accident reports. And since I'm better with the walk, shall we take a look at them?"

"That's way over my pay grade," said Troy. "You'll probably need to ask Colonel Dempsey to get access."

"Okay. How do I get in to see him?"

Troy raised an eyebrow. "Knock on the door."

"Really. I thought someone would be managing his schedule."

"We're pretty informal around here," Troy said with a shrug.

"In that case, let me grab my notebook."

When we got to the Operations Room, Troy removed a piece of paper that was taped to the door and read the name on the outside. "It's for you. Fan mail from some flounder."

"Thanks, Bullwinkle," I replied, surprising myself by pulling the name from my memories of the old cartoon series. Troy showed the same reaction, releasing a single laugh.

"Handwritten from the colonel," I said after opening it. "You do keep things casual. Looks like he wants to see me."

Troy pulled back and stared. "You think Drew said something to him? Something that would discredit you, if you complained?"

The thought had crossed my mind, but it didn't seem likely. I doubted Drew had the creativity to come up with anything convincing in the few minutes since it had happened. Apparently, however, I was pondering the issue too long as Troy added, "It's probably nothing. Colonel Dempsey probably just wants to welcome you to the program.”

“There’s one way to find out,” I replied. We went into the Operations Room where, thankfully, I found that Drew was gone. I collected my notebook and left for the colonel’s office.

When I knocked on his door, I heard someone say, “Come in.” I did, finding an imposing-looking black man behind a large, wooden desk. It was Lieutenant Colonel Dempsey unless the service dress jacket with a silver oak leaf hanging on a coatrack belonged to someone else.

“Dr. Sam Price,” I said, as I extended my hand.

Even seated, I could tell he was tall, but when he stood to shake my hand, I would have guessed him to be at least 6 feet, 5 inches. And though his job put him behind a desk, he stayed in shape. Adding his close-cropped hair with a touch of grey, his ramrod-straight posture, and the steady gaze he focused on me, he fit my concept of a military officer to a T.

In some ways, it felt like a waste for a man with such a presence to be in command of so few. But as soon as the thought came to the fore, I realized my error. Although there were only about a dozen people on the JACC test range and despite the informality he preferred, he was the face of a state-of-the-art weapon system research and development program. Over the life of it, he was overseeing an effort costing a half-billion dollars or more.

“Lt. Col. Ray Dempsey. I believe I heard you go by Doc.”

“It’s a nickname from work, where there are far fewer PhDs than you deal with every day. Doc or Sam is fine, sir.”

“So, Doc, what do you think of our operation?”

“It’s quite impressive. Before I left St. Louis, Dr. Mark Dillon at Air Dynamics briefed me on some of the unclassified parts of the program. And now that I’m cleared, I’ve had a chance to watch a practice session for the upcoming live-fire demonstration and to work with one of your Operations Coordinators, Troy Sayers." Figuring there was no time like the present to make my request, I added, "To get a better idea of the challenges of his job, I'd like to look at the accident and incident reports."

"Mark Dillon? Smart man. I've never met anyone who knew as much about automatic target recognition as he does."

Dillon seemed to have a universally good reputation on the program, which boded well for the information I'd received. I also noticed, however, that he hadn't responded to my request. I hoped that didn't mean there would be a problem.

But before I could ask, the colonel launched into a well-rehearsed summary of the program—its history, the involved military organizations, and the program's place within the Omega Systems structure. Then, he overviewed JACC's rather formidable capabilities. While his words were quite similar to what Mark Dillon had told me, I also noticed references to the system's autonomous capabilities. I wasn't sure if this was new information or if my expectations had colored what I had gleaned from Dillon.

The colonel had hardly completed his overview when he turned the tables on the discussion rather dramatically. "So, as we put more and more artificial intelligence into a system like JACC, do you see that causing any particular training issues?"

Fortunately, the question came up regularly, not just for military systems, but any place where an AI and a human needed to act collaboratively to achieve a common goal. "Not issues necessarily, but a change in methods. Training developers working on a system like JACC need to think in terms of team rather than individual training. And specifically, it's a team where one member is human and the other's a machine."

"What's that mean in practice?" asked Dempsey.

If I'd known the man better, I might have come back with a joke. The one that came to mind was about an instructor telling the machine it needed to loosen up if it wanted to work with humans and then handing it a screwdriver. But maybe it wasn't the lack of familiarity so much as the slight edge of nervousness I felt that guided me; I went with something much staider.

"One fundamental principle of team training is that each member needs some background on the roles and responsibilities of the others. So, in this case, the human needs to know what the machine is expected to do and when, as well as what to do if it doesn't. And the reverse is also true, with the machine jumping in when the human forgets or is too slow. There are a lot of extremely simple examples of this already—things like automatic collision avoidance in cars. The machine expects the driver to hit the brakes before running into someone, but it takes control when necessary.

"Of course, the interplay of man and machine gets a lot more complex when the task is more difficult and things are changing rapidly. So, take the car of the future. It's driving when it gets a notification of a traffic backup. It recommends a different route. The driver approves it but so slowly that the car has already passed the exit. Now, it's trying to figure out how to do a U-turn and things fall apart."

"And those are the kinds of problems you expect?" asked Dempsey. "Poor management of the tasks the human needs to handle?" I didn't hear condescension in his tone, just curiosity.

"That's probably still too simple, but yes, I think it has the right flavor for Jack and the pilot working together. Jack understanding how humans react will be important. But the Operations Coordinator's job seems a little different. Mind you, this is just after a couple of days here, but the coordinator seems more like a driver monitoring a car on cruise control. He has several things to watch— the waypoints, altitude, the status of each air vehicle's propulsion and other systems—but it's all preprogrammed and the system rarely fails. His challenge may be more like those of a driver on a long stretch of empty highway with nothing to do."

Dempsey stared at me a moment, making me wonder if I'd conveyed my concerns. Finally, he said, "You mean like falling asleep at the wheel?"

"Maybe not falling asleep but losing focus. Letting his mind wander. It's so fully automated, the coordinator's part of Jack's missions may become boring."

His forehead wrinkled. "But that's not something you can fix with training, is it?"

"If the job can't be changed, then training becomes the last line of defense," I replied.

The statement was something of an informal credo around Ruger-Phillips, having a couple of meanings for us. It recognized the importance of training in ensuring the appropriate and safe use of the products we supported. But it also implied that all too often, operation had been considered little in the design of equipment, and we were supposed to untangle a hopeless mess with training. Fortunately, that didn't seem the case on this program.

"The problem I mentioned is generally known as vigilance decrement, and I think we can reduce it with training. But before we get any further into that, I should verify that this is actually a problem. And that's why I wanted to look at the incident and accident reports."

Dempsey gave a quick nod of his head. "That makes sense." He opened his desk and pulled out a pad of paper. After a moment of writing, he handed me a sheet. "There's a copy of all the reports in one of the file cabinets in the Conference Room. That's the number on the cabinet and the combination. You can read the reports there and make notes, but don't remove any of the papers from the Conference Room."

Dempsey paused. I nodded to indicate I understood and he continued. "I believe you'll be briefing us on your initial findings in about ten days. Assuming vigilance decrement appears to be a problem, we'll hear your thoughts about it then?"

"You will."

"Good. Anything else come up in your first look at the coordinator's job?"

"I wondered if he shouldn't be taught something about JACC's weapon systems, just so they could be used in self-defense. If a coordinator gets pressed into service during a battle, about all he can do is run."

Dempsey nodded but not in agreement. "That's not likely."

He paused again, perhaps considering what he could say. Even with my clearance in place, there was "need to know" to consider, and perhaps he didn't think I needed this information. But after a moment, he said, "Jack has extensive self-defense capabilities he uses in battle. In addition to standard countermeasures, he uses ground clutter to hide his position and he changes locations rapidly and in no apparent pattern. He can also return fire, assuming that's authorized by the rules of engagement. All of that is being made available for the ingress and egress phases as well—that is, when the coordinator is flying."

"So, in effect, the coordinator will have all the same tools as the pilot."

Dempsey frowned, the lull in the conversation much longer this time. Finally, he said, "I've heard the talk about the coordinator just being a babysitter. It's hard to miss. But you should know that his job, or something that looks much like it, might be all that's left in six months or so. That job didn't get such an ostentatious title without a reason."

This time, it was me who needed a moment to collect his thoughts. This was, of course, the scenario where all of Jack's considerable capabilities for autonomy were not only fielded but also made available for every phase of a mission, takeoff to landing. He'd fly to the battle zone, assess the situation, instigate actions, and return when fuel got low. If that happened, Jack would need little except a babysitter, a coordinator for the entire time.

How likely was that? I wondered if anyone knew. "I understood that there was that possibility from talking with Mark Dillon. I'll keep it in mind when I'm preparing my recommendations."

"That would be good," Dempsey said, "because we know it's coming. It's a progression that's been occurring for a while now. If you load an infrared image into a fire-and-forget missile and launch it, you're telling the machine to go find the target and neutralize it. If we let Jack match his sensor readings to something in his database, it's a step forward, but it's not that much different."

Seriously?

"That step seems huge to me." The words were out of my mouth almost before I knew it, but if Dempsey was troubled by them, it didn't show. "It's just that the databases that control Jack are created far from the battlefield, potentially distant in both time and miles."

I probably should have kept quiet. Dempsey's comment about fire-and-forget weapons had gently nudged the discussion away from training and into policy, while I had just shoved it with both hands into a realm that had nothing to do with my job. After the colonel's now-familiar pause to reflect, he said, "In a sense, that's true. Who and what are threats to Jack and the United States will be largely determined by policymakers sitting hundreds of miles from the fight, weeks, if not months, in advance. Things change, of course, and Jack's systems can be updated almost as fast as humans can be briefed on new developments.

"What's different, however, is the lack of a final human review of the situation. Is that target really the one Jack's hunting? Are there extenuating circumstances? In the call between letting Jack act or putting a human in charge, we end up trading off the somewhat brittle but fixed logic of a machine and the less predictable reasoning of a person. Humans may second guess and be slow, or even fail to act. Or they may act, only to suffer from the memory. Or perhaps they develop feelings of omnipotence from their vantage point in the sky. There are a lot of ways human decision-making can go wrong. What do you do?"

The way he said it, the question wasn't rhetorical, so I provided the answer I'm certain he was expecting. "I don't know. But aren't you putting a lot of power in the hands of a small number of people? A few individuals could set up Jack so he tyrannizes a population rather than protects it."

"And this small group has enough political clout that they can set policy inconsistent with public welfare? Or, are they getting unauthorized access to classified weapons to enforce their will?"

This guy has given these issues a lot of thought.

I guess the fact I had no immediate response showed on my face, and he continued.

"I suppose it would only take one rogue programmer to poison Jack's logic or database. But he or she better plant that Trojan horse now because once Jack's fielded, the software would be protected just like all other software connected to one of our classified weapon systems. Which gets us back to the small, politically powerful group that can create public policy. And that's politics, which is a bit outside my purview at the moment."

I rubbed my forehead. I'd been pushing my thoughts, trying to find an issue that tipped the scales, making the lives Jack might save worth the risk the program posed. Or the opposite. But the only thing I'd found was that Dempsey was no stranger to these questions. That made sense, given his role. But somehow, it seemed like these matters were more than just part of his job. Like it was personal. But I couldn't put my finger on why I felt that way.

After a few moments of silence, Dempsey asked, "Anything else you'd like to discuss—training or otherwise?"

I grinned. He'd either allowed me to stray from instructional issues on my own or I'd taken the bait he'd offered. Either way, he'd been in control, and I had ended up with few conclusions but a lot to ponder. "Not that I can think of," I said.

"In that case, come by if other questions come up. Otherwise, I look forward to hearing your recommendations in a few days."

After I left, I went back to the Operations Room. Troy was at his desk, and Drew was still missing. Perfect, in my mind.

"So, Drew talk to Dempsey and trash you?" asked Troy.

"Not that I could tell. Nothing about the Deadman's Gulch fiasco came up."

"So, what'd you two talk about?"

"Well," I said slowly, "sorry, but you're not getting that weapons training we talked about."

Troy drew his lips into a tight line and nodded slowly. "That's okay. At least you asked."

"I did. And the reason you won't get it is because Jack's going to defend himself. In fact, coordinators may get access to most if not all of Jack's final capabilities, leaving nothing unique for the pilot. It sounds like you might end up running the show."

A slight smile came to his lips. "That works, too."

THE DAY, THURSDAY, JANUARY 14

Operations Center, JACC Test Range, Nevada, 10:02 AM

I turned toward Troy, staring in disbelief. "Drew? How the hell could Drew be flying? I mean, he's ...."

"Dead," he said for me.

"Yeah," I replied softly. I was sitting beside Troy in front of his console, exactly where I had dropped when Jack fired on the Maintenance Building. I glanced back at the threat map, watching helplessly as the machine continued its deadly advance toward the next target, Information Systems. He'd be there in less than ten minutes.

"I don't get it. The guard told you that Marshall and Dempsey showed up with the VIPs, but Drew wasn't with them. And I don't see how he could have known the shot was coming early enough to get out of the Mobile Command Center." But I knew the error of my thoughts the moment I voiced them. I put my hands on the sides of my head as if I was trying to squeeze out the misconceptions that lived there.

"That wouldn't have done him any good, would it?" I said miserably. "If he ran, Jack would have chased him down with the machine gun."

"Yeah, he would," confirmed Troy, "if Drew was the enemy. But I'm not sure he was. He could have faked that shot and if so, he's still alive. Still flying."

I thought back to the attack on the Mobile Command Center. Although it was only minutes ago, it felt like days. Could I be distorting the facts already, letting a simulation take on the mantle of reality in my memory? But then, the rumble of the distant explosion, the vibration of the building was too real and too recent to deny.

"The missile was real," said Troy, as if reading the confusion in my mind. "It's where it hit that's the fake."

"But that would mean ...." It still seemed impossible and it took me a moment to work through the implications. "That would mean you can aim a real weapon and a simulated one at different targets because the simulated one hit the mobile center and destroyed it."

Troy nodded without saying a word.

"And the real missile hit safely away from the trailer?"

"Exactly." But after a moment, he said, "Oh, shit."

"What?"

Troy looked down at his keyboard, rubbing his forehead with a hand. "We had an accident on the range ... although now, I'm wondering if it was."

He looked up at me and took a deep breath. "It used to be impossible to fire both a simulated and a real weapon at the same time. It was something about both functions using a lot of the same software code. But then, we had this scheduling snafu. We had to run two weapon tests, one right after the other, using Bogey Town as the target for both. There wasn't any time to rebuild between them. So, the software guys did a quick hack to allow both real and virtual missiles, each with its own aimpoint. We could simulate our terrorist town getting blown back to creation, while the real missiles hit twenty yards away. And from an observation point a quarter-mile away and all the smoke and dust, no one could tell the difference."

"And that hack was still in there for the live-fire demo today?"

"It was," said Troy, "and that's what I'm getting to. It was supposed to be gone, deleted, but the guy that was supposed to do it—Garcia was his name—he died in an accident before he finished. He was working late, and the next morning they found him dead in one of the maintenance bays. The cops said it was an accident, but jeez, now I'm wondering."

"The Military Police?"

"Them, the locals, and a police detective from Las Vegas. They had the range shut down for two days, the Maintenance Building for a week, but found zilch."

I stood from the chair. I needed to walk, perhaps to use up the last of the adrenaline pumped into my system from the attack on Maintenance. Or perhaps it was to expend the few new drops that came from the last revelation. My mind flew through a chain of logic, resulting in a muttered "Damn" under my breath.

"You think the cops messed up?" asked Troy.

"Possibly, but it's not ...." I stopped mid-thought. My pacing had taken me back to where I was looking over Troy's shoulder at the threat map. "Jack just keeps creeping up on them, doesn't he? What, maybe seven, eight minutes before he gets to IS? I wish there was something we could do."

Troy turned back to his console. His hand flew forward, pointing at something like a Wi-Fi symbol on the screen. "Look. That's the pilot's icon. Somehow, Don's got the coordinator's console looking like a pilot's." He was practically shouting.

"And he can get control?"

Troy paused. "If anyone can do it, he can." My question had wrung some of the excitement from Troy's voice, although he still sounded upbeat. "Everything's documented, of course, but there's a world of difference between documentation and intimate knowledge and Don has the latter. He was the system architect, even wrote a bunch of the code. Getting the console to transmit opens the first door." Enthusiasm had continued to bleed from Troy's voice as he spoke.

"There's a security handshake that needs to happen next," Troy said. "The problem is, he'll be transmitting the same signal that makes us look like the enemy to Jack. Unless ...." He drew the word out in thought. "Unless he can tweak that signal somehow. I'm just not sure anyone has done that before. Or even if Don knows exactly what Jack wants to see."

We both stared at the display in silence, willing the designation for the Information Systems Building to turn to friendly.

"I need to send an email."

The thought had come out of nowhere, apparently surprising Troy as much as me; he had jumped when I spoke. He turned to look up at me, and I tipped my head toward the computer in the corner. "Sure," he said. "It's all yours."

"In case you want it, I'll just be a minute."

"No, I'm good."

He probably thought I was going to email family, say my goodbyes, just in case. But I wasn't. I wasn't going to admit it was the end ... to them or anyone else because I didn't believe it was. And besides, a note like that to family felt more melodramatic than necessary. I had no unfinished business with my mom, dad, or brothers. Somehow, I suspected Troy felt the same about his kin.

But I felt quite differently about Nicole. Everything about us was unfinished. I sat down at the workstation. My words came easily as if she was sitting across from me. In a matter of a minute or two, I was done.

When I returned to my pacing ground—the space between Troy as he sat at his console and the wall—I checked into the status of IS's peril. Jack had continued his slow but seemingly inevitable march.

"You started to say something about whether the police blew the call on Garcia," Troy said after a few moments of me staring over his shoulder.

I sat down, but he didn't turn from the console. "Yeah, I was. So, what was Garcia like?"

Troy shrugged. "Hard to say. He was a short-timer and an outsider. Around here, there are a bunch of companies with part-time coders with security clearances. He was from one of those shops. Why?"

"So, no track record, no enemies on the program. Not much to make the police suspicious. It's a lot harder to find something when you're not looking for it."

"So, you agree that Garcia was killed?"

"I think it's possible. But what's interesting is where you get if you assume he was and reason from there. Do you know who scheduled the two weapon tests so close together?"

"Nope. Not something I'd hear about."

"How about who authorized the software hack for the different aimpoints?"

Troy ran a hand through his hair and released a single laugh. "I haven't got a clue, but my guess is it didn't go beyond Col. Dempsey and Dr. Marshall. A decision like that would have been made locally." His voice began to trail off as a frown replaced the blank look that had been on his face. "I don't see where you're going with this. If Garcia's death wasn't an accident, then Drew killed him so he could hide behind the simulation smokescreen."

"Maybe," I said slowly. "But I'm ending up at a different conclusion. Just a couple more questions. You said the police decided his death was an accident, but did they suspect anyone?"

"Not that I know of. And frankly, I doubt it. The night Garcia died, nearly everyone was on the range. Garcia was by himself in the Maintenance Building working on the software. We were in this building, brainstorming ideas for the live-fire scenarios. But people were coming and going till the wee hours. So, the cops talked to everyone, but no one for long."

"Who organized the brainstorming session?"

Troy stared at me a moment, his frown growing. "We get all our direction from Marshall, but that has little to do with where it comes from. I suggested something to him once, and two days later, he presents it at a staff meeting like it was his idea."

I nodded, knowing that fit my impression of the man. "I'm still thinking that Jack is stuck in the autonomous search-and-destroy mode," I said, having completed my questions. "That could have happened either because Drew screwed up in all the excitement or a software glitch. As for Drew being behind this? I'm doubting it. I'm not sure he's bloodthirsty enough, for want of a better word."

"I'm not so sure," replied Troy.

What's he done now?

My face must have asked the question for me as Troy said, "One night, he told me …. Let me back up. We were out drinking, and I was drunk. I'm sure Drew was, too. Anyway, he was talking about growing up in west Texas and hunting and guns. At one point, he said something about humans being the only big game on this continent that he hadn't bagged. I thought it was a joke and said something about going to Africa so he could have other options. But now, I'm not so sure he was kidding."

I wasn't certain what to make of Troy's story, if anything. After all, I had been drinking with plenty of guys who declared, under the influence, that they were going to dump their girlfriend or quit their job or start practicing for a marathon. The next day, they would be back with the same woman, working at the same place, and hitting the donut shop rather than the track. Drunk men talk; it doesn't necessarily mean anything.

But on the other hand, I was certain no one had ever told me that humans were on their hunting "bucket list." Did Drew have the insight and authority to create schedule conflicts and orchestrate this slaughter? Did he even have the patience to plan it? I doubted it. But on the other hand, he could have just seen an opening. That seemed more likely.

I massaged my temples with my fingertips, working at the tension that grew with each revelation about our possible adversary or adversaries, biological and/or mechanical. If nothing else, Troy's story had caused me to reorder my suspects. Jack was still first, but Drew had moved up to second. Both of them had motives—Jack because he was driven by his programming and Drew because of some sort of sick fascination with hunting or being in power or something similar. That left serial killing by committee in the third spot. But if it was a group, what did they hope to achieve? To discredit autonomous AIs?

My mind had just started to churn on that possibility when Troy yelled, "Jack's attacking!"

I looked on helplessly as four missiles flew into the Information Systems Building and detonated. That was more firepower than he had used at Maintenance and IS was only about one-third the size. There was no doubt. No one could have survived that attack; that is, unless all the shots were fakes.

ONE DAY EARLIER, WEDNESDAY, JANUARY 13

Operations Center, JACC Test Range, Nevada, 6:17 AM

After some initial surprises on the JACC test range—finding Jill here and being killed virtually at Deadman's Gulch being the primary ones—the job had settled into a comfortable routine. Preparations for the live-fire demonstration had taken priority. Troy's part in them, however, was small from the beginning and had shrunk every day. It wasn't that the scenarios were getting longer; it was that Marshall kept increasing his time on stage, squeezing Troy out. As of today, the schedule showed the coordinator with three minutes under the spotlight.

The positive of Troy's diminishing role, however, was that it gave us more time to work together. And frankly, it wasn't wasted.

Part of my learning curve involved terminology. Misusing words or phrases or failing to use them when appropriate separated the knowledgeable from the uninformed, and Ruger-Phillips paid me to be in the former group. And like every program in the military, JACC both shared terminology and acronyms with other programs and had its own vocabulary. I was somewhat familiar with rotorcraft aviation lingo, which was one source of the shared verbiage. But unmanned systems was another, and I knew nothing of it. And then, JACC had its jargon.

So, while "a flight squawking the right IFF code" didn't give me heartburn—the aircraft was broadcasting the correct Identification Friend or Foe signal—something like "Jacking the HS game" produced nothing but head-scratching at first. But after seven days on the range, I could recognize the latter as Jack's unique defensive maneuvers against a heat-seeking weapon. Evidently, the program took that capability to a new level—not that I knew what the old one had been.

The bulk of my work on-site, however, was verifying that the training provided the knowledge and built the skills necessary to the Operations Coordinator. On that front, I had no qualms. I had eaten, slept, and breathed the *Training Needs Analysis and Curriculum Development* document for seven days. I had nearly memorized all the incident and accident reports, not that there were many. And Troy and I had discussed his job for something like thirty-five hours. I was ready to present my initial findings to Marshall and Dempsey.

At precisely 6:30 AM, Col. Dempsey entered the conference room carrying a cup of coffee and a pad of paper. Dr. Marshall followed closely on his heels, holding the same two items and a third that looked like an external disk drive. Unfortunately, the parade ended at that point without Troy. If the discussion got deep into the minutia of his job—extremely minor details that I wouldn't be expected to know but that they wanted to discuss nonetheless—having Troy here would be a boon. He knew the limits of my knowledge and wouldn't hesitate to join the meeting as necessary.

I wasn't the only one disappointed by the attendance, however, as Col. Dempsey said, "I was hoping that Don Williams would be able to attend. He's in for the demo, and I thought his perspective on the automation created for the Operations Coordinator might be helpful.

Unfortunately, he's busy with other matters. So, I guess we're all here."

The words were no more than out of his mouth when the door opened and Troy walked in. He was met by a stern glance from the colonel. "Now, I believe we're all here. Doc, the floor's yours."

I had enough experience with public speaking to know that I tended to start slow. When I got to the meat of the talk—what most people thought of as the boring details and mind-numbing statistics—the energy in my presentation would increase noticeably. I am a research geek, and I've never tried to hide it.

To counter my sluggish openings, I had added a few general remarks about my background and training. Since it was canned, I could practice and at least be smooth, if not passionate. I covered that material. Then, I described the current state of the coordinator's job and its potential to subsume the pilot's responsibilities soon. This wasn't news to either man, of course, but it helped establish my understanding of the field ... and it got me to the good stuff. The data.

The first part of this material was standard fare involving slight mismatches between training standards and the program's curriculum. Had the topic been finance rather than instruction, it would be the typical bean counter's report—much ado about pennies. But there would be individuals at Omega Systems and in the military who knew the value of checking the details and making sure they were correct and complete. As for my current audience? They were getting a workout reaching for their coffee cups.

With no questions on the minutia, I soon reached the final topic for my talk, vigilance decrement. I suspected it would elicit some discussion, and I wasn't disappointed. The term was hardly out of my mouth when Marshall asked, "Like daydreaming?"

Before I could answer, Col. Dempsey said, "A deterioration in the ability to remain vigilant to critical information over time." Marshall swung his head around to look at the colonel, as did I. His response was too close to the formal definition to be anything else, which he confirmed. "I looked it up online after we talked."

"But we already have eye-tracking in place," said Marshall, turning back to me. "I'd say it's like some of the high-end cars with drowsiness detection systems, but that would be an insult to Jack. His system is self-calibrating. It's unaffected by glasses or contacts. It even monitors eye blinks and pupil dilation. Too wired, too drowsy, not watching, whatever—any of those happen and an alarm goes off."

Knowing how the consoles were equipped, I'd anticipated his reaction. "Maybe you've had the experience of reading a page in a book and then realizing you have no idea what it said?"

Marshall stared at me for a moment. "Yeah, I suppose."

"Well, after a while, the scan patterns you're teaching coordinators will get like that. Just because their eyes are moving through the displays, it doesn't mean they're thinking about what's there."

"And you don't think the normal 'kick 'em in the butt when they screw up' approach will keep them motivated?" asked Marshall. "Always worked in the past."

"More pep talks and reprimanding coordinators for mistakes will only take you so far," I replied. "And that's because vigilance decrement isn't really about a lack of effort. But this should be a lot clearer after we take a look at the data."

I found the numbers compelling, but then, that was part of my researcher's psyche. In this case, however, it seemed clear that automation had rendered the coordinator's job completely mind-numbing.

"Okay," Marshall replied, doubt clear in his tone. "Let's see what you have."

Overall, the Operations Center was rather Spartan, but it had one minor extravagance; the conference room had a dual projection system. I made use of it now. On one of the screens, I showed a listing of 93 extended-flight missions the program had flown to date—over 1,000 hours on the simulation or in the air. I had selected these flights because they focused on things like aircraft durability or mission tactics, rather than the coordinator. In other words, Troy did nothing but monitor, hour after hour. I asked the colonel to select a date. I started the video from that day, skipped past the takeoff, and muted the sound. I said nothing about what was on the screen but left the recording playing silently. It was easy to see Troy's eyes as they systematically scanned the displays, just as he had been taught.

Fortunately, there were eleven other scenarios where, amid hours of doing and seeing nothing, Troy was supposed to detect a problem. I say "fortunately" because without those flights, we might never have known that vigilance decrement was an issue. Troy had made mistakes on three of those eleven.

I posted a summary of those three cases on the other screen and went through them individually. In one, a flight of four aircraft was leaving after a seven-hour, close-air-support mission. At one of the waypoints on the return home, three of the Jacks turned; one did not. Troy continued to scan his displays, but it was several minutes before he realized he was watching only three blips on the moving map. Even Marshall chuckled. It was difficult to see the wayward Jack against the ground clutter even when you knew it was going to happen.

During this part of my talk, Troy stared at his shoes. He had agreed in advance that the discussion was necessary, although, of course, not easy for him to watch. But by the look on Marshall's and Dempsey's faces, he had nothing to worry about. They seemed quite impressed with his resolve. Their eyes kept going between the silent video of the flight on one screen and the chart that summarized the 216 seconds where Troy had missed a single, isolated piece of information in 1,117 hours. I'd even done the math for them; it was 216 seconds of information and 4,020,984 seconds of nothing.

At the end of my review of the incidents, Marshall raised a hand in mock surrender. "I'm convinced. I'd swear you paused that video except I saw the map display changing. But I think we've hit the limit on automation. And system reliability is already better than just about any other program." He paused, looking off into the distance for an instant. Then, he sat forward, his expression morphing to a scowl. "You're not suggesting we make Jack less capable, are you? Just to give the coordinators something to do?"

"No, no, not at all," I said, surprised he thought I might be considering anything like that. "Col. Dempsey told me he thought the trend toward smarter machines in the military was inevitable, and I agree. We're not going to take a step backward." Marshall leaned back in his chair.

"I just want to make it more likely that coordinators catch problems even after their attention is nearly spent. What I am suggesting is often called training to automaticity. You're probably familiar with what happens when you drive the same route, say to work, day after day. After a while, you get to the point where you hardly think about it? Some people call it, being on automatic pilot. In psychology, that's automaticity."

Neither man said anything, but I noticed two, nearly imperceptible nods. "And if a problem pops up during your drive—a car cuts in front of you, brake lights come on up ahead, someone steps off the curb—you snap back to the here and now and slam on the brakes."

Dempsey chuckled. "I hope that's true, but sometimes I wonder. I can get all the way home and not remember much about the drive at all."

Good. They understood the concept ... or at least, the colonel did. Now, it was time to answer one concern that was almost certainly in their minds.

"With the current simulation, you can implement this training with very little cost because what I'm recommending is that you use it to present problems at a fairly high rate—like one every few minutes rather than once every few years." I saw, more than heard, Marshall snort. I figured he'd like the exaggeration. It was his style.

"The issues should spring up in different subsystems unpredictably. Maybe have two problems overlap or have the same subsystem fail a second time after the coordinator just responded to it. Throw in some faults in the console itself, like a flickering light. Anything to keep the coordinators on their toes and make them sensitive to potential issues. Then, add a scoring system, so they know how they're doing. Since they know problems are coming, they probably won't miss any, but they can be scored on how long it takes them to notice—their response time."

"And you think this will help them pay more attention?" asked Marshall.

I wanted to agree. I wanted to build the feeling that we had a shared understanding of the problem and ownership of a possible solution, but I couldn't. "Almost. I want to make detecting these problems more automatic, so when the coordinators have little attention left to invest, they'll still notice them. It's like taking months of near car collisions, flashing brake lights, and daydreaming pedestrians and putting them into a couple of hours of training."

"And that's the duration you're suggesting?" asked Dempsey. "A couple of hours?"

"There's no precise formula, Colonel, and people will differ, but it'll probably take three or four times that. To get a better number, I'd recommend watching the scores when the training is first being tested. When the testers start, they'll be repeating the rules to themselves, just like any new coordinator would do. 'Check that altitude is to plan.' 'Verify the spacing among aircraft.' 'Check operating temperature.' Every novice starts by silently rehearsing the procedure in their head. That's why their reactions are slow and prone to error. And when their scores stop improving rapidly, they've started overlearning and automaticity is developing. Soon, they'll be reacting almost before they realize there's a problem."

"You know, that almost sounds like fun," said Marshall slowly. "Problems springing up all over the place. Coordinators needing to stay on their toes and react to them. Might even get some friendly competition going."

"It might," I said, keeping my voice neutral. In fact, I'd hoped someone would come to that conclusion. By adding things like pace, unpredictability, and scoring, some training developers had been able to transform rote practice into interesting challenges. The best examples looked much like games, and people would play them for hours. And because video gameplay, in general, was believed to reduce vigilance decrement, I was hoping to get the additional boost as a byproduct. True, research had found other factors that affected vigilance, but I doubted the program wanted coordinators wired on drugs.

The nearly imperceptible nods of a few moments ago became more demonstrative, and Dempsey started scribbling notes. Marshall leaned back and began doodling in the margins of his notebook. Or maybe he was making annotations there, but I doubted it. I glanced at Troy who grinned back at me. He thought it had gone well.

In this unplanned break in the talk, the fourth incident I had found in the reports flashed through my mind. It had nothing to do with vigilance decrement, but that wasn't the reason I'd omitted it. I didn't include it because it involved a pilot, not a coordinator. It involved Drew, and it made for some vaguely unsettling reading.

It had occurred about three months earlier, just before Col. Dempsey arrived at the range. The program was testing the integration of Hydra 70 rockets. During the flight in question, Jack was carrying some inert practice rounds. After test firing one, Drew put Jack into its simulated search-and-destroy mode as Marshall had directed. After a few minutes of flight, the aircraft detected a large animal. That alone was a bit unusual. With the fences, the relatively higher density of humans on the range, and the infrequent but nerve-shattering use of real munitions, wild animals usually gave the place a wide berth. But not this time.

Drew became fascinated with the creature, which turned out to be a coyote. He took control from Jack so he could, in his own words from the initial report, "... track Wiley through the desert." Yes, he'd named his quarry, perhaps in honor of the *Looney Tunes* character, Wile E. Coyote, or maybe just because the adjective fit. He'd even changed Jack's automatically assigned contact number to the name he'd bestowed on the animal. It was no wonder that everyone on the range now knew the incident as the Wiley case.

To this point, Drew was guilty of little beyond a bit of overexuberance. In his later statement about the incident, Marshall termed the pilot's actions "unexpected" but to this point, "... fully consistent with his directive to take every possible opportunity to test JACC's systems against naturally occurring impediments in the test range environment." Apparently, he wrote the same way as he spoke.

Drew's actions, however, became less defensible when the animal approached the range's outer fence. At that point, Drew launched the remaining Hydra 70 practice rocket, and the key question became, what was his intent? In Drew's initial remarks, it sounded like he had fired on impulse. He had tracked the animal for nearly two hours, and as it neared the boundary of the test range, he took the shot rather than letting it "escape."

Having grown up in a rural area where hunting was common, I had several friends who found it irresistible to take a shot at a bird, a rabbit, a squirrel, or whatever else happened to stray in front of their gun sights. Typically, they gave no thought to what would happen should the animal be wounded. Drew's initial account sounded much the same; it sounded like poor impulse control.

But by the next afternoon, when investigators conducted the formal interview, Drew's justification had either changed or was refined, depending on how one judged the truthfulness of his statements. Now, he claimed he been operating under a misperception. Because the software was evolving to accommodate new weapons, he had believed that firing the rocket before Wiley escaped was the only way he could capture the event on video. And, of course, the program would want the incident recorded, since it highlighted Jack's capabilities.

To remedy the problem of pilots not keeping up with rapidly evolving software, Marshall added a daily, ten-minute standup meeting with all of the pilots. The outcry from the program, however, didn't subside. Others held that it was a pilot's responsibility to know all the nuances of the system, old and new, and Drew had been derelict in that duty. He was placed on leave with pay until a final decision could be reached.

About two weeks later, a formal statement was released by the Air Force, and nothing I'd read to that point prepared me for its contents. It said that the incident was the result of human error with extenuating circumstances—the weapon loadout screen had been misaligned. The explanation seemed almost surreal. How did a slightly off-center display cause someone to take a shot at a coyote? But later sections clarified ... at least somewhat. The screen problem wasn't a causative factor but rather, a contributive one. Struggles with the display had diverted Drew's attention, and he had failed to recall other methods for recording the action. The rationale nudged my opinion of the explanation from surreal to strained, but the JACC program and the Air Force were satisfied. Drew went back to work the next day.

As I neared the end of the incident report, I wondered if Col. Dempsey knew about Wiley. But as I turned to the last page, I got my answer. What I was reading was a copy of the report sent from Omega Systems headquarters in Pittsburgh to the colonel. Not only did Dempsey know about the case, but apparently, he had scheduled at least two meetings with Drew to discuss it. I wished I could have been a fly on the wall for one of those.

Unless Dempsey was commending Drew for his skill.

Where had that thought come from? Whatever its source—a connection surfacing from my unconscious, an extremely unlikely possibility generated in the name of comprehensiveness—it was unsettling. But before I could consider it further, Dempsey looked up from his notebook and cleared his throat. "You have more on vigilance decrement?"

"No, sir. And that was my final topic unless there are questions."

Dempsey glanced at Marshall, who turned to me.

"Not a question so much as an observation," said Marshall. "I thought the coordinator's training was foolproof because the job didn't give them any latitude for mistakes ... but then, training's not my thing. And the idea of using training to deal with boredom? Fascinating, because frankly, training's usually one of its causes."

The comment was somewhat insulting, but Marshall had a way of saying things—like he was sharing a secret with a best friend—that made it seem less offensive. And there was the fact that his criticism was valid. A lot of training was boring.

"But you should probably know," Marshall continued, "we may soon do away with vigilance decrement entirely."

What the ...?

Without turning back the clock and letting pilots and coordinators fly, there was only one way that was possible—no human oversight. I turned to Dempsey hoping for some type of denial, but he was looking elsewhere. He was scowling at the Omega Systems Program Manager.

Marshall held out a hand toward the colonel. "With the Air Force releasing an announcement yesterday about our next phase, we can keep this discussion white world."

If the colonel's scowl softened, the change was slight.

"And since Dr. Price pulled one rabbit from his hat, I thought it wouldn't hurt if he knew where this program was going," continued Marshall. "The future might influence his findings about the coordinator's current training."

The scowl softened, but perhaps only because the colonel raised his eyebrows. He turned to me. "What Dr. Marshall is talking about is the final phase of the program. If program progress is satisfactory in this phase," Dempsey said, emphasizing the word 'if', "we'll be moving to a final research and development objective. That objective is to enable flights of four or six Jacks to work collaboratively to complete their mission. If that influences your findings for the current training curriculum, then, yes, please document your thoughts."

With a slight tip of his hand, Dempsey turned the floor back to Marshall.

"As Col. Dempsey said, we're about to start testing a capability that allows a group of Jacks to support each other, watch each other's backs. If you attack one aircraft, you have to deal with them all. They'll share strategic and tactical information. They'll find the bad guys and by triangulating, they'll know their position to a gnat's whisker. And if one of the Jacks is damaged and can't self-destruct, his buddies will take care of the issue. So, there will be no vigilance decrement because after Jack is given a battle area, a database of threats, and the rules of engagement, no one will be watching. Well, no humans, anyway."

The one word in his long declaration that caught my attention became my question. "Testing?"

"Excuse me?" replied Marshall.

"Maybe I'm over-interpreting, but you said you're about to start testing. You didn't say, you were about to start design and development."

Marshall chuckled. "Nope, you didn't misunderstand. When we were first developing Jack's capabilities, we were constantly shifting between software coding and testing in the simulation or on the aircraft. And as you've seen during our practice sessions, those abilities have been perfected. This new capability isn't about creating new abilities but, rather, organizing and coordinating the ones Jack already has among several aircraft. It uses Jack-created strategies and tactics rather than data from the environment, which means we could develop the software almost completely in the lab. And we have."

Marshall picked up the device he had brought with him and raised it in the air. "So, after a successful live-fire demonstration tomorrow, we'll be flying the demo aircraft back to Maintenance where he'll join three others. There, we'll load the contents of this disk drive onto all four and go directly into testing."

I didn't know what to say about aircraft working together other than the obvious—no, I don't think this capability will affect my recommendations. What more could we teach coordinators if this vision becomes reality—résumé writing skills for when Jack puts them out of a job? Sarcasm, however, was inappropriate. So, I said, "I understand. And when I get back to St. Louis, I'll give this capability some thought."

After that, the discussion ended quickly. Both men thanked me and left, followed closely by Troy. He said something about needing to use the restroom, but his words hardly registered. I had said I understood when Marshall finished his description of the final R&D phase, and I did ... after a manner. I understood that despite living unmanned systems for seven days and studying them for seven nights and a weekend, the adjustment in my thinking hadn't been enough. Not nearly enough.

I'd gone from near-total ignorance of their existence to guarded acceptance of their research objective to become autonomous. But I'd also taken comfort in Mark Dillon's belief that the live-fire demonstration was most likely an overstatement of Jack's true abilities. Such demonstrations often showcased a specially built system for a handpicked scenario. That relief, however, was illusory. While Marshall was prone to hyperbole—exaggeration was his stock in trade—Col. Dempsey had no such proclivities, and he foresaw a near-future with only limited human oversight. So, my worldview had come to incorporate that prospect, too.

That had been my concept of unmanned systems and the JACC program until this precise moment when once again, it changed dramatically. The final step in the program, if it occurred, would give the world a devastatingly efficient weapon devoid of all human oversight. It would be a weapon system that would support others of its kind, making them more than the sum of their parts. Somehow, I couldn't shake the image of a pack of wolves and the way they would nip at the heels or the unguarded flank of their prey. Eventually, their quarry would fall from blood loss and exhaustion. Would a pack of Jacks be that much different?

So now, with Marshall's disclosure of the program's final phase, even the thought that we were "on the cusp" of a revolution in warfare was an inadequate adjustment to my reality. That was because we had, in fact, moved well into this new world.

The Nevada Desert, 6:53 AM

Drew adjusted the rifle in the crook of his arm and pulled the bill of his cap down with his free hand to shade his eyes. The sun was just starting to crest the rise to the east, sending fingers of light stretching across the desert. Even with the feebleness of the early morning rays, he could feel the warmth on his face. In the sky, three thin lines of wispy, white clouds spanned the horizon like waves breaking on a brilliant ocean of orange and blue.

"Idiot," Drew muttered to himself. He'd gone hunting to forget about work for a few hours, but the goal was proving elusive. He couldn't put Troy and that idiot, Doc, out of his mind.

Before Doc arrived, Troy had been okay. He'd been decent at his job, and he knew what he was. A coordinator. A babysitter. Someone who didn't have what it took to be a pilot. And though they both knew Drew could fly circles around almost anyone on almost any unmanned system, Troy never seemed to let that fact bother him. They had their places, and Troy had known his and had accepted it.

But in the week and a half since Doc arrived, everything had changed. The two of them had talked endlessly about what a coordinator did. It felt like a month for a conversation that should have lasted less than a minute. And this whole idea that Doc could train coordinators so well that they could do their job without thinking? Of course, they could. There was nothing to think about.

But Troy's mind wasn't the only one Doc had poisoned. There was also that cute girl working with the maintenance guys, Jill. She'd shot him down the very first time he talked to her. She said something about getting married, but she wasn't wearing a ring. And when he pointed that out, she said it was getting sized. Doc had to be behind that; she was too smooth, too quick with her lies. He'd probably told her about Deadman's Gulch. Probably said he was in all kinds of danger when in fact, nothing could have gone wrong. No one died from having their picture taken.

"You'd piss your pants if I pointed Jack at you, wouldn't you, Doc?" Drew said to no one but the empty desert. He chuckled at the thought, then told himself again to forget about them. He started down the bank of a shallow wash, all but the very bottom already bathed in sunlight.

He could have gone to Doc's talk today. He'd been invited. Of course, he had. A pilot's perspective on anything to do with Jack would always be in demand. But he didn't care about training for a job that didn't need any. And besides, the talk was the perfect opportunity to slip out of work for a couple of hours and do a little hunting. Since arriving at the range nearly a year ago, he'd found dozens of opportunities to play hooky. He'd come to think of it almost like a perk of the job. The big boys got busy; Drew got some time picking off game at a hundred yards. He'd even hit a hawk in flight once.

Climbing out of the other side of the wash, Drew found himself breathing harder than he would have liked. He was getting soft. He spent too little time in the desert and too much sitting in the Ops Center. That, however, was by choice, because while he enjoyed lining up a shot with his rifle, it was nothing compared to the kick in the butt he got from drawing down with Jack.

Most of the hunting he did with Jack was picking off the manikins in Bogey Town, of course. Initially, that had been fun, even when he had only simulated weaponry. But by now, he'd seen their positions and their pre-programmed movements so many times, the thrill had been replaced by boring routine. And firing virtual bullets at real animals was completely unsatisfactory. He'd shoot and they'd scamper away as if nothing had happened ... because, in their world, nothing had. He'd considered asking one of the software engineers to develop simulated animals that would die gruesomely with virtual bullets. Surely one of them was a frustrated game developer at heart. But in the end, he hadn't asked because he could call none of them a friend.

That left his memories of stalking Wiley, the coyote that had wandered onto the JACC test range. With a prey that seemed to sense it was being hunted and an almost-real weapon, the quest had been a near-mystical experience, like nothing else he had ever done. Unfortunately, the memory was fading. And since that day, actual ordnance had been scarce. It wasn't as if the program was giving him live ammunition for his private use. All he'd come up with was a few machinegun rounds that remained after a test, and when no one was watching, he'd left a saguaro cactus or two missing an arm.

Of course, the scarcity of real weapons was about to change. Tomorrow, he'd have a fully loaded Jack at his command. Despite the rising temperatures, a chill ran through his body with the thought.

Drew paused on the edge of the wash, scanning the terrain. Nothing moved save the illusion from the faint ripples of heat rising from the desert floor. With more time, he was certain he would have found something, but Doc's talk wouldn't last forever. He'd better get to work. Marshall would undoubtedly want to practice his talk for tomorrow one more time. Or two. Or ten. The man never seemed to tire of his voice. But then, he kept the program sold and the program gave him Jack. He could daydream through Marshall's pitch as many times as it took. Drew turned to go back to his car.

There was no doubt, tomorrow was a big day, and the risk inherent in the event had robbed Drew of his sleep. It had been about three months ago when Marshall had first told him that the program might cut back on pilots, might even eliminate the job. Drew had thought that the old man was mistaken; that couldn't be true. But when Dempsey arrived, he had said the same. The possibility was troubling, but unless they cut everyone, he'd have a job. He was, after all, the best.

Then came the rumors that the program might be terminated. Something about a problem in the last phase, before he was even part of the team. How the hell could they punish him for something he hadn't been a part of? And when Dempsey lent further credence to the rumor—not by confirming it but just discussing the possibility at one of his staff meetings—Drew's concern became anger. He hated being at the mercy of these clueless, political hacks. They held him hostage with the one thing that made him feel alive.

Then, seemingly from nowhere, a solution to that problem had materialized. It was a plan born of desperation, but clearly, it could work. That knowledge should have let him sleep. And it would have, except for one thing. If the government morons were stupid enough to cancel the program, there'd be hell to pay. And those images were the stuff of nightmares, not dreams.

Guard Station, JACC Test Range, Nevada, 2:00 PM

"Bet he won't miss this one," Dempsey muttered to himself as he took a seat in Conference Room One. With the live-fire demonstration tomorrow, his boss, Col. Newberry, would want to verify that everything was in place. Of course, if they traded places, he'd feel the same.

Dempsey dialed. Newberry answered on the fourth ring. After he identified himself, Newberry replied, "Hi, Ray. What's the news from backwater Nevada?"

Dempsey thought about saying that the use of "backwater" as a derogatory description of the Nevada desert was inappropriate, but he thought better of it. Newberry might see it as an excuse for another tirade about the inappropriateness of his career path. Or, at least the one his boss thought he had chosen.

"Our primary activities this last week have focused on the live-fire demonstration. The contractor team flew practice flights on both scenarios each day and they went well. I've received drafts of the three contractor presentations. The ones for the pilot and the coordinator are short. You could describe both of them as 'just the facts.' Dr. Marshall's talk, on the other hand, is considerably longer and heavily slanted toward vision and costs should we not pursue the technology."

"Soapboxing, as usual."

"Some, but it is his job," replied Dempsey slowly.

"It's his job to keep the program sold, not expand his role through the use of intimidation. Send me the draft."

"Yes, sir," replied Dempsey.

Although describing the cost of ending a program was part of "keeping it sold," it was Marshall's reputation for stating possibilities as if they were fact that was earning him Newberry's additional scrutiny. It was, of course, a wasted effort for his boss to review the draft. Marshall would never stick to it once his foot was on stage. It was, at best, a shadow of what he'd say, but there was no reason to tell Newberry that.

"Is Representative Alison still attending? He's got some pull in the House Armed Services Committee, so his thumbs-up is crucial."

"As of yesterday, the visit was still on Alison's schedule."

"Good. Keep him happy."

This was vintage Newberry. He had found enough dirt on the program to get a one-month stop-work issued and had probably strained his arm, patting himself on the back. Now, the news was about to break, and Alison could very well be the one that delivered it. No one would be happy about that. So, what Newberry meant was, let them be upset by the slap on the wrist I'm delivering, but don't let it expand. Newberry wanted Jack in the U.S. arsenal as much as anyone … well, once it was stripped of its autonomy, that is. He had no interest in a machine that could think for itself.

"How's the work of those two civilians coming?"

Dempsey expected thoroughness from his boss, but this level of interest surprised him. "Good, sir. I received a report from the Maintenance group. They had nothing but positives on the woman who's working on the task analysis. And the man looking at coordinator training? He briefed us this morning, and everything was reasonable."

"She attractive?" asked Newberry.

She was but to say so implied support for Newberry's insinuation, and he didn't care to do that. His hesitation, however, apparently spoke when his voice didn't.

"Never mind," Newberry said. "The other one, Price. He bothers me a bit. He hasn't been at Ruger-Phillips long. Worked a couple of jobs but then got put on a desk for a few months, and it's not clear why. I just hope he's not trying to make amends for a screw-up, looking for a problem with the training that only his company can fix. Wouldn't be the first time a defense contractor tried that ploy."

Now the reason for his boss's interest was clear to Dempsey. Many of the Ruger-Phillips employees had previous military experience; that was just standard operating procedure for companies with military contracts. Newberry undoubtedly knew one of them, and this tidbit on Price had come from the company rumor mill.

"I didn't see anything in his talk that looked like a smear campaign," replied Dempsey. "But I'll keep an eye on him."

And then, an idea struck him. "To answer your earlier question, the woman is quite attractive. A real girl-next-door type … although I think the guys are paying attention to their jobs, not just her." Dempsey figured the denial would make Newberry even less likely to accept the situation at face value. "But the interesting thing is that they know each other—Price and this woman, Henshaw. Quite well, actually ... if you get my drift." With few places to go in the evening and a small, tight-knit group, even history made the rounds quickly on the JACC test range.

"Damn, that's one helluva coincidence." The line went silent. Even without Newberry saying, "I'll check into her," Dempsey knew it was mission accomplished. It was just one more thing to sidetrack his boss at a time when every distraction helped.

Finally, Newberry asked, "Anything else, Ray?"

"No, Colonel. That's all I have."

"Okay. Keep a leash on Marshall and his team tomorrow. I'll call in the afternoon for a debrief."

"Good ...." But before he could finish his farewell, the line went dead.

Dempsey leaned back in his chair and stared at the clock on the wall. It was 2:40. Technically, he didn't need to leave the range until 3:00 to meet with Stephen Gerhardt, but his patience was in short supply. He was anxious to do something, to take the next step.

He had decided what had to be done nearly two years ago, and since then every waking hour outside of work had been spent making his vision a reality. But now that he was on the cusp of this future, the waiting between steps had become nearly unbearable. And worse, his forced plodding stood in stark contrast to the speed of change in the world beyond the JACC test range. There, things were happening in a blur.

First, there had been the accident with the Harpies. Firing them, he was certain, wasn't a mistake, but where they had landed might have been. And then there was Newberry, running his own, private witch-hunt, seeking to prove that Marshall had pushed the JACC system into the current phase before it was ready. What a major blunder it would be if Newberry's largely trumped-up charges yielded a three- or four-month pause in the program. And finally, there was the game Marshall was playing with the live-fire demonstration. He was pushing the bureaucrats hard, almost daring them to terminate the program. That trick could easily backfire as well.

But even more ironic, the myopic efforts of these two men might interact. Marshall's ultimatum with Newberry's insinuations could yield a result that neither of the men wanted—a permanent shutdown of the program. Dempsey almost wished he would be around to see it if that happened, but he knew he wouldn't be.

His mental accounting of these possibilities bothered him, but that concern paled in comparison to his fear that there were other, unknown forces in play. While he had immediate and unfettered access to everything related to JACC, news outside the program was often delayed and frequently distorted, even if it involved the military. Newberry, for example, had known about the Harpy incident eleven hours before he'd heard a whisper. And now that the time to set the final sequence in motion was measured in hours rather than days, that kind of gap in the information flow could be disastrous.

Fortunately, he wasn't alone. Stephen Gerhardt was his eyes and ears everywhere he couldn't be. The man ate, slept, and breathed the state of their world, examining in microscopic detail events and people he hardly recognized. But that was what he was paid to do. Well paid.

Dempsey stared at the clock again. Only four minutes had elapsed. Maybe he should leave now and use the time on the other end to collect his thoughts? He needed this next meeting to be conclusive. Gerhardt had to be pushed from the hedged positions he formed so easily, the shades of gray he found so comforting, into Dempsey's stark world of black or white. Kill or be killed. Go or no-go, because if it was a go, this would be the last time he would meet Gerhardt as a Lt. Colonel in the U.S. Air Force. There might be secure phone calls or encrypted emails while he was still in uniform, but the time to sit across the table and hash out the details would end today.

One final glance at the clock and Dempsey muttered to himself, "Close enough." It was time to start a long, boring drive to a backstreet bar not far from the Vegas strip. It was time to start the rest of his life.

The Golden Nugget Motel, Nevada, 5:23 PM

I dropped into one of the overstuffed armchairs in the motel's lobby, its bright, floral pattern in stark contrast to the muted shades of brown and green outside. The receptionist behind the counter grinned and gave me a knowing nod. He was the same person who had manned it the first night I'd picked up Jill for dinner. I figured his gesture was in appreciation for the attractive young woman who was about to join me. Or maybe it was just in recognition of the fact that, whatever we were up to, I had mastered my unease. Tonight, I could have kicked back and put my feet up on a footstool, except they didn't have any.

After a moment, Jill entered the lobby from one of the side halls and was now looking over her shoulder as she headed toward the front door. When I caught up, she said, "Evening, Doc," and turned her head for a peck on the cheek.

"You look great." And she did, wearing a dark blue, slightly-above-the-knee-length dress. "But I don't think you had to dress up for this barbeque restaurant," I said, smirking.

"I packed it and it's not like I can wear it on the test range." The statement made perfect sense—a dress wasn't the attire for climbing around a maintenance bay—but her tone implied she had either missed that I was teasing or something else was bothering her. She continued out the door before I could ask. "Do you mind if we go back to Betsy's? I know you had your heart set on barbeque, but I don't feel like anything that heavy tonight."

"Sure. Betsy's is fine."

Once we were seated in my rental car, Jill asked, "How well do you know Drew?"

"Drew? The pilot, Brandt Drury?"

It was an ill-considered question—I doubted we had any other Drews in common—but I was confused. I didn't even know she knew him. I caught a nod from the silhouette in the seat beside me and then, "Yeah, him."

I started the car and backed out of the parking spot, using the maneuver to give me a moment to organize my thoughts. I needed it because I didn't know exactly what to make of Drew. "I don't know him well. He's a pilot like I mentioned, and my project only involves the training for coordinators. But we did have something of a run-in on my second day here."

I proceeded to tell her about my simulated assassination at Deadman's Gulch. By the time I finished, I was parking at Betsy's. I'd expected some mild ribbing—what, can't take a joke—at least for the first part of my story, but Jill had been quiet for the entire drive. I glanced over, catching a faraway look on her face in the red glow of the neon sign in the restaurant's window.

"Something happen between you two?" I asked to break the silence.

"You could say that."

She went quiet again. I waited for a minute before asking, "Want to talk about it over dinner?"

"No, it's better I tell you out here. It was two days ago, at the Maintenance Building. Jack had just landed after one of the practice sessions, and the guys were refueling and loading more ordnance. I stay out of the way when they're doing that, so I was sitting in a back office when Drew came in. He seemed nice enough. Introduced himself and we talked for a while. Then, he asked me to dinner. Sorry, but I used you as an excuse—told him we were eating together."

"Not a problem," I said. She knew that, but the smile and slight nod said it was good to hear anyway.

"After that, he suggested I dump you so we could get to know each other better, as he put it. He was being a bit pushy, so I told him I was engaged. That didn't work any better. It was like he took it as a challenge. He started getting up in my face, saying he could guarantee a good time. Fortunately, one of the maintenance guys came in and he left right after that because I was starting to get pissed."

I'd seen Jill angry before, and she could handle herself in a verbal battle. But it was the thought that the fight might involve more than words that brought me up short. "Are you all right?"

"I'm getting there," she said. "Anyway, word got around the shop that Drew and I had been arguing, and two different guys came up to me today to say I should watch my back. Apparently, he likes to intimidate people, which fits with your story. But they thought he might be capable of going through with his threats. Before he came here, he flew drones as a hobby, but rumor has it, his were specially equipped."

"Put a beefed-up camera on it so he could get close-ups of his neighbors? The women in particular?"

"That much is fact," Jill replied. "He's shown his drone with the camera to anyone who'd look. Some of the pictures, too. But it was the rumor that he'd outfitted it with a gun that got him into trouble. The guys think Omega Systems transferred him out here as a lesson. Get him out of their hair and away from civilization, except they think it had the opposite effect. He loves all the firepower he has now."

I blew out a long breath, starting to pull my thoughts together about what we could do, but Jill wasn't finished. "Last night, about two in the morning, someone knocked on my door."

I had turned toward my old friend, leaning in as she told her story. But with her last statement, I felt my head jerk back as if her words had slapped me in the face. "Jill, this is freaking serious," I blurted. "Did you call the police?"

Jill slowly shook her head. "No, I didn't. By the time I checked the peephole in the door, there was no one in the hall. So, I made sure the deadbolt was locked and went back to bed. But I can't say I slept much."

"You want to change rooms? Or even motels? If Drew can't find you, he can't ...." I didn't finish, not wanting to hear the words. And besides, if she moved, she'd be farther from me, and that didn't seem like the best plan. "Or I could sleep in your room tonight. Tomorrow night, too, and then you'd be headed home. Maybe you could change back to your original travel plans and leave tomorrow?"

"Easy there, Doc," she said. "We don't even know it was Drew, and I'm not letting some anonymous sleepwalker bumping into my door scare me off. I'm staying till Friday. I'll just keep both locks on and my phone handy whenever I'm in the room. But I would appreciate it if you'd walk me back there after dinner."

"Of course."

"Good. Tomorrow, I'm watching the demo from the Maintenance Building. I have the word of two of the maintainers that they won't leave me alone with Drew if he happens to come by afterward."

"What about the drive between the range and the motel?" I asked.

Jill released a single laugh, sounding more nervous than amused. "I don't think he'd carjack me in the middle of the day."

"No, I don't suppose he would," I replied slowly. "What I think will happen is that you'll get a mysterious flat tire, and he'll come along to rescue you. Or your radiator will overheat, and he'll just happen by with a can of water." She frowned but said nothing. "Look, it's probably perfectly safe, but why take the chance? We'll have breakfast tomorrow, and then I'll follow you to the range. Same on Friday, when we head to the airport."

"I can't decide if your imagination is running wild or this is just more of your compulsive thoroughness."

"Compulsive?" I said, feigning hurt feelings.

"Yes, compulsive ... but in the best possible way. You're constantly sifting through all the noise, and somehow, you find an answer. You did that in school all the time ... which, by the way, is why everybody hated you."

I chuckled, knowing there was some truth to Jill's words. "So, let's take full advantage of my obsessiveness. Commuting's decided. Now, how about I be your personal bodyguard for tomorrow night's festivities?"

"I was just going to lock myself in my room and pack," Jill replied.

"You don't want to miss the big victory celebration, do you?"

She rubbed the fingertips of one hand over her forehead. "It would be nice to congratulate everyone. Or console them, if things flop."

"Bite your tongue."

She grinned. It was a welcome change in the prevailing mood. "I may take you up on your offer. We can talk about it tomorrow after the demonstration, but now, I'm starving. Let's go eat."

We went in. If Jill was still thinking about Drew during dinner, I couldn't see it in her face or read it in her body language. For my part, I focused on her anecdotes about the maintainers she'd met, and I reciprocated with tales of Troy flying Jack. But I wasn't fooling myself. My compulsion, as Jill had called it, was working in the background. Occasionally, some tidbit of her run-in with Drew surfaced in my mind, and I knew my unconscious was silently twisting and turning those new pieces, checking for fit in the puzzle I was building of the man.

THE DAY, THURSDAY, JANUARY 14

Operations Center, JACC Test Range, Nevada, 10:11 AM

After seeing the Information Systems Building laid to rubble, Troy and I fell silent. He sat, staring at the display on his console as if hoping to rewind the events of the last few seconds. I was looking over his shoulder, fantasizing the same thing, but it did no good. Jack just continued his march, leaving behind a pile of smoking rubble and dead bodies.

Who could do something like this?

The question wasn't academic; it was practical. If we knew who was coming, we might figure out how to evade it or him. I started the mental roll call of my suspects.

Jack was still at the head of my list. Perhaps he was out of control because of a bug in the software. Or maybe it was operator error. But whichever, he was now locked into a cold machine calculus that required our death.

Then, there was Drew. Maybe the pilot was driven by psychological forces that were beyond my grasp. Perhaps he felt omnipotent with Jack to do his bidding. For all I knew, Drew heard voices telling him to kill us. And since it was possible he was alive, he remained firmly lodged in second place.

The third position was the most shadowy of all the possibilities—that some other person or persons were orchestrating this massacre.

If so, they had regular access to the program because, even if the killing was a crime of passion and opportunity, they had been around enough to keep up with the changing software. Marshall fit the description. So did Dempsey, but motive was my problem in either case. Both men had something to gain if Jack succeeded, but what did they achieve if the system failed so spectacularly?

A software engineer who wanted to sabotage the program also fit the description. All that was required was a Trojan horse, some benign-looking code that took control of Jack when Drew tried to shut him down after the demo. But there were major issues with this scenario. Under it, Garcia's death had been an accident and the existence of the software hack that could have kept Drew alive in the Mobile Command Center was just a coincidence. Additionally, the saboteur had wanted to discredit the program so badly, he had probably forfeited his own life. All of the primary software developers had been killed including their chief. It was obvious why this option rested firmly in last place.

But in the end, every entity, man or machine, that I considered led to the same result—I didn't know if he, she, or it was the killer. If I held the datum, that one particular piece of evidence that would unmask the hunter's identity, it eluded me.

"I still can't believe Drew is doing this alone," I said to break the silence that hung in the air between Troy and me. "He runs on impulse, and this has all the earmarks of some careful planning. Or a total technological screwup, I suppose." I couldn't select one possibility even to start a conversation.

Troy turned to look up at me. His eyes narrowed. His forehead wrinkled. "What the hell difference does it make? If it's Mother Teresa at the controls, we'll be just as dead."

"But knowing who it is might give us a leg up. Something we could exploit to get out of this."

"Yeah, good luck with that. For Jack, killing us will be like shooting fish in a barrel." Troy pushed back from the console and strode from the room without a backward glance.

I couldn't blame him. But I couldn't join him either. My mind wouldn't allow it. It continued to churn at the slim prospects left us. Many of them could be realized if we had the time and the freedom to act—the software could be verified, the police could reopen the investigation into Garcia's death, a clinician could talk to Drew. But in terms of what could occur in the next twenty or so minutes before Jack reached us? All those avenues were blocked.

Those blockages, however, weren't producing fatalism in me. They weren't whispering in my ear to give up. Rather, they said, "reformulate the problem." Come at it from a different direction. If I couldn't figure out who was systematically picking us off, perhaps I could come up with a defense. What could Troy and I do to thwart Jack, whoever or whatever was at his controls?

Unfortunately, the data I had on that question was limited as well. There was virtually no information on Jack's offensive capabilities in the coordinator's training. I'd been over that void with Marshall and Dempsey enough to be certain it existed and why. And I hadn't picked up much during my time on the range, mostly because I rarely spoke to Drew and he was the one who would know the most.

Troy, on the other hand, would have soaked up more during his time on the program, but he wasn't talking. He would, however. Of that, I was nearly certain. He just needed a few moments to get his mental arms around our situation, and then, he'd be back. And if not? Well, I'd have to convince him that fooling the mind in the clouds was our best hope.

In the meantime, I decided to review what I knew about Jack's capabilities. Unfortunately, recalling that information from my talk with Mark Dillon more than three weeks ago wouldn't be easy. I didn't have notes. I'd never even thought about our discussion. So, some of what he had told me would be gone, forgotten. Other parts might be there in gist but not in detail. And still more of what I would swear were Dillon's exact words would be pure fiction, false memories created by later information or my expectations.

All of these mental processes served people well every day. They made sure our minds weren't overwhelmed by stored detail or paralyzed by conceptual inconsistencies. Unfortunately, in the current context, those inherent, mental simplifications might result in our deaths.

As I recalled the discussion, much of it had dealt with Jack's physical capabilities—speed, maneuverability, onboard weapons— and that of its sensor package. It felt pointless, however, to dwell on those facts as they just made Jack seem invulnerable. Then, we'd talked about artificial intelligence. Dillon had said that the concept was a moving target; yesterday's astounding achievement was tomorrow's mundane feature. And we'd talked about how AI, at least on Jack, was rarely patterned after human mental processes, although it often accomplished the same thing. Vision was the example we had discussed.

Once through what I could recall, I found nothing we could use as leverage against Jack. He could identify living entities at great distances, determine the entity was human within seconds, infer the danger he/she posed, and eliminate the threat with exacting precision. There seemed no weak links in the process. At the same time, however, it felt like I was missing something. But what? I got no further than sensing the void in my mental picture when Troy returned.

"Sorry, Doc. I can't say I feel any different, but I shouldn't have walked out."

That was all I could ask. "No worries. It's great to have you back because I'm stumped on a few things—like Jack letting those construction workers walk away earlier. It seemed to make sense when we told them to move away slowly. But thinking back on all the times we watched Jack running a simulated search-and-destroy mission, I thought he'd always classified them as hostile?"

While I talked, Troy had walked back to his console and sat. Now, he turned from the equipment to look at me, his head shaking. "I've seen it both ways. Sometimes, Jack takes them as foes, sometimes as friendlies. It probably depends on things like the history of their movements and proximity to other hostile forces."

I nodded, although it wasn't the response I had hoped. Jack thinking he saw lots of bad guys on the range might get him to waste shots, not that I knew where we'd get these sacrificial targets. But if he wouldn't, it was time to explore something else. "I didn't think the attack at the Maintenance Building looked right."

"Yeah, you mentioned that. And I still say, you don't know exactly where those missiles hit. You're trying to read a difference of a few yards with missiles flying faster than the speed of sound on computer hardware that has its own set of delays and inaccuracies."

I raised a hand. "Yeah, and I remember you saying that, too. And while I'm not sure about that part, I was thinking about something else—the strength of the attack. It seemed pretty feeble, especially compared to IS."

Troy frowned and turned back to his console. After a few moments, he faced me again. "Maybe you're right. Either IS was overkill or the attack on Maintenance was weak. But since I've never seen Hellfires used against anything other than our ramshackle buildings in Bogey Town, I'm not sure which it is."

"We could assume each and see where that gets us," I said. "If the attack at IS was overkill, that means it was probably a human at the controls. Jack wouldn't understand the concept of saturating a site just to be sure."

"Probably not," said Troy after a moment. "And if the attack at Maintenance was underkill—if that's a word—maybe it was because a human backed off, didn't want to kill everyone. Or if Jack was flying, maybe it would have taken too much ordnance to destroy the building. Does he try to conserve firepower so he can finish a mission?"

"I don't remember hearing anything like that, but maybe he has something like a shock and awe tactic in his arsenal. Throw some missiles out there, and by the time the dust settles and the ringing in the enemy's ears stops, he's back with a new loadout."

"Yeah, could be," said Troy. He was talking to me, but his thoughts were elsewhere. I could see his eyes darting around the room like he was searching for something. The scan stopped and he stared at me.

"Another thing that might explain why IS was hit so hard is the fact that they were transmitting, trying to establish contact. Maintenance wasn't. Maybe the signal increased Jack's estimate of threat. After all, war runs on information. So, at a minimum, we should power down everything in the Operations Center before Jack gets here. Maybe we can look harmless."

"I don't think so," I said slowly. "With the history of electronic emissions from the building and two heat signatures inside, Jack's not going to ignore us. I think we have to be outside somewhere, leave your console on, and hope that he lobs two or three missiles into the building."

Troy nodded a couple of times. "I think you're right, but don't get your hopes up. He won't waste a bunch of missiles on this building. One with a fuse set to penetrate the roof would crush and incinerate everything inside."

I didn't need the image because it brought to mind something I'd seen when I was five or six years old. Another boy had put some insects into an empty soda bottle, dropped a lighted firecracker in, and put a stopper on the top. When the firecracker exploded, the stopper went flying. And when the smoke cleared, all you could see was splattered bugs all over the inside of the glass. I suppose we were lucky the bottle hadn't shattered, but the image it had left was bad enough.

"Like I said, I think we need to be out of here but not running. We saw what happened to Richter."

Troy nodded. "So, Jack sees electronic signals as a bad thing. Maybe we can give him a bunch of transmitters to worry about rather than a bunch of people."

"We have other consoles?"

"No, but we have some old equipment racks with transmitters in back. I think I can find some power converters, so we can run them off a car battery."

"There are four cars in the lot since Col. Dempsey took his. And two sets of keys—yours and mine."

"Three," said Troy. "Drew keeps a set in his desk. It would be better if all the cars weren't parked so close together. One shot might take them all out, but I guess we gotta hope for the best."

"Yeah, I guess," I replied because nothing more profound came to mind. "I probably can't hotwire Marshall's car, but I can pull the battery if you have some pliers. And with a knife, I can strip the wires on the power supply and wrap them around the battery terminals. Any chance you have those two things?"

"I do." He pulled the tools I needed from a cabinet.

"And the keys?" I asked. Troy fished his set from a pocket and tossed them to me. He started toward Drew's desk to get his. "I'll set up the cars while you get the transmitters."

"Sounds like a plan." Troy turned to leave, then turned back. "You know, this isn't going to work if Drew's flying Jack. He'll just ignore the cars and come for the two heat signatures that look like us."

"Maybe not," I said. Troy frowned in reply.

"Let's say Drew's doing this because, as you said, he's never hunted a human. Well, now he has. Maybe he'll have second thoughts by the time he gets here. Maybe he doesn't need two more trophies. Who knows?"

I kicked myself mentally for the last statement. I didn't have much of an argument, which was highlighted by the pathetic "who knows" summary. But at least the chance of success was greater than zero, and that appeared to be enough for Troy. "Meet you in the parking lot as soon as I can," he said.

We both left the room on a trot. At least we were going to fight to the end.

Operations Center, JACC Test Range, Nevada, 10:14 AM

"What the hell did you do to Marshall's car? And where's yours?"

I took the easy question first, pointing a thumb to where my rental sat near a turn in the road about 25 yards away. Marshall's car was closer at about ten yards, which is probably why it had caught Troy's attention. Or maybe it was because the hood was up, the driver's side window was shattered, and the front end of the car was sitting in a shallow ditch.

I raised a hand toward Marshall's vehicle. "Warned you. I missed the day they taught hotwiring in graduate school. Or how to get into a locked car, for that matter. I had to break the window to get to the battery. Then, I let it roll down the hill to put some distance between it and the others. Without the heat of a running engine, I figured that was safe enough."

Troy snorted. "Guess we're lucky it got that far. But how'd you move your car? That's uphill ... as much as we have hills."

"Drove ever so slowly."

"Damn, Doc. What happened to, it's safe enough without a running engine?" Troy shook his head and shrugged. "I could only find three transmitters, counting the one I'm leaving on my console.

So, I guess we'll put one in your car and the other in Marshall's." He paused to force a grin. "Gotta cover the damage you did, right?"

"Right." I appreciated his attempt at humor but didn't like the direction our plan was headed. "Maybe we should pull the transmitter out of your console, too. Surely the building has enough history for Jack to take a shot at it, even if there are no active emissions. Then, he'd be down four missiles, not three."

"Nothing to lose," replied Troy. "I'll go get it, and we can put it in my car. It's a piece of junk anyway and Drew's car might survive." I doubted it since they were parked side-by-side, but you never knew.

Troy handed me the two transmitters. "The power converters go here." He tapped a standard plug on one of the devices. "But don't turn them on yet. We'll wait until Jack is closer."

"Okay. I'll meet you at your car in a few." Again, we took off at a run.

* * *

By the time I had hooked up the two transmitters and returned to Troy's car, he had just finished putting the third on it.

"How long do we have?"

"About thirteen minutes," Troy replied after checking his wristwatch. "Now, the only question is where do we hide? I think the storeroom might be our best bet if we want to stay in the Ops Center. It's small, but we can isolate ourselves from the rest of the building and the door's solid. Otherwise, we could just try to walk away. Maybe, with enough distance before he arrives ...." Troy didn't finish.

"Of those, I like walking. If we've gained guilt by being close to the Ops Center, maybe distance reverses the trend."

"Maybe," said Troy. "But I like hiding in the storeroom. Even if distance makes us look less threatening, we're defenseless out in the open. If we sit tight in the storeroom with my console off, there's nothing in the building but a couple of little heat signatures."

"Signatures that have been in the building all morning, operating a ...."

Little heat signatures?

"That's it," I said to myself.

"What's it?" asked Troy, but I couldn't speak.

My mind was too busy racing through how this possible deception might be implemented and where it could go wrong. And admittedly, there were a lot of places it could fail; it was about as airtight as a screen door. But of all the ploys I had considered, it had a strength no other had. It was built on what I recalled to be one of Jack's features. Hopefully, my recollection was correct because there was no way to verify it now.

"To deal with all the information that Jack receives, he does a quick, initial check of the possible targets using infrared returns. If the heat signatures are small, he ignores them as a small animal of some type."

"Or a kid," said Troy. "Separating children from grown-ups was a big deal in our second scenario."

"Right," I said, although technically the initial look from the infrared would have occurred well before the second scenario started. To digress to discuss that now, however, would be a waste of what little time we had.

"So, how do we look small? I can think of a couple of possibilities. One is to use glass. If you've ever seen an infrared picture of a person with glasses, the lenses look black. Infrared doesn't pass through glass easily. So, if we did something like pop the windshields out of a couple of cars, we could cover half our body with them. The problem is that Jack would probably detect the obstruction between him and us. And when he uses other sensors to check us out, the jig would be up."

"Okay. What's the other?"

"Basically, the same thing, but with water. We dig a hole, fill it with water, and get in. There's still an obstruction, but it's something that seems natural. Like kids, playing in a mud puddle."

Troy rubbed a hand over the back of his neck, letting his gaze travel around the area. "In the desert?"

"There's still some water, even here. And hopefully, Jack isn't sensitive to inconsistencies in the environment."

"Not what I meant, Doc. The ground around here is all sand and rock. By the time we come back with a second bucket of water, the first will be gone."

"Which is why we can't use a bucket brigade. Marshall has been having trouble with the car he drove today. It's been overheating and I saw him filling the radiator with a hose one morning. We just have to find it. If we keep the water running, we should be able to keep some in the holes."

"You check his trunk?" asked Troy.

I hadn't since this desperate plan had just formed in my mind. We jogged over and popped the trunk. There it was. "I'll get this ready. You want to see if you can find something to dig with?"

"Sure." We split up again.

After I attached the hose to the faucet and rolled it out across the lot, I discovered that Troy had been there and gone. Three boards lay on the gravel where he had dropped them. The hose reached about ten feet beyond the edge of the parking lot. I would have liked to be farther from the building, but at least we were beyond the ground packed down by years of car and truck traffic.

The door to the Ops Center opened, and I looked up to see Troy heading my way at a trot. "These may work better." He was holding up several thin, metal plates, perhaps covers from boxes that held electronics.

"Yeah, probably," I replied when he joined me. "I thought we could dig here. Two holes, but they need to be close enough together that we can toss the hose back and forth."

Having two rather than a single hole was probably meaningless. A missile lobbed into either would probably kill both of us, but I wanted to take advantage of whatever slim chances the situation allowed.

We both fell on our knees and started to scrape at the rocky soil. After only moments, Troy asked, "So, if graduate school didn't teach you to hotwire a car, I doubt it taught you about infrared sensors on unmanned systems. How'd you know that stuff?"

"I did learn that from school. Well, sort of. We learned that people only see a small part of the electromagnetic spectrum. That made me curious about what we don't see, including infrared." I paused my tale to catch my breath. Digging was a lot harder than I'd expected.

"Anyway, there are a bunch of everyday items that let you see or use infrared. Things like infrared cameras, night vision goggles, some types of motion detectors."

Troy snorted. "Everyday items, huh?" He paused for a lungful of air. "Your every day must be different than mine."

I stopped and stretched my back, wiping the sweat from my forehead before it reached my eyes. Even though the temperature was in the mid-40s, my shirt was already soaked. Troy had been right. Digging a hole here was nothing like digging one in St. Louis. This was pickaxe country; it was not a place where you could pry out clumps of soft, black soil with a board. In St. Louis, the biggest problem would have been all the tree roots; here it was rocks the size of my fist and larger.

I discarded all my tools except for one small metal plate, and I started using it and my hands. Three fingers were soon bleeding, but

I was making progress. Then, I uncovered a large, flat stone that extended halfway across my hole-in-the-making. I could either widen the opening so I could dig around it or I could pry it out of the wall. I decided on the latter, and after a few moments, it came loose. Unfortunately, when it did, the wall collapsed, turning my somewhat cylindrical hole into a ragged, bowl-shaped depression in the ground. I grabbed one of the boards I'd discarded earlier and made quick work of the loose gravel that had accumulated at the bottom. At least with that done, it didn't feel like I was moving backward.

"Time?"

"About seven minutes," Troy said. I glanced his way and would have laughed except I probably looked the same. The area around his eyes was relatively clean, giving the impression that he was looking through the eyeholes of a mask composed of salty grime.

"Better get the transmitters going. I'll get my rental."

By the time I jogged back from my car, Troy had already returned. He was standing at the bottom of his hole, flinging metal plates full of sand and gravel. "Maybe three more minutes and then water," I called as I got back to work.

"If I can last three more minutes."

I couldn't find the breath to answer. The pain in my shoulders, arms, and hands was becoming unbearable. I needed a distraction. Generally, the time I spend jogging goes by in the blink of an eye, even when I am tired and sore, because I use it to review the day's challenges. Had that technique been working today, I would have been oblivious to everything because I had nothing but challenges in my thoughts. How to defeat a killer machine or a homicidal human were at the top of the list, although excavating a particularly stubborn rock with a sharp edge took priority with some regularity.

Unfortunately, daily challenges weren't distracting me; they were adding mental fatigue to the physical, so I tried the opposite. I cleared my mind and focused on the mechanics of removing each handful of sand, each rock that lay in my way. I worked by propping myself up on my left hand, while I used the right to scrape at the bottom of the pit. One, two, three. I kept count of each scoopful, as I rose and tossed it over the side. When the pain became unbearable, I switched positions—right hand holding me up while the left dug.

I tossed a scoop of sand on the growing pile outside my hole and watched it dissipate in a series of miniature landslides down the sides. The color caught my eye—red. I flipped over my left hand to find a jagged gash across the palm. Maybe I'd caught it on the edge of the flat rock? Maybe from the board?

"I've had it. I'm starting the water," said Troy between gasps.

It hadn't been the full three minutes, but I just nodded, thankful that I, too, could stop. I walked over to the edge of Troy's hole just as the water started pouring in from the hose. I waited for its level to rise. And waited. The water was draining as fast as it entered. Had we done all this for nothing?

But after another moment, the hole began to fill. Troy returned and jumped unceremoniously into the growing puddle, then picked up the hose and let the water run down over his head.

I wandered back to my project. I was intending to dig for the minute or so I had until Troy's hole was full, but I couldn't muster the strength. I sat on the edge, the muscles in my arms and shoulders trembling from exertion.

"Your turn," said Troy as he tossed the hose to me.

I rinsed off and sat down, cross-legged, in the bottom of the hole. The water from the hose was warmer than the air or the ground, but they soon stole its heat. Depleted of energy, my body wasn't producing much warmth. I started to shiver. A glance at Troy told me he was in the same state. I rose a bit and saw that his knees were about to break the surface of the water, so I tossed the hose back to him.

"Jeez, it's cold," Troy said. "Ah, shit. Jack's here."

I looked in the direction of his gaze and saw a speck on the horizon. All thoughts of my physical discomfort vanished. All I could think of was making myself invisible. That was a desire I hadn't experienced since grade school when I didn't know the answer to my teacher's question. I tried to relax every muscle, allowing my body to conform to the irregularities of the bottom of my hole. Much like grade school, however, it wasn't working. I felt completely exposed, sitting out in plain sight of Jack on the nearly flat desert floor in a hole half-filled with water.

Jack moved closer as if to size up his helpless prey. Troy tossed the hose back to me.

"You think Drew is looking at us on his video feed right now?" he asked. "And laughing his ass off?"

"Don't know, but if he is, I hope he's saying, 'I'm gonna cut these pathetic losers some slack.' I mean, isn't sitting in this dirty, mudhole enough punishment?" The quip, however, belied my feelings. I was scared, but at least we hadn't given up, hadn't surrendered to helplessness.

Jack altered his course slightly, heading for my rental car. It appeared that this part of the plan was working. At least, that was what I thought until he was about twenty yards from the vehicle. Then, he opened fire with the chain gun. I didn't realize the devastation a gun of that caliber could wreak until the flames subsided and the dust settled a bit. The car was shredded. The middle of it was resting on the ground, the ends propped up on wheel rims and burning tires.

"Top off," I said, tossing the hose back to Troy. It wasn't necessary to say our transmitting decoys were failures; Troy could see that for himself. After my rental, Jack demolished Troy's car, with Drew's catching fire to become collateral damage. Then, he started toward Marshall's.

"Damn. Someone must have cut the power to the building," Troy hissed over the sound of metal popping in the heat. My head snapped around to the Ops Center. Sure enough, the lights on the outside of the building had gone dark. "And we're losing water pressure."

I spun back around to see that the gush from the hose had become a trickle. "They don't pump water out here, do they?"

"No clue," replied Troy. "All I know is we're going to be high and dry real quick."

Jack fired on Marshall's car with results similar to the first two. Then, he turned to a heading that would take him directly to us.

I strained against the rocks at the bottom of my hole, arching my back so I could force more of my torso under the water. There was a lower spot to my left, and I placed my hand and half my forearm into the liquid. It wasn't much, but it was just that much less exposed skin radiating heat.

I could see Jack now, although the light of the sun was almost completely absorbed by the dull gray of his finish. The muzzle of the machine gun protruded slightly, Jack now in a fighting configuration. At any moment, I expected to see a line of flames leap forward, ending my life. But would the inputs from my eyes even register in my brain before the end? I doubted it.

My eyes tracked back and forth between the water and Jack. It would only be a matter of moments before my legs and my left arm poked out. But likewise, it would only be moments before Jack passed by. It would be close.

Finally, Jack flew over.

I stayed down until he disappeared behind the pile of rocks and sand I'd left by the side of my makeshift puddle. I peeked over the top. Jack was continuing to shrink into the distance. I released a long breath, hearing the same from Troy.

With the reprieve, senses that had been blocked by the danger returned to me. The stench of burning rubber and spent ammunition hung in the air and left a bitter taste in my mouth. My arms and shoulders were screaming in pain and shaking from the cold. My hands ached from the minor scrapes and scratches that covered them. Surprisingly, the gash on my palm didn't hurt that much. Then, a flicker in the corner of my eye caught my attention.

"The power's back on," I said mostly to myself.

And then, the possible significance hit me—how will Jack react? Maybe he won't notice. But a peak over the debris told me my hope was ill-founded. He had already turned and was coming back. I was fully out of the water now. Soon, Troy would be, too. When Jack got back, our gambit would be over. We'd lost.

At a distance of about thirty yards, Jack launched a missile. I watched with the hope it was aimed at the building, that I would live another second or two. There was a second flash as Jack launched again. And then my world went black.

THE DAY AFTER, FRIDAY, JANUARY 15

Las Vegas Regional Medical Center, Las Vegas, Nevada, 9:11 AM

Sometime later on Thursday morning when Jack came to kill us, I was surprised to find I was still alive. And, to the best of my recollection, I made the same startling discovery several more times Thursday afternoon and into the evening. I wasn't lucid, but my thinking was clear enough to be amazed I was still walking the earth. Or lying in bed, as was the case.

Now, by the angle of the sun, it was morning again. Friday, I hoped. I tried to sit up to check out my surroundings, but that was a mistake. I was either too weak or too sedated to do more than gently ease my head off the pillow. Even that, however, was too much. Pain shot from the top of my forehead to the back of my neck near my shoulders.

I tried to reach up to massage my temples, but my right arm wouldn't move. I tried again, only to vaguely register a dead weight connected to my shoulder where my arm should have been. I couldn't turn my head far enough to see. What was wrong with me? But in my alarm, my left hand came up to my face. I reached across my body to find my right arm in a cast from about the middle of the palm past my elbow. A sling held it tight to my torso. Exploring further, I found bandages covering the top of my head and down onto the right side of my face. But unlike my numb, right arm, every touch sent shooting pains through my body.

The ache was spreading … or my senses were returning. My left hand hurt. I held it up in front of my face to find a bandage across the palm. And with that sight, an image of a gash popped into my mind's eye, and everything came back to me—the methodical way Jack hunted us, the explosions, the death. But where my memories ended, a flood of questions came to take their place. Who or what had been after us? And why? How had I escaped? But most insistent in my concerns was the question, who besides me still lived?

"Please, let Jill be alive," I mumbled. It came out as a hoarse rasp, barely understandable even to my ears.

I carefully turned my head without raising it. On one side of my bed was a rack of equipment quietly humming. On the other, a rolling tray table and a chair. Beyond them, another bed—empty—and a window.

I turned from the window. The door into the room had a glass pane and a man was looking through it. A doctor? But when he stepped in, he was wearing a uniform. Not police. Not military. It looked like he belonged to a private security service. What would he want with me? I tried to ask, but even less sound came out this time.

"Good, you're awake. Let me get someone." He left, returning moments later with a nurse in tow.

"How are you feeling?" she asked.

Since medical personnel knew you were either suffering or loopy with painkillers, I figured they asked that to see how difficult you'd be. If you said "fine," they would expect little trouble. You were going to take care of yourself. But if you said, "how the hell do you think I feel," which is what I usually wanted to say, they'd know it was going to be a long shift, probably for both of you.

"Okay, considering." I croaked. I thought that was a good, middle-of-the-road response.

The nurse winced. "Sounds like you need a drink."

I thought better of trying to speak and managed a slight nod, then took a sip from the glass of water she offered. After swallowing several times, I said, "Jill Henshaw?"

The nurse's eyes narrowed, and she glanced at the guard.

"Gone, most likely." He shrugged to complete his reply and left the room.

"Gone?" I don't think my head was raised that much, but it fell back onto the pillow as a wave of guilt, pain, and disbelief came over me.

"I don't know why I thought he'd know anything," she said, shaking her head while glaring at the closed door. She turned back. "He means gone from the hospital, not the world. None of the fatalities were women."

Her words were like a sprinkle of water on dormant seeds; my relief sprung to life. The release, however, was partial, since "none were women" just meant she hadn't died. I looked at the nurse, hoping for more. She was adjusting the machines monitoring me and spoke after noticing my stare. "Some people checked out yesterday with just minor cuts and bruises. The woman you asked about might have been one of them."

My relief grew, nourished both by her words and my returning memory. If anyone had come out of this incident with just minor cuts and bruises, it would have been the people in the Maintenance Building. Still, I wanted something more definitive than "she might have been one of them."

"Young woman? Dark hair, brown eyes?"

"Sorry, but I wasn't on duty. I'll see what I can find out." She jotted something on a pad of paper.

"Troy Sayers?" I asked, my throat still sore but recovering.

She looked up from her writing, her face seemingly caught between impatience and sadness. "That's not a name I know." She paused, melancholy winning the battle over her expression. "The names of the deceased haven't been released, so all I can say is that he's not my patient."

That told me almost nothing. He was not her patient because his injuries were different than mine or because he wasn't anyone's patient? I nodded, knowing that line of questioning was at an end for now. "What's with the guard?"

"Someone seems to think you need protection from the press." She shook her head, looking disgusted once again. "As if we can't do our jobs."

The press?

I suppose that made sense. They'd want to know what had happened, maybe even as much as I did. The nurse turned back to me. "Do you know where you are?"

"Didn't you give that away when you said people had been checked for injuries and released?" She stared, telling me a question to answer a question wasn't sufficient for her. "Some sort of medical facility, probably a hospital and probably in or near Las Vegas." I hoped that answer made her happy because it was a lot of talking on a throat that felt as raw as hamburger.

Apparently, it did because she smiled. "You're in the Las Vegas Regional Medical Center."

"What's wrong with my arm?"

The nurse rolled something over my forehead and down toward my chin. I must have frowned because she said, "It takes your temperature. Next, blood pressure." I felt a collar tightening around my good arm.

"You came in yesterday suffering from hypothermia, a blow to the head, a broken right arm, a dislocated right shoulder, and a variety of cuts and bruises over your hands, arms, and face." I almost expected her to add, "and a partridge and a pear tree," but the list was complete. "Your arm has been set, and it has been placed in a sling to immobilize your shoulder. Your head's been bandaged, and we'll probably keep you here overnight to make sure everything's okay."

"What happened yesterday?"

With the look she gave me, I think she was hoping I could tell her. What she said, however, was, "I don't have any details. We've only been told there was some type of accident. As soon as the doctor clears you, you have several official visitors who may be able to help with that question. The doctor should be by shortly, and in the meantime, I'll see what I can find out about your friends."

She left, and a few minutes later, the doctor arrived. While he gave me a quick and somewhat rough check of my injuries, I repeated my questions. But if the nurse knew little of what had happened out on the JACC test range, the doctor knew even less. Or he had been told to act that way. The thought was a bit paranoid, but on the other hand, there had been a major disaster at a military facility. No one at the hospital was talking. There was a guard on my door, allegedly for my protection. And official visitors were waiting to debrief me. Even without the head trauma and the residual of painkillers in my system, suspicion seemed appropriate.

After giving up on the who and what questions, I asked the one on when. When could I leave? He said he wanted to hold me overnight for observation. When I asked if that meant I was leaving on Saturday, he replied, "We'll see."

About the only thing the doctor seemed certain about was that I could receive visitors—if I wanted. Of course, I wanted visitors; I was starving for data, for grist for my mental mill. So, when he left, I said, "Please send them in." Marshall was the first through the door.

"You're looking better," he said. "Yesterday, you were somewhere between white and gray when they brought you in."

"Just happy to be alive," I said as Col. Dempsey and Troy appeared at the door.

"Troy. God, it's good to see you."

"You, too, Doc." He glanced sideways at his bosses, looking a bit uneasy perhaps because I was ignoring them. I didn't care. Other than a few small bandages and a bruise or two, he was largely unscathed.

The forced smile that had been on Marshall's face faded to sadness. "Dr. Price, I'm truly sorry for what happened to you. While we do everything we can to be safe, accidents like this are just part of the job. But you didn't sign up for this."

"What happened?" I asked.

Dempsey and Marshall gave each other a look, then Marshall spoke. "We don't know yet, but most likely, it was human error."

Dempsey cleared his throat. Marshall looked at him and then turned back to me. "We'll be fighting an uphill battle figuring out what went wrong. Jack wasn't transmitting to us, so we don't have those logs. And we lost the people best equipped to check for a software bug, which is another possibility. Fortunately, I have a copy of the code, and Omega Systems has a lab in New Mexico. I'm taking it there tomorrow so we can dig through it, line by line. If there's nothing there ... well, the error lays with what's left."

I'd actually been asking who'd survived rather than who was to blame, but his response was enlightening anyway. If the problem wasn't in the code, then Drew was flying. I couldn't see how anyone else could know Jack well enough and had found a way to get to the command center undetected to take control. That being true—and I wasn't certain it was, given my somewhat fuzzy mental state—the carnage was most likely the result of pilot error. Drew in his haste and carelessness had killed himself and several others. But before I could clarify my question, Marshall continued.

"The complexity of figuring this out is why we wanted to talk to you. Can you give us a day to check out the facts before you talk to anyone? And by anyone, I mean the press."

I hesitated. It wasn't the request, but rather, the timing. They weren't starting to verify the software until tomorrow. What would they have in a day?

"One day won't tell us much," he said, almost as if reading my mind. "But by tomorrow, we'll have a complete accounting of what's known, and that'll be a good start in keeping the rumors down. Otherwise, the theories will range from a terrorist plot to space aliens."

I nodded. "Yes, of course I can keep quiet. I don't remember much anyway. But what about the other people on the range. It sounds like some of the software people didn't make it?"

Marshall's gaze dropped to the floor. I half expected him to say, everyone was killed, but it was Dempsey who spoke. "Your friend, Jill Henshaw, is fine."

The remaining uncertainty about her fate and the guilt I harbored deep within me escaped in something between a laugh and a sob. I squeezed my eyes closed against the tears. "Thank you, Colonel. And the others?"

"Three people with her at the Maintenance Building survived. We pulled the last one out around midnight." He paused, perhaps not wanting to move to the sad news. "Unfortunately, the man who tried to drive away from Maintenance .... You remember that?" I nodded. "He died. The bodies of three software engineers have also been recovered from the Information Systems Building, and we expect to find a fourth. And Brandt Drury is missing, probably dead." A look of sad resignation covered Dempsey's face.

"Drew's missing?"

"The full investigation at the Mobile Command Center site will start later today."

Marshall was still looking at the floor, but his head was slowly shaking. Then, I heard him whisper, "What a loss."

Dempsey cleared his throat before continuing in a more upbeat tone. "I understand you're already lobbying your doctor to leave tomorrow."

"Guilty, sir. I can recover at home as easily as here. Probably better."

"Well, take your time. I've talked to your boss, Ken Waters. He said you shouldn't leave until you feel up to it. I also wanted to add my apology to that of Dr. Marshall. Casualties during war are the price we pay for freedom. Casualties during times of peace, however, have no excuse. JACC was going to be closed down temporarily for a review, but with this disaster, the closure may become permanent." He paused, his look faraway for a moment. "I also know what you and Troy did to survive, and I applaud your ingenuity."

"Thank you, sir."

Do you thank someone when you save your own skin? It felt odd, but the mental fog was rolling back in. Perhaps it showed because Dempsey said, "Get some rest, Doc." He departed, Marshall following him out with a nod goodbye.

Troy stepped forward and pulled a sheet of paper from a back pocket. "I'll leave you to get some rest, too, but first, I have this." He handed me the sheet. My name was on the outside in Jill's handwriting. I looked up at Troy. "She wrote it yesterday, asked me to give it to you when you were awake."

"Thanks." I opened the note and read it.

Dear Doc –

I wish I could have stayed until you were out of surgery and awake, but I need to get home, return to sanity. Sorry, but I'm taking my scheduled flight on Friday. But on the positive side, I'll be seeing you in a couple of months anyway for my wedding. And bring Nicole. I'd love to meet her.

I'm fine – just some scratches and I got most of those from my own clumsiness, trying to find a hiding place from Jack. Your doctor swore you'd be fine, too, or as close to a guarantee as you're likely to get from a doctor. When I get back, the first thing I'm doing is telling my boss, no more task analyses for the military. Once in the line of fire is more than enough for me.

As strange as it may sound, I also wanted to say thanks. Just knowing you were on the range, fighting for your life, kept me from panicking, kept me fighting for mine. It was shades of graduate school again, except a heck of a lot scarier. You helped me get through.

I'm lucky to be alive and I'm going to enjoy every minute of it from now on.

Love,

Jill

I felt a smile form on my face, a warmth spread through my body. The Jill I knew already loved life, making me wonder how she was going to squeeze any more out of it. But if anyone could, she would be the one.

I looked up at Troy. "I'd like to talk, have a million questions. But I'm fading fast."

I think I finished the sentence, but maybe I just dreamed it. I fell asleep with Jill's note clutched in my hands, her words floating in my thoughts. "I'm lucky to be alive."

Las Vegas Regional Medical Center, Las Vegas, Nevada, 3:37 PM

"For someone with a million questions, you sure slept a long time."

I blinked a bleary eye at the form sitting next to my bed, knowing it was Troy from the voice. "And it must be a very slow workday for you to be sitting here, watching me sleep." I rolled onto my back and rubbed my eyes with my hands. Blinking wasn't getting the job done.

"Slow? We're shut down, remember? And besides, I'm still getting used to the idea that you're alive."

"Ha, ha, very funny," I replied as drolly as I could manage.

"I'm not kidding."

I rolled back to my side to look at my visitor, wondering if the last cobwebs of sleep and sedation were keeping me from spotting the tells that this was a joke, but I found nothing in Troy's face.

"Seriously, Doc. You slouched over in the hole and didn't move a muscle. And it wasn't like you were sleeping, with all the crap that was going on. I thought you were a goner."

I'd never had anyone tell me they thought I was dead, and the effect was a bit unsettling. Had I been close? But another question was even more pressing.

"Uh, Troy, I didn't just dream that Jill got off the range okay, did I?"

He smiled. "Nope, not a dream. She's fine." He nodded his head toward the table. "There's her note. You still had it in your hand, but I rescued it." I'd also forgotten about the note until he mentioned it.

"By the way, I guess you were right, Doc. The missiles that hit Maintenance were mostly on the north end of the building. She and the others were lucky. They were on the other side."

Lucky?

The word felt wrong, but it took me a moment of concentration to figure out why. If Drew was flying, it wasn't luck. He would have known humans from manikins if he'd watched which contacts moved back and forth and which stayed fixed. And if he'd had enough killing at the other sites or just had a moment of remorse, he might focus his shots on the lifeless dummies. Or perhaps sparing the maintainers had always been part of his plan and he just avoided all of them? It was a flimsy line of reasoning, but it was possible.

"Were there a bunch of manikins in the north part of the building?"

Troy flipped an open hand toward me. "Who knows? But I do know that two consoles and three aircraft were there ... and no real people, which is the important thing."

"Yeah, true," I agreed, although I wished he had the less important piece of data, too.

"I know you've been pressing the doctor to let you go home ... not that I blame you. So, I checked you out of the motel. Your stuff is in that closet over there." He nodded with his head. "So, whether it's tomorrow or next week, you're set. And your company changed your flights to tomorrow but said they can change them again if you don't feel up to it."

"Thanks, Troy. I'm surprised the motel let you in."

"When most of your business is from the NTTR, a request from a colonel goes a long way. Or at least, implying one asked does."

I chuckled. "You didn't have to do all that, but I appreciate it. And as for tomorrow or next week, it had better be tomorrow or I'll go crazy." He returned my grin. "So, I'm a little fuzzy. What did happen on the range, there at the end? Last thing I remember was Jack launching a couple of missiles at us."

"Not really at us. Those shots hit the Ops Center." A frown flickered across his features and then disappeared when he looked at me. "Before one of the guards picked me up, I got as close as I could. Nothing but rubble and twisted metal, all burnt so bad I couldn't tell a desk from a door." He gave a single, sardonic laugh. "That would have been us if you hadn't come up with the dunk-yourself-in-the-freezing-water plan."

"Actually, that plan was yours."

"How so?" Troy asked.

"You said something about Jack hunting us was like shooting fish in a barrel, which by the way, isn't as easy as it sounds. You have the refraction of the light to deal with and the resistance of the water to the bullets. And that got me thinking about what didn't go through water easily, including infrared."

Troy chuckled. "Yeah, quite the insight I had without knowing it. Anyway, I didn't see it happen, but I guess something hit you on the head from the explosion. That's what the doctors said. Whatever it was must have knocked you out."

"Jack just turned tail after that?"

"I wish," he said. "It would have saved me another ten seconds of pure terror before two Apache helicopters appeared. Someone must have figured out how to make them look friendly because Jack didn't pay any attention. They spread out and opened up at the same time. Jack might have been able to dodge some of that fire, but with two streams from different angles, he didn't have a chance. They dropped him about thirty yards from where we were sitting."

He got a faraway look. I waited for a while but finally broke the silence with a question. "They find Drew yet?"

"Not that I've heard," replied Troy, shaking his head as if chasing an image from his mind. "Col. Dempsey mentioned the dig at Maintenance?" I recalled the colonel's comment and nodded at Troy's questioning look. "The guy they pulled out was pretty banged up, but he'll be okay. They found what was left of Marv Richter and got most of the bodies out of IS sometime very early this morning. And flights over the range are continuing but no other survivors so far. I suppose they'll find what's left of Drew at the Mobile Command Center any time now." Troy shuddered.

"Sorry, Troy. Sorry about the friends you lost."

"Thanks, Doc."

"So, they think Jack was stuck in ...."

Troy cut me off. "Your nurse warned me. No long talks because you need your rest. And I don't think I want to cross her." He exaggerated a grimace, which puzzled me. The last nurse I remembered was a tiny thing. But then, my first-grade teacher had been small of stature, too, and no one wanted to be on her bad side.

"Besides," said Troy, "this is one of those marathons. They'll get to the bottom of what went wrong, eventually." I nodded but not in agreement.

I wouldn't leave the slight discontinuities in this story unexamined, even in the short term. I couldn't. I'd never been able to do more than hide unfinished business in the recess of my mind for a time. And now, there was no reason to do even that. Troy was pulling out his phone, probably to play a game so I could rest. It was the perfect time to bring the issues into the full light of my attention so I could pick at loose ends, run assumptions to their logical conclusions.

I quickly reviewed what I knew. First, the possible actors in this drama were both easy to list and completely uninformative. It was either Jack, Drew, or SOGG—Some Other Guy/Girl. If it was Jack, it was either a human error or a software bug that had turned the weapons system into a stone-cold killer. If it was Drew, the cause lay somewhere in his psyche, but I'd never unearth it; that was out of my league. And the SOGG? That possibility was as vague as it sounded. It was probably someone on the range, but I had no other clues. And since Jill was the only female and she hadn't done it, the SOGG was actually "some other guy." And that was all I had.

"I think I'll go try my luck on the slots."

Troy's words broke into my thoughts, and I sat up in bed, first holding my head, then chuckling at both myself and Troy. "The slots? I thought you knew better. No one gets lucky against the machines."

"Some of us do," Troy replied. But I hardly heard him.

I am lucky to be alive. No one gets lucky against the machines.

The memory of Jill's words and my statement to Troy collided head-on in my thoughts, producing cognitive dissonance—a mental discomfort due to holding inconsistent beliefs. How could both of these premises be true? How could Jill have been lucky when Jack held all the cards? True, we had considered the possibility that he had lobbed a couple of missiles into the building to keep the occupants pinned down, but wouldn't a better-placed shot be even more effective? It made no sense unless Jill's escape wasn't a matter of luck. She had been allowed to escape. And if that was true, Jack wasn't flying.

I'd gotten to this point before, but what came from the dissonance of my thoughts was a way to test this idea. "Before you go, do you have the screenshots of the pilot's displays with you?"

Troy frowned. "You can see them on the range, but I can't give them to you here."

"But you have them?"

"You're going to get me canned."

"They're not classified by the military, just Omega Systems proprietary. And I only need to glance at them. You can sit right here, make sure I don't transmit any pictures with my phone."

"You don't have a phone, Doc."

I groaned. I'd forgotten mine was gone ... or never knew. But I could tell Troy was weakening. After a moment, he pulled his phone from a back pocket, turned it on, and pressed a few buttons.

"Yours survived?"

"Some of us are smart enough to keep their phone out of the water ... although I think yours got smashed before you drowned it." He grinned and handed his phone to me. "That's the latest version."

I started paging through the screenshots. He had most of the interface on his phone, which meant it would be a while before I found the half-dozen or so steps I wanted to review. "I'm looking for the procedure to put Jack in the autonomous, search-and-destroy mode with either simulated or live weapons. You have that on here?"

"Yeah, sure." He took the phone from me and started flipping through the images. After a moment, he leaned over and said, "Here, watch. There are four steps to get into simulated weapons mode." He paged through them. "And there are six steps for live weapons." He displayed that sequence.

"Good, but can you go through them again?"

He did, but before he'd finished, I'd reached a conclusion. "Can you see if the colonel is still in the building, and if he is, bring him here? And if he's gone, find out how we can contact him."

"What?"

"No time to explain. I'll tell you when you get back."

Troy stared only a second, then turned and hurried out of the room.

Las Vegas Regional Medical Center, Las Vegas, Nevada, 4:03 PM

If what I was thinking was true, the shooting was over, but the plan was still in play. And most importantly, time was our enemy. We might have a day or two, but hours, maybe even minutes were more likely. And if the colonel had left the hospital, the window of opportunity shrunk even more. I stared at the clock on the wall. I wished the hands would move faster so Troy could return, and I wished they would move slower so that we had more time. Unfortunately, neither wish was coming true.

Finally, Troy returned, and he had the colonel with him. But even as the man entered, I could see he was in a very different mood than he had been in earlier. He looked like I felt—frazzled and exhausted. Troy took a seat, while the colonel stood looking down at me.

"Troy said this was important, but I can't stay. The press is being as patient as we could hope, but we have a flurry of official inquiries. I have to get back to the range."

"I understand, sir, and I'll be quick." And then, almost as if I was trying to make a lie of my promise, I paused. I had to because this was going to be tricky, and I probably had only one chance to get it right.

"I have a hypothesis." I'd settled on that word rather than a guess. It sounded better. "But it's based on speculation that puts some people in a very bad light. Maybe even treason."

"You want to tell this to the Military Police?" asked Dempsey.

"There's some of them in the building?"

"No, but I can have someone here in a couple of hours."

"Too long," I replied. "If you think there's any merit to my concerns, you can get things started. If not, I hope I can count on your discretion."

"We protect those who, in good faith, report possible cases of government malfeasance."

His response sounded rehearsed—like it was right out of the manual on dealing with reported cases of waste, fraud, and abuse. But he also sounded sincere. I nodded. "I don't believe Jack was out of control. I think Drew was flying."

Dempsey rubbed his chin. "I wouldn't be divulging anything to say we have a few questions for him if he's alive."

"So, he hasn't been found?"

The colonel paused again, showing the same, deliberate behavior I'd come to expect. "Not yet, but we'll have a full forensic team at the Mobile Command Center site soon. This mystery may disappear when we do. So, tell me why you suspect Drew other than the run-in you had with him at Deadman's Gulch."

"You know about that?"

"Not until recently, but yes."

I wondered how he had found out, but it seemed a better question for later. "Troy, can you bring up those screenshots we were looking at before?" He looked somewhat pained, but I suspected his relatively minor infraction—if this could even be considered one—would be completely forgotten by the time we finished.

While Troy brought the pictures up on his phone, I went back through the attack on Maintenance. Like Troy, Dempsey confirmed that the missiles weren't evenly distributed. Apparently, that had become an accepted fact. And when I said that Jack wouldn't hold back, wouldn't avoid the humans on purpose, Dempsey just nodded. But then, he knew that already. It was time to break new ground.

"Troy, please take the colonel through the steps to put Jack into the autonomous search-and-destroy mode with and without live weapons."

When Troy was done, I said, "There are only two steps that are the same for both modes, the first two. After that, they are completely different, and this is how the software has been for at least the last two months while you were practicing for the live-fire demo. During that time, Drew probably used simulated weapons several times a day, maybe a couple of hundred times total. And during the same period, I doubt real weapons were used much at all."

"Probably never," said Dempsey. "We test-fired munitions. We used them during some of the demonstration practice sessions. But full autonomy in search-and-destroy mode with live weapons? We don't run Jack that way for obvious reasons."

"Which makes it extremely unlikely that when Drew was busy in the aftermath of the demonstration, he activated live weapons by accident. If he was distracted, if he couldn't concentrate, he would follow the path he's used over and over again. Jack would have ended up firing simulated missiles."

I was used to Dempsey's contemplative pauses, but this one went on for what felt like a full minute. "Is this the same effect you described in your briefing—automaticity?"

"An extension, more or less," I said. "When you have to deviate from behavior that has become automatic, you have to think about it, you have to concentrate on taking a different path. Otherwise, you just do what you've always done before."

He nodded. "I'll keep all this in mind." He leaned forward to stand.

"There's more."

Dempsey looked at me, blinked a couple of times, and settled back into his chair. "Okay. Go on."

I gathered my breath and my wits. "I don't think he acted alone."

I could see Troy flinch out of the corner of my eye, so I glanced at him. He'd gone as white as the sheets on my hospital bed. But when I turned back to Col. Dempsey, he just stared at me. I wasn't sure if he had developed a calm exterior as part of the job or if he already had suspicions about the attacks. But whatever the reason, I couldn't detect a reaction, positive or negative.

"If I'm right, someone put a great deal of thought and planning into this attack," I said. "Take the argument in the Mobile Command Center after the demo. No one could have known for sure it was going to happen. So, the plan must have had a contingency built into it. If the politicians loved the demo, everyone goes home happy. If they didn't ... well, we have what happened."

"There was already a plan to stop work for a month," said Dempsey. "But they wanted to extend it. Six months was mentioned, but so was a permanent shutdown."

"So, after that setback, the shooting started. And for Drew to be pulling the trigger, the software hack that allowed real and simulated weapons to have different aimpoints had to be in place. That required more planning."

"So, you knew about the software workaround?" said Dempsey.

"It came up when we were talking." I could have given Troy credit for recognizing the importance of this fact, but I wasn't sure he wanted the limelight at the moment.

"So, let me get this straight," said Dempsey. "After Dr. Marshall and I left with the politicians, Drew fired a real and a simulated missile, the latter hitting the command center and the real one landing somewhere close by. Then, he proceeded to kill Marvin Richter, destroy most of the JACC Maintenance Building, destroy all of the Information Systems Building and everyone in it, and nearly kill you two?"

When he laid it out in one long statement, it sounded a bit far-fetched. But that was my belief in a nutshell. All I could think to say was, "Yeah, that's my guess." Unintentionally, I'd downgraded my "hypothesis" to a mere guess.

"Did you talk about Alan Garcia, too?" asked the colonel. Dempsey was working out the implications on his own, although I was surprised he'd come up with the name so quickly. But then, a civilian dying on a military installation under his watch would make the details memorable.

"We did," I replied. But when Dempsey continued to stare, I knew he wanted me to explain. "It seems possible he was killed so that the software that allowed two aimpoints would still be on Jack."

"I see. Anything else?" asked the colonel.

I was hoping that by this point, he'd be volunteering his thoughts, but he wasn't. Maybe he thought my story was ridiculous, just the delusions of an over-stressed, partially sedated victim of a near-death experience. Or maybe he held the same views but wanted to hear me voice them. Either way, I had no choice but to finish.

"It's possible that the planning goes back even further. Someone got the program into a bind in the first place, so the workaround had to be created. Someone scheduled two weapon tests too close together."

"That was me," Dempsey replied.

I wasn't prepared for that response, and it took me a moment to recover. "Maybe that was a lucky coincidence for them? Or maybe the scheduling conflict was somehow orchestrated outside your purview?"

"Maybe," Dempsey replied, but he didn't elaborate. "So, it couldn't be Drew alone. He couldn't influence scheduling or software development." He paused. "Are you suggesting James Marshall is behind this?"

"If it happened this way, he's in the best position." In fact, Marshall's position wasn't any better than the colonel's, at least when only authority over the program was considered, but I'd decided to trust Dempsey.

"And why would he and Drew do something like that?" asked Dempsey.

Previously, I thought Dempsey could have joined in the speculation, but he hadn't. But now, he had to have this answer. What did it mean that he was still asking questions? Perhaps rather than just giving me the rope to hang myself, he was letting me fabricate it before I swung? All I could do was trust that my hunches would be held in confidence.

"Maybe they did it so they could make Jack into exactly what they want? When Congress and the public take a closer look at what's going on, they could demand that Jack be stripped of his autonomy, his intelligence. It's happened before, as I understand it. But if they take Jack elsewhere, Marshall has a free hand to experiment and Drew always has a system to fly. But," I said stretching out the word, "I'm betting they did it for the money."

I paused to give Dempsey a chance to react. He didn't, but Troy's frown grew.

"At first, I was surprised that the standard operating procedure for a damaged aircraft was to destroy it," I said. "But both you and Dr. Marshall have made it clear that the value isn't in the hardware. It's in the software, in the intelligence built into the aircraft. Considering what was lost yesterday, there aren't many working versions of that software left. Every aircraft on the range was demolished—the one flying, the three in the Maintenance Building, and the two in the Information Systems Building. The software repository in the IS building was also lost. That leaves the software backups, which are probably in Pittsburgh, and I'm betting those have been corrupted."

"That's not possible." We both turned to Troy. He probably didn't realize he was thinking aloud until we looked at him, and now, he was turning red.

"A program manager with a technical background working behind the Omega Systems firewall?" Dempsey said, raising an eyebrow. "Sorry, Troy, but it wouldn't be that hard for him to do."

"Marshall also has the software for the next phase, the extension that lets groups of aircraft coordinate," I said. "He has a lot he could sell if he gets away with this." A silence hung in the air a moment, my heart accelerating during the interim. "That is, of course, if he did it."

"With Don Williams being killed in the IS attack, whoever buys that software will be months ahead of the US military," said Dempsey. "Maybe years."

It was his first statement consistent with my thoughts, and I breathed a sigh of relief. At least the colonel understood the possibility. Whether he believed it, however, I couldn't be sure. He stood but to pace rather than leave. After a couple of laps, he said, "So, in your view, Drew focused his fire on the aircraft in the Maintenance Building to ensure their destruction and several people escaped as a result. But at Information Systems, he had to make sure everything was obliterated—aircraft, software, people?"

"Sadly, yes," I replied. "That would be necessary for the plan to work, although I hadn't thought about the effect of killing Williams."

Dempsey paced a couple more circuits. "Everything seems to fit, but it's all circumstantial. There's nothing to directly link either Drew or Dr. Marshall to anything that happened on the range or earlier." Dempsey paused, running a hand over his close-cropped hair as he looked at me. "I'm going to have to go. I'm already overdue at the range, but I'll check out your story as soon as I can."

The colonel started toward the door but turned back before reaching it. "I understand we have to move quickly, but it may be some time before I have anything. In the meantime, you and Troy need to keep these ideas to yourself. Especially, you, Doc, because if they turn out to be unfounded ... well, your career would probably be over and there's nothing I could do about it. Do I make myself clear?"

Troy and I answered in the affirmative, and he turned and left.

The colonel's warning was troubling, but I was more worried that five strides down the hospital corridor he would have forgotten everything I'd said. Who knew how many leads he was following? Was my hypothesis a close second in his mind? Or maybe it was a distant twelfth? And what would he make of a clue built on psychological research? It wasn't like predicting human behavior based on the effect of automaticity was something he did every day.

"What do you think?" I asked Troy. Some of the blood that had left his face was returning, but he still looked shocked.

"Not sure. The timing works, but isn't it a lot easier to believe that Drew just messed up? He was a great pilot, but sometimes, shit just happens."

That was exactly what I feared Dempsey was thinking. But as I looked at Troy, I knew there was something else on his mind. "What?"

"Why do you suspect Marshall and not Dempsey?" he asked slowly. "I mean, they both have the same things to gain—money, power. And, yeah, I know Marshall's a bit of a blowhard and the politicians were threatening a longer stop-work, but he's kept this program sold. And as long as he does that, he's in the driver's seat. He calls the direction of AI in weapons for this program."

Troy had probably exaggerated Marshall's potential influence on technology, but frankly, I'd struggled over the question of Marshall vs. Dempsey as well. If Drew was involved and had a co-conspirator, it could be either. They both knew Drew. They both had a strong, direct influence on the program. Dempsey had even admitted he was the reason Jack could aim simulated and real weapons at different targets. But on the other hand, Marshall could have sabotaged the software backups in Pittsburgh much more easily than Dempsey. Unfortunately, I didn't know if they were ruined; that was only a guess.

In the end, I'd gone with my gut. And although my life is driven by data, by weighting the pros and cons in a mental spreadsheet, going with a feel was not uncomfortable. That was because I'd learned that what happened in the recesses of my mind mirrored what happened in the foreground. It just took time to unearth the reasoning in the former.

I must have pondered his words too long because Troy spoke again. "I'm worried that if yesterday was a heist, you just told the mastermind the noose is tightening."

"I'm worried about that, too. But I don't think so." Unfortunately, I could think of nothing more to say to ease his mind.

Las Vegas Regional Medical Center, Las Vegas, Nevada, 8:42 PM

Some have said that I'm like a dog with a bone; I never let a problem go. To me, there's an ancillary trait to persistence. It's patience because much about being persistent is having the resolve to see something through. In my current situation, however, I was finding it impossible to be patient.

No one was phoning. Not Troy. Not Col. Dempsey. Not an investigator from the Military Police. No one. All I wanted was a call saying "yes, Marshall and Drew staged everything, and thanks to you, they're safely in custody." Okay, that's too much to ask so soon—or ever—but a call saying "we're checking" would be nice. And if it was from Dempsey, it would have been even better. Then, at least I'd have confirmation that he was one of the good guys.

But in the absence of anything like that, the images that were pushing into my thoughts were troubling. I saw Dempsey walking down the hospital corridor mumbling, "Poor guy. Hallucinating from the stress." But that wasn't as bad as the one with him breaking into a sprint for the airport as soon as he reached the hospital's front doors. And then there was the picture of a young Dempsey and a young Marshall in a grade school yearbook. How could I have known they'd grown up together and were best friends through college? Of course they had conspired with Drew to steal Jack, and now all three were streaking for the border in a stolen car.

Logically, the chance that any of these visions was accurate was small, but that didn't hold them at bay. I needed someone, perhaps Troy, to call and say Dempsey was still on the case, not running from it.

"Ah, damn," I mumbled under my breath. I was lying there in my hospital bed waiting for a call without a phone. Troy had told me of the fate of mine. Or maybe I had known it; I still couldn't remember.

Of course, Troy knew how to reach me. It would just take some patience with a hospital receptionist or more patience with the hospital's automated system—"please listen carefully because our options have recently changed."

What the hell did they give me for the pain?

Patience wasn't the only characteristic that had gone AWOL. Where had my concentration gone? My thoughts were all over the map. I needed to do something to make them stop jostling for position. I picked up the receiver next to my bed, dialing a number I knew by heart. Troy didn't answer, so I left him a message.

Maybe I could dispel my concerns about Dempsey if I talked to him. And the pretext that I just wanted to let him know how to reach me would cover the real reason for a call. Trouble was, I didn't have a number for his personal line, which meant I'd have to leave a message at the range.

When that call went through, I heard the familiar please-listen-closely message. Surprisingly, however, it was true. None of the current options involved voicemail to a specific person. They all seemed to go to the same pre-recorded message about the incident that was heavy on adjectives—tragic, devastating, disastrous—but actually said nothing. There was an option to leave a message to a general, voice mailbox with the promise that it would be forwarded to the proper authorities. That was better than nothing and I made use of it.

After I hung up, however, the number for a direct line to the JACC guard station popped into my head. That had to be better than some anonymous, unmonitored mailbox, so I dialed. Surprisingly, a human answered. "Criminal Investigations Special Agent Willsmore. May I help you?"

"FBI?"

"No, Dr. Price. That's a U.S. Military Police Corps rank, although I understand the confusion."

"Oh, okay." Then I processed the part where he had used my name. "You know who this is?" It wasn't the most perceptive of questions I realized after the words left my mouth.

"I know the name that comes up on my display. Dr. Sam Price, correct?"

And I was worried they couldn't find me. "That's right. I was trying to reach Col. Dempsey. Can you connect me."

"Sorry, Dr. Price, but that's not possible," Willsmore replied.

"He's not there? On the range?"

There was a slight delay before the agent said, "No, sir. He's not."

"That's strange. He said he was headed there when he left the hospital."

"Sorry. Maybe he'll show up later."

This information was concerning. Dempsey could have driven to the range more than twice in the nearly five hours since he'd left. "This is important. Is there any way you can contact him?"

The pause this time was longer. "I have a number but only for emergencies. Colonel's instructions. Is this an emergency?"

Was it?

I couldn't decide. My unease wasn't a matter of life and death although letting a serial killer escape was. But what were the chances Col. Dempsey was behind Jack's killing spree? Earlier, when my mind had been clearer, I'd thought he was trustworthy. And a lack of information wasn't new evidence. It was just that. A void.

"Dr. Price. Are you still there?"

"Yes, sorry. No message. I'll try to reach him later."

I hung up the phone and turned to the window. The reflections of headlights on the street below slid across its darkened surface as the images of doubt crept back into my mind. If the colonel hadn't gone to the JACC test range as he said he would, what else had he fabricated? Part of my mind said this logic was flawed—he could have been there and left for all I knew—but the image of Dempsey racing out of the hospital parking lot returned. I couldn't wait any longer. I was going to have to check on the colonel myself.

The closet where Troy said he'd put my suitcase was just feet away. I'd grab my bag and go into the bathroom to change. If anyone came, I'd stash the clothes and put my hospital gown back on before I came out. If not, I'd wait until I heard people passing in the hall and then, blend in as they left the hospital. I'd take a taxi to a convenience store to pick up a phone and then go on to Dempsey's house to set up surveillance. I knew where he lived. Troy and I had driven by once. And even though I didn't have the exact house number, I'd recognize it.

I sat up, swung my feet over the edge of the bed, and slid off. That, however, was a mistake. My world blurred, the edges of it disappearing into darkness. Somewhere an alarm went off. I crumbled to the floor and dropped my head into my hands. The alarm grew louder—or maybe my ears cleared. It was coming from the instrument rack near my bed. I turned to stare at it, trying to make sense of what was happening.

A sound behind me caught my attention and I turned. My nurse was standing there. "Are you okay?"

Some order returned to my thoughts—enough that I realized she'd know if I lied. "I think I almost blacked out."

"Probably. Your blood pressure dropped. Let's get you back in bed."

I thought about saying I needed to use the bathroom to disguise what I'd been doing, but that no longer seemed important. I looked up at her from the floor. She appeared even smaller than I remembered. "Maybe there's something I can use to steady myself?"

"Sure." She disappeared into the hallway. When she came back, she was carrying a walker.

I grabbed onto it and struggled to my feet, helped by the nurse but hindered by the fact that I had only one good arm. Once standing, I caught a glance of myself in the mirror on the back of the bathroom door. I was clinging to the walker like it was a life preserver in the middle of the ocean, my knuckles turning white. Every scrape and bruise that wasn't bandaged stood out in bold relief against my nearly bloodless face and neck. The sling holding my broken arm in place looked a bit like half of a straitjacket.

I started laughing. I didn't look like a man who was going to slip through the halls of the hospital unnoticed, hail a taxi for his getaway, and then stake out a suspect by sitting on a public street. I looked like a man who was lucky he hadn't face-planted two feet from the bed.

"Something funny?" asked my nurse as I crawled into bed and pulled the covers up around my neck.

"It just ...." How to explain it? "It just looks a lot easier in the movies."

TWO DAYS AFTER, SATURDAY, JANUARY 16

Las Vegas Regional Medical Center, Las Vegas, Nevada, 7:46 AM

Eleven. That was the eleventh shadow to appear at the bottom of my hospital room door and then disappear after the nurse had said, "The doctor will be right in". It wasn't that I was in a hurry to leave; I was desperate. My palms were sweaty. I jumped at every sound. I'd even stopped the debate between easy falsehoods and the truth, going with the lie to anyone who asked how I felt. "I feel great." In fact, I felt awful, but then, I'd been waving off the pain pills all morning. I wasn't sure about the airline's policy on loopy travelers, so the drugs could wait.

There was something besides my desperation to leave that was clear in the light of a new day—the delusion under which I'd operated the previous evening. Now, I felt that my images of Dempsey as the mastermind behind the massacre were just that— delusions. Tidbits of information that my unconscious had used to trust him were surfacing in my thoughts. Or perhaps resurfacing because they seemed familiar. And while they held nothing definitive, nothing conclusive, they showed a student of machine intelligence, not its wanna-be master, or worse yet, its slave. Of course, I'd still welcome confirmation of my beliefs, but I didn't need it nearly enough to break out of the hospital and set up a stakeout.

A television on the wall was playing quietly. I was hoping to catch the latest news about the attack on the test range, and it looked like I was about to be rewarded. I turned up the sound. "... word last night of a training accident on the Nevada Test and Training Range that took at least five lives. The program involved was the Joint Aerial Combat Capability, the latest in a line of highly advanced, unmanned aerial systems. No additional details are available at this time. Release of the names of the deceased is pending notification of next of kin. A formal statement from the government is scheduled for noon today."

After two days, I'd expected more from the news, but then, the JACC Program was trying to keep a lid on the rumors. And even the information the reporter gave—at least five had died—wasn't informative. Did that number include Drew or was the fifth the software engineer Dempsey said they expected to find in the IS Building? The announcement at noon might clear up those questions, but by then, I'd be on an airplane. At least, I hoped that's where I'd be.

"Sam Price." I spun from the television to find the doctor standing in my door. "So, how are you feeling?"

"Great! I feel great!"

Take a breath.

Blurting that I was the picture of health wasn't going to help, but if the doctor noticed anything unusual, he didn't mention it. Rather, he busied himself with my chart, while I held my breath. I wondered if the nurse had recorded the fact that she'd found me floundering on the floor last night. Perhaps she had because he frowned several times. But then, maybe he was recalling a fight with his wife this morning. I could only hope.

"Okay, let's take a look," he said. After several more minutes of poking and prodding, measuring and pondering, he said, "I see no reason you shouldn't be on your flight this morning." Even I could hear the increase in my heart rate on the monitor. The doctor just smiled. He probably saw this reaction all the time.

After that mini-ordeal, the morning passed in a blur. It was a teeth-grinding, beads-of-sweat-on-the-forehead, pain-filled blur as I pulled on a shirt and jeans with one hand. But it passed, and soon a nurse was pushing me to the door in a wheelchair.

I felt like I was running for my freedom, not just flying home.

St. Louis Lambert International Airport, 5:53 PM

If the morning had been a blur, then my afternoon was a blink of an eye—a three-hour-plus blink of an eye while I was in a dreamless sleep over Utah, Colorado, Kansas, and most of Missouri. That was probably because before takeoff, I'd given up fighting the discomfort in my shoulder and taken a pain pill. And now, despite the additional shuteye, I was shuffling toward baggage claim at the St. Louis airport, seemingly unable to make more speed than an amble. I was feeling much older than my 27 years.

"Doc." I knew the speaker long before I found Ken in the crowd.

"Ouch, Doc. What happened to you?" Ken asked when he got closer, his face twisted in a grimace.

"You don't know?" I could tell by his expression, he didn't. "I left before I got the details, but there was supposed to be a press conference about the attack at noon."

"Attack?" Ken's jaw dropped. "There was something on the news around 2:00, or so I've heard, but I've been in meetings." He paused and shook his head a couple of times. "Sorry. I haven't been ignoring your situation, but Col. Dempsey said you were fine ... or would be, anyway. And I figured I'd get the straight scoop from you. But an attack? What I heard was that someone had tried to steal a classified government weapon."

"Was it Brandt Drury? The guy that was trying to steal the weapon?"

Ken shook his head slowly. "No. I don't think that was the name."

"Dr. James Marshall?" Even though I'd pointed the finger at Marshall, a little surprise crept into my voice thinking that I might have been right. But Ken's head continued to shake.

Please, not Dempsey.

My concern didn't last long. "No, it was someone named Jack something or other."

I couldn't hold back the single chuckle. "Sorry, Ken, but that's J-A-C-C, Jack."

The look on Ken's face went from confused to amused. "Okay, yeah, I guess it wasn't Jack unless the aircraft was stealing itself."

"Well, that's not impossible," I said slowly, bringing the confusion back to Ken's features. That story, however, could wait until later. "But you heard the word theft in the news report?"

"Pretty sure but not on the news," Ken replied. "It was just a conversation in the hall. This story is getting around at work. Guess I should have listened closer."

He tapped his forehead, then pulled a phone out of a pocket and unlocked it. "You've got a message that might answer some of these questions."

"You didn't listen?"

"Enough to know it's Troy Sayers. We talked earlier about your flights, but this one was for you. He said something about losing your office number, although I'm not sure why he didn't call your cell."

"Because it died out on the test range." Ken blinked a couple of times but didn't ask. Instead, he handed me the phone.

"Hey, Doc. Sorry, lost your number but had this one for your boss. Hi, Ken." There was a pause. "Actually, I still have your number, but I figured it would take too long to hunt down all those scraps of charred paper blowing around the desert." He chuckled at his quip. "Anyway, by now you have the tale, right from the military brass. I'm still having trouble believing it. Give me a call when you have a chance. Later."

"No answers there," I said as I handed the phone back to Ken. "Except there is some sort of official news release. I'll have to call him back."

"Well, if your cell was destroyed, you want to use mine?" He held it out. I didn't know if Ken was being generous or if he was as anxious as I to get the whole story ... although I suspected the latter.

I was about to thank him when his phone rang. He answered with the standard Ruger–Phillips' greeting, listened for a few moments, chuckled, and said, "No, we're totally in the dark, but he's right here." He started to give me the phone but stopped when the person on the other end started speaking again. Ken listened. "Yes, absolutely. And thanks. We'll be back on in just a moment."

Ken started walking. "It was Col. Dempsey. He's offered to fill us both in if I put him on speaker." When we reached a relatively quiet side hall, Ken pressed a couple of buttons. "We're back, Colonel. And all ears."

"Thanks, Ken. And, Doc, it's good to hear you're safely back in St. Louis."

"Good to be here, sir." I kept it short, knowing that neither Ken nor I were that interested in small talk at the moment.

"So, yesterday, Doc, when I kept trying to leave the hospital, that was because we were launching a manhunt for Drew."

"So, you already suspected him?"

"We did. Even though we hadn't been able to check what was left of the Mobile Command Center, it was clear that a missile had hit nearby. Jack wouldn't miss that badly, so like you, we thought that shot might be a smokescreen, something to make us think Drew had been killed in the first attack. Then, a second missile—one that didn't show up on any of the JACC displays—destroyed the van. That would give us something to sift through while Drew made his escape. But rather than letting that happen, we declared him a person of interest and put out an alert."

"And the programmer who died before he could fix the software, Garcia—are the police going to reopen his case?"

"I suspect so, but that's in the future. We still don't have all the answers on this one. So, after getting the alert out, the investigators took a look at Marshall." Dempsey paused, and I heard a single, soft laugh. "Me, too, no doubt. But they had a viable suspect in Drew and a plan that was complex enough it didn't appear to be a frame but not so complex it couldn't work. Sitting here now, I wonder if we would have become so embroiled in the search for Drew that Marshall would have just slipped away."

"So, you started watching Marshall after we talked?" I asked.

"Not immediately, but one thing that bothered me, in addition to the long-term planning and the effect of automaticity that you mentioned, was the sophistication of the software that had to be created to make this plan work. It was well beyond Drew's capabilities. And with most of the software team dead, Marshall was one of the few who could have pulled it off."

Out of the corner of my eye, I saw Ken recoil when Dempsey mentioned the deaths. Apparently, that part of the story had been missing from the office rumors.

"Then, Marshall started acting strangely ... or at least, it seemed that way to me. He was telling anyone who'd listen that Drew was innocent, and the problem had to be in the programming. And he was going to New Mexico to manage the line-by-line review of the code that would prove it. I told him he needed to stay around and help with the local investigation. He balked; we argued. Finally, I pulled rank. By then, I was almost certain he was involved somehow, so I got the MPs to keep an eye on him. They caught him leaving his home around 2:30 in the morning, two disk drives with the stolen software in the trunk."

"And the software backups?" I asked.

"Everyone said they looked fine at first," Dempsey replied. "But when they tried to download a file, it started some sort of virus that ripped through the entire directory. That was one example of Marshall's programming expertise."

"And Drew was with Marshall when the police stopped him?"

"No," Dempsey replied and paused a moment. "No, and we're not entirely certain what part Drew played. What we believe is that Marshall promised him something—money, power, his own Jack— if he'd destroy the aircraft in the Maintenance Building. He did, and he did it in a way that let the people get away. Unfortunately, before that, Marv Richter tried to escape by car and was killed by a missile. It isn't clear whether Drew knew that something like that was a possibility from the start, but whatever the case, he didn't stop Jack from killing Richter.

"After that, we believe Drew put Jack into the autonomous search-and-destroy mode—the mode we thought the aircraft had been in all along—so it would continue to look like a smart weapon out of control. Maybe Drew knew that was a death sentence for the people in IS. Maybe not. But in any case, he didn't know that the act was a death sentence for him. The modified software on Jack, the code Marshall had changed, turned the Mobile Command Center into a threat. Jack launched on the center and Drew was most likely killed, although the identification of the remains isn't complete."

There had been a delayed explosion after the attack on Maintenance, and now it was clear why Troy and I hadn't been able to connect it to anything on the display. "Remains?" I said. "So, there was a body at the mobile center?"

"There was," Dempsey confirmed. "So, it looks like Marshall created a couple of layers of deception. He made Jack look like a rogue smart weapon, the result of a software bug or human error. Or, if the investigators saw through that ruse, they might buy that the massacre was the work of a deeply troubled pilot. That would hold up until we found the body, but either way, Marshall would have time to slip away. And that's pretty much what was in the press conference, minus the allegations of responsibility ... and our possible mistakes."

"Good call," said Ken.

"We thought so," came the reply over the phone. "Now that you know the story, the reason I called was to say thanks. Thanks, Doc, for keeping two more deaths off my conscience. And thanks for trusting me. You probably saved us days, maybe even months tracking down Marshall. And who knows, he might have escaped entirely."

"You're welcome," I replied, at a loss for more to say about the unexpected praise. "As for trusting you, you treat artificial intelligence with respect, rather than something to be trifled with."

The delay on the line was long enough that I wondered if I had said something wrong. But eventually, Dempsey spoke. "It's interesting that you said it that way because I've used almost the same words."

He cleared his throat and paused a beat. "You're going to hear this eventually. Well, you will if you follow Nevada politics because I'm retiring from the military to run for a seat in the House of Representatives. It was a tough call because I'm leaving behind a lot of good friends and comrades in arms. Some of them will see this as a betrayal because military use of AI will be one of the key planks of my platform. But I've been meeting with the head of the southwest district of my party, Stephen Gerhardt, and we agree, the time is now."

I could tell something was on Ken's mind. He kept shuffling his feet, looking away at the empty hall one minute and toward the phone the next. I wasn't sure what his concern was, however, until he spoke. "Are Nevada voters concerned about AI? Seems like all I hear about is healthcare, taxes, and jobs."

Dempsey didn't hesitate. "No, Nevada voters aren't concerned, but doesn't that need to change? At an annual international conference not long ago, the artificial intelligence community posted an open letter about the threat posed by their technology in military weapons. It was co-signed by several well-known public figures including Elon Musk, the CEO of Tesla; the physicist, Stephen Hawking; the social theorist, Noam Chomsky; Apple co-founder Steve Wozniak; and more than a thousand others involved in the research and development of AI. They warned us, but we're not listening.

"Don't get me wrong. An AI that tries to overthrow humanity is probably years away. Putting self-awareness and self-replication into a machine isn't a trivial task. But if we wait until they can repopulate and see the benefit of doing so, it'll be too late.

"And even using today's technology, we could create a '*War of the Worlds*' type situation easily. Research programs have proved that machines can operate independently or cooperate to solve complex problems. Unmanned combat systems have shown that they can find and eliminate our enemies. If we combine those abilities, we have lethal, autonomous killing robots. This isn't science fiction—it's reality.

"And even these current-day variants could be so coldly efficient and impersonal that abuse is almost guaranteed. They'd be pirated and sold on the black market. They'd be reverse-engineered so that inferior, but still deadly, replicas could be built. They'd be stolen so the wealthy in power could suppress the poor.

"So, whether I'm elected or not, the party will be calling for a Congressional task force to study the use of AI in weapons. We're not saying the capability should be banned. We're saying it should be studied and studied closely. Perhaps we'll find that the current safeguards and training standards are sufficient. More likely in my opinion, we'll find that additional oversight and measures against their proliferation are needed, much as what we have for nuclear, chemical, and biological weapons. I can't foresee the outcome, but I already see the need for the dialogue."

When I first met Col. Dempsey, I felt he was an imposing presence—dignified, confident, well-spoken. However, in the nearly two weeks I had known him, I'd rarely heard him string three sentences together. That is, until now. If there was to be a national debate on this topic, he was the person for the job.

"It sounds like a monumental task but one worthy of the effort," I said. "I wish you every success."

"Likewise," added Ken. "And if Ruger-Phillips can help in any way, please let us know."

"I will," he replied. "But now, I've kept you two long enough. Doc, thanks again. And if either of you gets to Nevada—or hopefully, DC— look me up. You're always welcome in my home."

After good-byes to Dempsey, Ken said, "Doc, I'm dying to hear about the two deaths you kept off the colonel's conscience, but I can wait. You should take a couple of days off, recharge, and then we can sit down in my office."

"I look that bad, huh?"

"Bad enough that I'm sure you need a ride home."

We headed toward baggage claim while I wondered if my suitcase was still riding the conveyor belt. Or maybe it had been tagged as suspicious and taken away. Perhaps I had spent too much time on an unmanned systems program, but I could almost see a bomb-disposal robot dragging my bag to the tarmac where they'd shoot it full of holes to see if it exploded.

As I rounded the corner, however, I found something I never expected—Nicole, with my luggage in tow.

"Should I stick around, give Doc a ride home?" asked Ken when we got close.

"I think I can handle that," she said. Ken nodded and walked away. Nicole turned to me. "Looking for something?"

I suspected she meant my bag, but that item paled in comparison to what I'd found. Through happenstance, I'd never done more than shake Nicole's hand in the eight months I'd known her. That knowledge, however, held no sway over my current feelings, the closeness that had grown over the hours on the phone and the thousands of words of email. I wrapped my arms around her and said, "Yeah, I was looking for you."

When we released the embrace, she stepped back, the smile on her face turning to a look of pain. Since many of the bandages were gone, all the tiny gashes from flying rocks, glass, and metal were visible. And the bruises? They were getting that lovely shade of green that is part of the healing process, albeit an unsightly part. Her look of pity, however, lasted but a moment. She took her hand and drew it down across my cheek.

"Do you think the same chunk of rock that caught you on the cheek also dislocated your shoulder?"

I smiled to myself. I didn't understand Nicole and probably never would. But even I recognized that in that instant, she had transitioned from concerned friend to analytic engineer. She was trying to picture the angles and forces of rock against flesh.

"Maybe. It's a bit of a blur to me. Say, do you want to get a beer? Alcohol doesn't mix with the pain pills I'm taking, but I could get a soda."

Her smile returned. "Wish I could, but I need to get home. I'll drop you off on the way. And that last email you sent when Jack was hunting you? It came yesterday."

"I meant every word."

I thought she might want to talk about it, but the look on her face said there was something else on her mind. She leaned in and kissed me softly, then turned and started down the hall. By the time I had gathered my wits, she was nearly ten feet away.

"Nicole." She stopped and turned around. "So, I guess I finally got my goodnight kiss." I tried to stop the grin from reaching my face, but it wouldn't be denied.

She tilted her head to one side dramatically, as if in thought. "No, you didn't. I kissed you, but keep trying."

I caught up with her, took her hand in mine, and we continued down the hall. "You can count on it."

ACKNOWLEDGMENTS

This book would not have been possible without the help of a number of talented individuals. First, I'd like to thank Ms. Janet Harrison for reading and providing numerous helpful comments on an earlier draft of the manuscript. And since this is a second edition, I'd also like to recognize all those who commented on the first. Thanks to everyone who took a moment to leave a review; I read them all.

Special thanks go to Dr. Liz Gehr for helping me watch my technical Ps and Qs. Any inaccuracies are mine; hopefully, they're all intentional to build the fiction.

The diligence of my editor is greatly appreciated. I'd never find all those pesky, extra commas without her help ... not to mention all the other slipups that are so easy to overlook when you know a story by heart.

Finally, thanks go to my talented daughter, Ms. Courtney Perrin, for the design and creation of the cover art. Maybe I can build a picture with words, but I could never do what she does with graphics software and a computer.

AUTHOR'S NOTE

I was concerned that during the writing of this book it would change from the thriller genre to inaccurate history overnight. That's because, unlike most of the novels I write, there is little stopping the events depicted in it from happening now. None of the technology described requires an earth-shattering scientific insight ... or even a small step forward in technical capability. The research results and the weapon systems programs that are mentioned are real, with the exception of the Joint Aerial Combat Capability (JACC), the subject of this tale.

And now that the book is written, hopefully, it will always remain in the fiction genre.

ABOUT THE AUTHOR

Bruce Perrin has been writing for more than twenty-five years, although you will find most of that work only in professional technical journals or conference proceedings. After receiving a PhD in Industrial/Organizational Psychology and completing a career in psychological research and development at a major aerospace company, he's now applying his background to writing novels. Not surprisingly, most of his work falls in the techno-thriller, mystery, and hard science fiction genres, examining the intersection of technology and the human mind now and in the future. Besides writing, Bruce likes to tinker with home automation and is an avid hiker, logging nearly 2,500 miles a year in the first six years of Fitbit ownership. When he is not on the trails, he lives with his wife in St. Louis, MO.

Thank you for reading *Mind in the Clouds*. If you'd like to help others find this story, please consider leaving a review on Amazon, Goodreads, or the website of your favorite bookseller.

For all the latest on my new releases, promotions, and book reviews, please subscribe to my blog: BruceMPerrin.blogspot.com